THE *Magic* OF LIGHT

A NOVEL

The Flint Hills Series
JORDAN ABITZ

Dedication

For the twenty-eight children that hold pieces of my heart.
I love you to the moon and back.

A Note from Jordan

I WILL NEVER GET over the fact that you now hold my dream in your hands. If you're holding this book, you are a part of that dream. I never imagined writing a story as deeply personal as this one. Several years ago, I sat beside my husband at the end of our bed with my heart on the floor. I felt like the biggest failure as a foster mom despite trying so hard to excel at this role. I realized that all my good intentions, kindness, hope, and love couldn't heal childhood trauma. There were things I still didn't understand, and despite how much I loved someone, I couldn't heal them. If love alone could heal someone, my love would have done so. I loved these children with my whole heart.

I remember talking to my therapist about how helpless I felt, and she told me it was okay to grieve the losses I faced. Several weeks later, my entire world shattered when a child tucked a stuffed animal into my hands and told me to keep it so I wouldn't forget them. I won't forget them until the day I die.

Experiencing secondhand childhood trauma was the hardest thing I have ever faced. After realizing that I lacked crucial research about childhood trauma, I dedicated myself to learning everything I could. I took classes, read books, and spoke with therapists. I learned that trauma requires multiple factors for healing, and while love motivated my actions, it was not a cure-all.

You can't love trauma away.

It was then my hobby of writing romance began to provide me with an outlet. Soren and Sawyer came to life through my words. This book will not contain vivid or graphic details of childhood abuse because it isn't about magnifying the trauma; instead, it's about the journey to healing. I hope it makes you smile and kick your feet with giddiness, and if it does bring you to tears, my wish is that it leaves you with hope in the end.

Love you, mean it.

Jordan

Content Warning

Childhood Sexual Abuse (Off page)

Childhood Physical Abuse and Neglect (Off page)

Panic Attacks

Attachment Disorders (RAD)

Food Insecurity

Addiction

Bullying

Grief

Prologue

Sawyer

(Age Fourteen)

Plink. Plink. Plink. The water dripped, resembling teardrops, from the leaky kitchen faucet into the stainless-steel sink basin. My heart raced as I quieted my breathing. The lock was harder to pick than I expected, but once it was open, I could escape to the bus stop in the next town over. *Just a little more and it should open.*

I gently shifted the straightened hairpin, willing my hands to stop shaking. *Come on.* As my fear of being caught grew, a bead of sweat trickled down the pearls of my spine, and an unconscious shiver overtook my body at the sensation. I stilled as I heard a creaking sound in the distance. Blood rushed in my ears.

I can't get caught.

I didn't know if I'd survive getting caught. Once I found what I was searching for, then I would be free. As free as I could be until they shipped me off to the next monster, because I knew they would find me at some point. They always did.

I had made this arrangement work for three months when I should have left after two weeks. The reason I had stayed was for the six-year-old twins, Anna and Justin. Their freckled noses scrunched and their square teeth that were a little too big for their faces shined when they smiled. I had made it my mission to make them smile. They were sweet, un-hardened from the life that stretched ahead of them. A life I knew all too well. Soon enough, they would build walls, and everything wouldn't hurt as it did now. The walls they most needed were the ones they would build around their hearts. Walls that blocked out any possibility of light. Fortresses that would keep them safe from the people who made them *feel*. Because sometimes the expectation of good was more heartbreaking than always expecting the impending downfall of bad luck.

I knew bad luck better than anyone. My life was a series of bad luck draws, broken promises, and moments where I simply fell through the cracks. I once thought the impenetrable walls I had built were the saddest part of my life. However, I have found safety in their protection, and it didn't matter if there was any light or not. I understood the darkness, or rather, I understood that darkness could not be understood and, therefore, it could not be trusted. There was no gray area with darkness. All that mattered was that I survived another day, because every day I endured was one step closer to freedom.

I had suffered in this hellish place for three long months only in order to prolong the warmth of sunshine for the twins. They had gained three more months of childhood, and I was stripped of three more months of mine. But when he had taken the only thing I had ever cared about, I knew I'd risk everything to get it back. I would willingly give over my small accumulation of mismatched belongings—everything except this. It was the only thing I had ever loved. It was the only thing that was truly mine. It had been gifted to me by the only person who had ever loved me, and it was behind this lock. I wanted to scream in frustration and pound my fists on the wall.

The silence returned, and I worked diligently on the lock with my sweaty hands. After a couple more minutes of working, I finally opened the latch that had been holding the lock shut. The moonlight illuminated the space, but not clearly enough for me to see into the cabinet, I reached my hand inside and felt around. There was an object that resembled Anna's tattered baby doll and another that had to be Justin's baseball from his dad. Their parents had been killed in a wreck, and when no extended family had been located, they ended up here with me.

I stretched my arm as far as I could, standing on my tiptoes as my fingers skimmed across a stack of papers along with something that resembled a thick envelope. I withdrew the envelope and saw a stack of money stuffed inside. I wanted to vomit, knowing that money was intended to buy me new shoes, but I immediately replaced it. I knew the last thing I needed was to be on the run with something that wasn't "mine," even if it had been intended for me. As helpful as it would be, it wasn't worth the risk.

I continued my search and finally found what I was seeking. As I pulled it out, it caught the light and reflected a dull shine. At that moment, I realized we were the same. I also only had a flicker of light left in me, and everything else was the grit that kept me alive. I placed it in my pocket as anger burned through my chest. I wanted to place the baseball and baby doll on the counter, but I knew that would only result in punishment for little Anna and Justin. I wouldn't let Mr. Phillips hurt them how he'd hurt me. If I could get free, I would tell anyone who listened about the hell it was to live with the Phillips, but until then, I had to get out.

I locked the cabinet so no one would be the wiser and quietly tiptoed toward the door. My small backpack was slung over one shoulder, filled with only the things I brought. I paused at the doorway, brushed a kiss to my thin bruised fingers, and pressed them against the chipped paint of the doorframe. I was too scared to kiss Anna and Justin's soft freckled foreheads, for fear of waking them up, so this would have to do. I willed their lives to turn out better than mine. One day, I would do everything in my power to protect kids like Anna and Justin, kids that were . . . just like me.

Chapter One

Sawyer

(Present Day)

THE SOUND OF GRAVEL crunched beneath my tires as I drove down a rural road in Rhodes County, Kansas. I rubbed my temple to ease the tension, but my eyes continued to burn from lack of sleep. The eye drops I had used before walking into court this morning, which claimed to "relieve redness within minutes," had worn off at some point in the last seven hours. I was running on four hours of sleep in the last two days, and I wasn't sure that any eye drop could fix that. I had already logged a good 1,900 miles within the last three days, and I had ingested enough caffeine to fell an elephant. Casting an occasional glance in the rearview mirror, I saw sad gray eyes staring back at me.

"I promise I'm doing the best I can, Connor."

We hadn't talked since we left the courthouse, and I hated this as much as he did. I had attempted conversation a couple of times by asking about the 1000-piece puzzle he had been working on at home, but he wasn't engaging. I didn't blame him. I hated small talk too, especially in moments when it seemed especially shallow in comparison to the unbearable weight of the moment.

"Yeah, whatever," he mumbled.

He rolled his eyes and turned toward the window. If only he knew how little influence I effectively had. People always assumed we were the powers that be, but most often, things depended on an entire team of individuals who might not see eye to eye. Additionally, there were the judges who were elected but lacked any knowledge of the laws they were expected to enforce. Good ol' boy judges with the right last names littered our state like most states, more concerned with keeping up appearances than keeping kids safe. Connor had lucked out with a judge that appeared to want the best thing for him.

I would "Yeah, whatever" too if I didn't know all the background information. However, there was not much that I didn't know about Connor Hanson. His dog-eared file rested in my caramel-colored, faux-leather tote bag in the front passenger seat. The thick, light blue folder stretched at the seams and spoke of his years in and out of foster care. Nine-year-olds shouldn't have this much heartbreak. Their biggest concerns were supposed to be about hanging out with friends and building Lego sets.

My childhood was far from ideal, I understood those heartbroken storm cloud eyes more than I wanted to. I wished I could fix this. I wished I could make parents love their children and always put their needs first, but sometimes that simply wasn't the case. Sometimes individuals like Connor came from a family tree riddled with addiction, and more often than not, the parents needed as much help as their children. Addictions were hard to break and even harder to break when someone hadn't made any measurable efforts. No one on the team was favorable to reintegration when they thought no steps forward had been made by the adults in the situation. It was only a matter of determining whether the effort was linked to a lack of understanding, challenges, or lack of follow-through.

I glanced at my reflection in the rearview mirror. My elbow-length, wavy blonde hair was in a French twist to make me appear older. Having what many deemed a "baby face," I always did everything I could to portray a professional appearance so that my opinion wasn't immediately discounted because of my age. I was consistently the youngest person in the room, and it had been that way since I had graduated early from college and was immediately hired as a social worker.

My makeup and clothing were flawless despite my lack of sleep. I'd watched hundreds of hours of makeup tutorials and videos on how to have "presence." The gist was to occupy the largest amount of space in a room, which was ironic considering all I wanted to do was take up the least amount of space possible.

I worked diligently to assess what life skills I was inadequate in and tried to fill that void with advice from strangers on the internet. You couldn't exactly walk up to someone on the street and say, "I don't know how to be a normal human. Can you help?"

People would see me as a freak more than they already did. These instructional videos were how I knew my makeup was on point, similarly to how I knew my gray pinstripe, slim, high-waisted trousers with a tucked in silk blouse and sky-high heels worked best on my body shape for business attire. I analyzed photos of completed outfits online and purchased my clothing accordingly, except for the occasional outfit that Talia talked me into. Her choices tended to be more bright, patterned, and sexier than anything I typically wore. To Talia's dismay, those outfits sat in my closet most of the time, untouched because the life of a social worker didn't require sexy outfits.

Even though I still exhibited the signs of being inexperienced in life skills, watching the instructional videos helped. I had to remind myself that at least I was a fully functioning, law-abiding human who tried to be kind and considerate. I had ten lifetimes of experience on how to be a vile one.

The headache that was a result of my French twist hairstyle throbbed as I glanced at my phone mounted on the dash. Fifteen percent battery. I inwardly cursed the fact that I had left my charger in my personal vehicle. I'd be lucky to make it to the respite home before it completely died. My eyes shifted back to the rearview mirror to check on Connor.

Court always triggered behaviors in him, as it did with many kids. The Martins, Connor's foster parents, were good people who took on tough cases and genuinely cared about the kids in their home. For their twenty-fifth wedding anniversary, they decided to celebrate and had been gifted a couple's trip. When events similar to this happened, another licensed foster home would be responsible for the child. Connor would be staying with the Baileys, a gentle retired couple that primarily only did respite for foster families instead of having one particular child in their home long term. Many of the families that used the Baileys for respite considered them to be grandparents, and the Baileys really had a heart for families that had a heart for foster care.

Once I dropped Connor off, I'd start my four-day weekend to burn off a vacation day from months of working overtime with no break. Social work was taxing in every area, but I loved making a difference, especially when it involved children.

"Why can't my dad take me home?!" Connor bit out. His harsh tone startled me.

"He can't right now. Kids deserve to live in safe homes. I'm sorry, buddy," I said gently as I glanced toward him. My heart ached for his situation.

His eyes narrowed, as his face turned red.

"I'm not your buddy. You don't care about me!" he spat. My heart caught because I genuinely did care. I thought about all the kids on my caseload daily, but I knew what he was saying wasn't personal. He was frustrated with the progress and I was too.

"It's okay to be disappointed, Connor, but it's not okay to be rude." I spoke clearly and calmly, knowing Connor thoroughly enough to recognize he was getting close to blowing his cool.

"I hate you!" he suddenly screamed and erupted in a combative volcano of anger.

Connor slung his arms around wildly, becoming aggressive, hitting things around him as he unbuckled himself and grabbed at the door handle. I had already been driving slowly due to the gravel road, but I immediately hit the brakes. The car slid to a stop as gravel dust billowed everywhere. Connor flung open the door, leaped from the car, and ran toward an open hay field as if the devil himself was chasing him. I shifted to park, hopped from the car and raced after him as fast as I could in heels, but he was already long gone. Damn. Panic built as I realized I could no longer see him.

I yelled out his name, but I knew it was pointless due to the distance. I spun around, studying the rural surroundings with no sign of life. It had been miles since I had seen a house or another vehicle. This portion of Rhodes County was especially rural, as it was mostly a patchwork of family-owned farms and ranches. I had no clue where I was because this wasn't the route I normally took to the Bailey's house. I trekked back to the work car where my cell phone was. Clutching my phone as I snagged it off the dash, I typed a quick message to my boss letting her know what happened. Surprisingly, the text had enough signal to go through. My cell signal kept dropping, but I was scared to turn off the navigation app, which depleted my battery even more.

This wasn't the first time Connor had run. He had a history of becoming combative during times of heightened emotions, but once he was calm, he'd apologize and be the tenderhearted boy I knew him to be. I attempted to call 911, but my cell phone signal wasn't strong enough for a call. Shuffling through the glove box, which served as a mini lost and found collection, I retrieved a hot pink ribbon, that had undoubtedly been left by a child. My heels sank into the soil as I tied it to a strand of barbed wire alongside the road. I knew the four-inch heels were impractical out here, but I was dressed for court, not chasing after a child through a field. The least I could do was mark a location for law enforcement to begin the search. I got back in the car and moved my cell around, trying to find a signal. Two bars. I froze and held the phone still, my arm almost fully extended, and dialed 911 on speakerphone.

Two rings.

"What's your emergency?" a female voice asked.

"My name is Sawyer Brannan. I'm a social worker for CPS, and I was transporting a minor when he jumped from the car and ran. I don't think he's injured. I'm not familiar with the area and I no longer have eyes on him. My cell signal is spotty, and my battery is low." This wasn't my first rodeo with runaway situations.

"Stay on the line and I'll get your location. What's the age of the child?" I could hear typing in the background as she spoke.

"He's nine years old," I responded as I actively scanned my surroundings hoping to catch a glimpse of Connor.

Suddenly, the phone chimed, indicating that the call had dropped. Hell.

"Ugh!" I huffed.

The only thing that was logical at this point was to turn around and find the house I had passed a few miles back. I crossed my fingers that they would have a landline or a different cell service that worked better out here. I couldn't merely sit here and do nothing, even though I didn't want to drive away.

I whipped the car around and sent rocks flying. This wasn't anything like the time Connor ran away at a mall or the time in the neighborhood. This time, I had no idea how to find him without getting lost myself. Connor would most likely try to find me again once he calmed down, but would he be able to find his way back? That seemed unlikely. The landscape was wide open, and hills rolled as far as your eyes could see. Gravel pelted the bottom of the car as I sped back to the last farmhouse.

Driving around a curve, I saw a large, beautiful white farmhouse with a wraparound porch. The house was something straight out of a dream. It was idyllic and the kind of peacefulness you could experience by simply looking at it. Off to the side of the house, a tire was hanging from a thick rope on a large tree branch.

Something felt vaguely familiar, which was disconcerting. I experienced that strange inkling again that I had the first time I drove by. It was as if I had been here before, but I didn't understand why. I currently had fifty-seven children on my caseload, but I knew with absolute certainty that none of them were connected to this house, and I lived forty-five minutes away. There was no logical reason why I should feel this way. Somehow, it felt older, perhaps something from my childhood, which also didn't make sense. I was exhausted from my unrelentingly stressful week, therefore I pushed the thoughts out of my head. I needed to find Connor, get him to the respite home, and then get some sleep. If the situation wasn't intensely stressful, I could have appreciated the beauty of the house and the perfect shade of sunshine yellow that the porch swing was painted. My cell signal kept fluctuating between one and two bars, but wasn't stable enough to call out. I parked and my heels clicked loudly on the wood as I hastily scaled the steps. I rapped on the door and tried dialing 911 again.

"What's your emergency?" Thank goodness.

"I called a couple of minutes ago. My cell doesn't have a good signal." I froze so the signal wouldn't change.

"Yes. Hold still and let me try to ping your location." I knocked on the door again.

There were five modes of transportation parked outside. Surely, someone was in this house.

Two pickup trucks were lined up next to the barn, along with a large green tractor on the far side. One truck appeared brand new. It was the nicest pickup truck I had ever seen, with glossy metallic forest-green paint. The other was an old gray farm truck with rust around the wheels. There was also a semitruck and another piece of equipment that I didn't know the name of, but it appeared to be something you could drive. I knocked on the door again.

"You're at my brother's house?" the dispatcher asked with an incredulous tone.

What? I had no clue where I was.

"I don't know where I am. I drove back to the closest house I saw."

"Okay. Hold on. We're a small department. I might be able to get you some help faster," she said, steadily clicking away.

I glanced at my phone's eleven percent battery. I needed to charge my phone. I would be the liaison between the office and law enforcement until Connor was found. I needed to keep in touch with the team, and I had to cancel plans with Talia again. We were going to celebrate the anniversary of her opening her therapy office two years ago. The celebration was a couple weeks delayed due to the chaos that I called my life. I rubbed my temple again and wished I had a hair tie to let my hair down and braid it. The weight of my hair tugging on the back of my head was going to be the straw that broke the camel's back. This headache was relentless.

"My brother is headed your way. He'll help you until a unit makes it. Hang in there for a few more minutes, and an officer is en route." She spoke confidently.

"Okay. Thank you."

I clicked off my phone and sat down on the top porch step. There was a chill in the air from an unexpected cold front in April. I needed a change of clothes. I texted Talia.

> I have a runaway situation. If this doesn't get resolved in a couple hours, can you please bring me a change of clothes? I'm sorry, but I most likely won't be able to make it tonight.

I saw three dots pop up immediately.

> Another runaway?! You have to be exhausted. Of course, I will. Where are you?

This is the second time I canceled on her this week for the same exact reason. I sent a pin showing my location.

> Got it! Anything else?

Talia is my best friend. My only friend.

> Hair tie. Tylenol. You can pick out the next two movies for movie night.

> Your debt can be paid in cheesecake. Cookie dough cheesecake. ILY.

The corner of my mouth tipped up in a smile.

> Deal. ILY.

Chapter Two

Sawyer

I LIFTED MY HEAD in time to see one of the most intimidating men I had ever laid eyes on. His tall frame stalked toward me with a scowl on his face. The intensity of his eyes made the hair on the back of my neck stand up before I could even see the color of them. I realized at that moment I didn't have my bag, therefore, my can of mace wasn't within reach. *Crap.* Such a rookie social worker move.

I was better than this. I was a planner. I prepared. I played it safe. I read the menu online before I went to a restaurant. I meal prepped for the week. I meticulously laid out my outfit the day before, down to the jewelry that completed each look. Every piece of my life was organized right down to the minute detail. At least the parts I could control. I told myself to relax in an effort to calm my nerves as I took a fortifying breath and stood on the top step. The man was easily over six feet tall and had the muscled body of a man that either performed physical labor or regularly hit the gym. A long-sleeve, waffle-knit, forest-green shirt stretched snugly across his broad chest, and dark wash Wranglers hugged his thick, muscular thighs. Despite the tension in the air, I couldn't deny that he resembled a cowboy in one of those pickup truck ads. Or was it a country boy? I wasn't sure. His chestnut, dark-brown hair was too long in all the right places, and there was a five o'clock shadow across his taut cheeks and sharp jawline. What drew me in, though, were his eyes. I'd never seen anything quite like them. Their intensity was unnerving. He got about six feet away from me on the ground at the bottom of the steps and abruptly stopped. I could sense the irritation rolling off him in waves and I resisted the urge to make myself small.

His stormy eyes raked over me, as if I were a threat.

"What are you doing?" Chill bumps raced across my body at his words. I wanted to take a step back but my feet were glued to the step. His voice was low and husky, as if it hadn't gotten much use today. Almost fierce, but still level. His jaw clenched, and my hands tingled. I knew the telltale signs that this was not headed in a good direction. I tapped my thumb against the pad of each finger, willing my body not to betray me. Until he spoke, I hadn't realized that I had stopped breathing. I sucked in a shaky breath.

"Hi. Uh . . . I-I'm Sawyer. I'm a social worker for CPS. I was transporting a child, and he jumped from the car about two miles that way."

I hitched my trembling thumb over my shoulder. "I'm not familiar with this area. Your sister said you could help me. I tied a ribbon to the fence where he ran." My voice sounded shaky with nerves.

There was something about his intense stare that made me unable to stop oversharing.

His eyes narrowed. His arms crossed over his chest and muscles rippled underneath. He took two steps closer. The action triggered black spots to cloud my vision. My thumb repeated the pattern across my fingers. I could still feel my fingers. As he moved closer, I caught a whiff of spearmint. *Body. Don't fail me now.* I itched to reach for the chain under my blouse to ground me, but willed my body to stay conscious. Something unrecognizable flickered across his face, but his expression hardened again.

"I don't have a sister," he retorted.

I had to get out of here. No one other than Talia knew exactly where I was, and she was at least forty-five minutes away. The dispatcher obviously didn't ping the right address because something wasn't right. Meanwhile, Connor was still running, and I didn't know how to find him. Could a week from hell get even closer to hell? What's worse than hell? The inner parts of hell? Standing next to the devil himself?

My eyes darted to my work car. I could hear my heartbeat in my ears. My hands continued to tingle, but I tried to ignore it as best as I could. I couldn't have a panic attack. Connor was depending on me, and I wouldn't let him down. If only they could be stopped that easily. I continued tapping my fingers and took another deep inhale. I heard the sound of cattle in the distance. I took in my surroundings as I attempted to keep my brain from shutting down. There were three porch steps between the man and me and another twenty feet to the car.

I leveled my voice the way I do when I talk to combative kids and adults and began walking down the steps.

"There must be some confusion. She told me this was your address."

I didn't glance toward him as I reached the ground, mostly because I could sense the weight of his assessing eyes as though they could peer into my soul. I had walked down the steps at an angle in order to be the furthest away from him as possible. Now that we were on even footing, I could tell without even sizing him up that he towered over my five-foot-seven frame from the sheer mass of his body. My four-inch heels helped, but this man was built like a brick wall. Twenty feet to the car. I could make it if I ran fast. Although, I crossed my fingers things wouldn't get to that place.

"Like I said. I don't have a sister." My eyes swung to his. "Now tell me what the hell you're really doing on my front porch." His voice thundered near the end. I couldn't help my involuntary flinch, and that made me justifiably annoyed. The hair on the back of my neck still stood at attention, but my lack of sleep, hunger, and headache caused me to hit my breaking point.

Tap. Tap. Tap. Thumb to ring finger. Thumb to pinky finger. If there was anything I couldn't stand, it was being intimidated or bullied, and this big jerk had hit my limit. I had suffered enough in my life from being bullied. I had promised my eight-year-old self that when I was an adult, I wouldn't stand by and let it happen again.

"Look, I don't have time for this! There's a nine-year-old little boy out there depending on me. My friend is coming here to bring a change of clothes so I can search for him, and law enforcement is on the way." I slung my hand out to the side. "I don't know why that dispatcher told me this was her brother's address, but regardless, you can stop trying to intimidate me." I narrowed my eyes at him. "The last place I want to be is on your freaking front porch! I simply want to find this kid and make sure he's safe."

Unwarranted tears pooled in my eyes but I *would not* cry. His eyebrows shot to his hairline as his eyes widened in surprise. I couldn't believe I divulged all that. I never let anyone see this side of me, but I was exhausted and I was channeling my inner Talia. She would be beyond proud of me because she wasn't scared of anything.

He was stunned and frankly, I didn't care. I wanted to locate Connor and make sure he was safe. Before he could say anything, a four-wheeler barreled into the yard, leaving a trail of dust flying. Another tall, muscular-built cowboy with whiskey-colored eyes slung his long leg over the seat and dismounted. His long, dark hair was pulled into a knot at the back of his head. A blue-and-rust-colored flannel long-sleeve shirt was buttoned across his chest. He nodded in my direction, and I saw it for what it was—good manners.

"Did she tell you the situation? Tess called Gene, and Gene called me since he's in town. Fulton's on his way."

Recognition flashed across the grumpy man's face. He regarded me again with eyes that saw entirely too much. I crossed my arms as if it were a shield against his inspection of my soul.

"Fuel up the side-by-sides. I'll grab some supplies inside, and we'll head out." He said all of this without taking his eyes off me. There was a sense of authority in his voice, but it lacked the gruffness he had inflicted on me earlier.

"Sure thing, boss." The man dipped his chin toward me again and mounted the four-wheeler, heading toward the backside of the barn.

The jerk turned toward his all-too-precious front porch without a word. I was relieved that there was someone else nearby. I walked toward my car, grabbed my can of mace, and slid it into the band of my pants since I didn't have pockets. I wasn't ever going to make that mistake again. My battery was at eight percent now. I couldn't remember the last time I had forgotten my charger. Usually, in any situation, if a list could be made for it, I had one. I survived thanks to obsessive organization. Organization made me have a sense of safety and control, and being safe meant everything to me.

I spun around as I heard the jerk walking down the stairs, his scuffed leather, square-toe cowboy boots loudly thudding with each step. He was now wearing a tan Carhartt jacket. A black backpack was slung over one of his shoulders. He walked straight toward me with that same intensity as before. Did he even walk? It was more of a stalk and completely intimidating. He stopped in front of me, appearing uncertain. I realized his eyes were indeed hazel. Green and blue that faded to golden amber at the edges. I'd never seen hazel eyes like his with such vivid colors. He rubbed his hand across the shadow of scruff on his chin.

"I'm sorry about earlier. I thought . . . " His jaw flexed and continued, "It doesn't matter what I thought. Tess, the dispatcher, is Gene's sister. Gene is one of my ranch hands that lives on the property. Again, I'm sorry. "

He extended his hand. "I'm Soren." His eyes never left mine. I tentatively offered my hand. His calloused palm engulfed my smaller one, and a spark shot up my arm. I had never experienced anything quite like that, and it was a bit unnerving. More than anything, I wanted to know what he was about to say.

"I shouldn't have snapped. I apologize. This is the third runaway situation I've had this week and I'm exhausted." I rubbed my temple as my headache continued to pound like a jackhammer against my skull.

"It's not your fault. Follow me," he commanded, walking toward the side of the large, white-painted barn that matched the fence along a portion of the road. I tried to keep up in my heels, but he realized he'd left me and slowed his pace.

"Do you have any other shoes?" he grumbled.

"No."

"I don't have anything to give you," he stated as he shifted the bag on his shoulder.

"I'll be okay. My friend is bringing me a change of clothes if we can't find him soon," I explained. I hadn't expected him to have shoes for me.

"Do you have a real jacket? It's going to cool off soon," he asked.

I shook my head. I hadn't heard about the unexpected shift in weather until I was in my Jeep headed to work this morning to pick up the office car. I had been listening to the local country music radio station when the DJ had mentioned the cold front coming in.

We rounded the barn to find the man from earlier with two red UTVs that had roll bars and bucket seats. He lifted his head in acknowledgment and gave a small smile. Something about him appeared genuinely kind. He was older than me, and I had a sense that Soren was older than him by a few years.

"Alright, I think we're ready to go. I'm Travis, by the way. Soren's foreman." He extended his hand and I took it.

"Nice to meet you. I'm Sawyer."

Soren cut his eyes to Travis while he removed a roll of barbed wire from the back of the UTV and placed it inside the barn door. There was a silent conversation with their eyes taking place that I wasn't a part of.

Soren walked toward the driver's side of one of the UTVs. Setting his backpack on the seat, he withdrew a thick olive green hoodie and tossed it to me.

"Put this on."

He must be accustomed to getting his way, but I didn't argue because there was already a chill in the air. His communication skills could use some work. Perhaps I could suggest a YouTube video to him. I amused myself at the thought. The length of the hoodie almost reached my knees. The sleeves went beyond my wrists, so I rolled them up to where my hands could stick out. The hoodie smelled of fresh air and spearmint. It was a scent I decided I thoroughly enjoyed. Sometimes I had a sensitivity to scents, but this smelled fresh and clean like spring.

Soren glanced at me and for the first time, I could see amusement glittering in his eyes at how ridiculous I must look in suit pants and heels with a hoodie on top.

"You're riding with me."

His tone brooked no argument. *Lucky me.*

He wasn't exactly rude now that he had realized I wasn't a threat to his precious front porch, but he wasn't exactly warm and fuzzy either. Travis quirked a brow, amusement clear on his face, before saying he needed to check on something quickly. He left and drove around the side of the barn. I climbed into the passenger's side seat of the UTV. This was the first time I had ever been on a UTV, but it seemed as if it would be fun to drive if the situation wasn't extremely serious.

Soren rounded the UTV until he was standing beside me. He extended the strap of my seatbelt and I stiffened. Before I even realized that I had moved, I splayed my hands wide open in front of my chest as if to prevent him from touching me. I wasn't exactly sure what he was trying to do, but his nearness was unsettling and throwing me off balance. He paused, his eyes narrowed as they flicked between my hands, and he reached around me and clipped the seatbelt into place. As he leaned, his eyes found my widened ones and he never broke eye contact. His exhale was warm on my cheek and sent shivers down my spine. He smelled the same way the hoodie did. My personal bubble was invaded, but he never touched me. His eyes were beautiful but they bore into me as if he could see all my secrets plain as day. I was not a fan. I preferred for my secrets to stay in their deepest darkest places. I broke eye contact because of the unnerving intensity.

"Always wear a seat belt." A muscle ticked in his jaw.

Did he have a thing about front porches and seatbelts? What a weird combo. This man was strange for sure, but I didn't have time to contemplate his bizarre behavior. I was worried about Connor which was how I had ended up in this place to start with.

"I can take care of myself," I clipped. My voice sounded cold even to my own ears. His nearness made me unsettled. Outside of Talia and her family, no one had ever invaded my bubble. It wasn't that I disliked physical touch, it was more that I was unfamiliar with it. At least the gentle kind that made me want to sink into the warmth of it.

I always took care of myself. Always had, always would. He analyzed me as if he saw too much again. Ugh. What is it with this man?

My fingers curled into my palms as my hands fell into my lap.

I saw the muscles in his suntanned neck roll as he swallowed. Soren tugged on the shoulder strap to make sure it was secure across my hips. I squirmed at the tightness. I pulled my phone out to check it, desperate to focus on anything other than him. Soren turned the ignition and it hummed to life. He drove us back toward the house, stopping next to the new truck I'd seen earlier to gather a few things from the cab. He turned and held up a phone charging cord.

"This should work. We have the same phone." Did he have some freaky ability to read my mind?

He handed me the charging cord that did indeed match my phone.

"Thanks." I wrapped the extra cord around the phone, plugged it in and laid it inside the cutout area on the dash. While I was doing that, he finished collecting whatever he needed, buckled, and shifted the UTV into gear.

"You said it was north?" He nodded toward the direction I had indicated earlier.

"Yeah, I think it's about two miles, but I'm not completely sure. I tied a ribbon on the fence to mark the place."

As we were turning out of the driveway, a black Rhodes County police SUV turned in. An older man, who mirrored a dad from any 1990s sitcom with permanent dimples, stuck his head out.

"Hey, Soren. Where are ya headed?" the officer asked.

"Sawyer, this is Fulton. He's a deputy with the Rhodes County Sheriff's Department." Turning toward the deputy that I now knew was Fulton, he stated, "She said it happened a little ways north. Travis will be right behind us. You can ride with him."

We drove off when Fulton nodded. Travis pulled up behind us and waited for Fulton to load up. We rode in complete awkward silence, and I prayed that the entire search wouldn't be this way. Soren shifted and stuck his hand inside the breast pocket of his coat and withdrew a chocolate chip protein bar. He cleared his throat and held it out to me.

"This might help with your headache."

I glanced up at his face as he watched the road. Our fingers brushed as I accepted the offering.

"H-How did you know?" This was completely unexpected, and I was taken aback by his attentiveness.

He simply ran a calloused index finger between his eyebrows without his eyes leaving the road.

"You have lines here." I likely had even more lines on my face now, furrowing in confusion as I studied the side of his face and cut-glass jawline.

"Thank you," I murmured softly. He dipped his head in response.

I tore open the wrapper and took a bite because I wouldn't pass on any food right now. I wasn't sure a protein bar would help the headache pounding in my skull, but it would certainly help with how hungry I was.

"His name is Connor." I took another bite and chewed. "He's angry with me because of the outcome at court this morning. He's a good kid. He's just extremely disappointed."

"What happened at court?" He glanced in my direction.

"I can't get into the specific details, but Connor had high hopes of returning to his dad, but his dad struggles with sobriety."

Soren cursed quietly under his breath and flexed his hands on the steering wheel. I lifted my hand to point toward the ribbon when it came into view.

"There's the ribbon marker." He came to a stop, waiting on Travis and Fulton to catch up.

"Which direction did he run?"

"That way." I motioned to the left with my hand. "He had made it to that tree before I lost sight of him and left to get help. My phone doesn't have a good signal out here." Soren squinted at the tree in the distance as Travis and Fulton pulled up alongside us.

"Travis, why don't you and Fulton take the north side of the fence? We'll take the south."

The men nodded, and I spoke up. "His name is Connor. He was wearing a light-blue, thin dress sweater and khaki pants. Please have patience if you find him. He doesn't handle loud voices well. I've known Connor for years. He's a good kid that has faced a lot of disappointment."

Soren's eyes never left my face as I spoke.

"If we find him and run into issues, we'll touch base," Fulton said. "Let's regroup here in two hours if we don't find him by then. I have a couple of other deputies driving nearby roads to make sure he didn't decide to walk along the road. They are also checking with neighboring farms. If you find any tracks or anything, let us know and we'll head that way. 10-4?"

My heart sank at those words. This wasn't the same as running away in a neighborhood where witnesses could direct us to his last known location or surveillance cameras that could have tracked his path.

Soren nodded, and we took off. He pulled off into the field, and other than two trees, it was all flat pasture that melted into gentle sloping hills. The tall amber-colored grass rippled in the breeze while limestone rocks sprinkled the rolling hills, much like glitter. Connor was nowhere to be seen, and the vastness of the space was overwhelming.

I folded the wrapper of the protein bar I'd eaten and glanced around for somewhere to place it since my slacks didn't have real pockets. I reached inside the pocket of the hoodie and found paper. I pulled out a small piece of torn notebook paper to see writing scrawled in pen on one side.

2931 > 1

My eyebrows met at the odd notation as I tilted my head to study it. Anyone in their right mind would know 2931 was a greater number than one. Soren reached his large hand over swiftly and snagged it from my fingers. He shoved it into his jacket pocket and kept driving. His unexpected movement caused my heart to race.

"S-Sorry, it was in the pocket of the hoodie. I didn't mean to pry." I clasped my hands together in my lap and bit the inside of my cheek. I hoped we'd find Connor soon. Soren let out a pent up slow exhale. I couldn't tell if it was from annoyance or something else.

"I'm not used to a woman wearing my clothes. I didn't realize it was still there."

The comment made my face blush, and I immediately felt as if I was doing something much more intimate than simply wearing a borrowed hoodie for warmth.

He stopped the UTV to reach down between us into his backpack and pulled out a bottle of water.

"Here." He held the water bottle out toward me as if it were a peace offering. His hazel eyes scanned my face, and he seemed to find what he was looking for. My face flushed deeper at his intense gaze.

"Thank you." In an attempt to break the awkwardness, after taking a sip, I asked, "Should we ask someone before we trespass through private property? I mean I don't know about you, but I don't really want to get shot out here."

My question made the corner of his mouth tug in an almost smile. He began driving again following the fence line. His eyes scanned the rolling hills.

"No, we're okay. I know the owner," he said after a pause.

"Oh, I guess that's easy to do when there aren't many neighbors."

He nodded in acknowledgment. Maybe it was my crappy day, but I was feeling feisty, or as my best friend Talia would say, "spicy." I was stuck with him for who knows how long. What could it hurt to talk instead of simply sitting here worrying the whole time? I could at least see if there was a personality underneath his intense, brooding, grumpy demeanor as I searched the landscape for any sign of Connor. At this point, I might be delusional from lack of sleep, but at the very least this would help me stay more alert.

"So what do you do? Of course, ya know, when you're not helping search for a runaway child?"

He quirked an eyebrow but kept driving.

"Not search for runaway children."

Deflection. Wit. Now I was curious. His dry answer sparked my curiosity. I was up for the challenge. As the go-to person in the office for challenging teens, I could play this game. He certainly wasn't a teen, but difficult. Ding. Ding. Ding. We had a winner. I changed tactics.

"What's in the backpack?" I nudged it with my foot. "And don't tell me this is the part where you reveal that's your kill bag."

He let out a sound something between a laugh and a scoff.

"A kill bag?" He quirked a brow at me again.

"Yeah, ya know, like a bag with killer-y things." His eyes crinkled slightly.

"It's not a bag with killer-y things."

He spoke the word similar to how someone would pinch the corner of a stinky diaper, holding it far away from them as they disposed of it.

"It's a first aid kit. Emergency supplies." He supplied as if bored.

"Ahhh, Mr. Prepared! Boy Scout?"

He smirked—or at least it could have been a smirk if his mouth moved at all, other than being in a flat line.

"No." He wasn't going to give me much to work with.

We continued driving but there was no sign of Connor anywhere. The hills stretched out endlessly ahead of us. It truly was one of the most magnificent places I had ever seen. The wind tugged a piece of my hair free and I tucked it behind my ear.

"This is a beautiful place," I remarked.

He nodded. "I've always thought so."

"You must enjoy living out here."

"Yeah." He paused and added in a somber tone, "When I was a teen, I hated it, but now I couldn't imagine being anywhere else."

I had never had a home anywhere as awe-inspiring as where he lived. I couldn't imagine ever wanting to leave. Places like this always screamed "family" at the top of its lungs, and it was a call I had always wanted to answer, but as I grew older, I accepted the reality that a family wasn't in the cards for me. Although, that didn't stop the longing, even if it was similar to attempting to capture fog in my hands. Everyone who had been in my life always slipped through my fingers.

"What made you change your mind?" I asked, wanting to know more than anything, because I couldn't understand why someone would feel that way.

He paused, his gaze fixed straight ahead.

"Time. Distance. Priority changes." The air was thick with a heaviness at those four words.

"What changed your priorities?"

As soon as I had asked, I knew I had pushed too far, but I wanted to understand how his life wasn't a dream, because that's what it echoed to me.

"Do you always ask so many questions?" he grumbled.

I felt gutsy and reminded myself that I had mace, though I highly doubted I'd need it. I continued, "Do you always deflect when asked a question?"

His head snapped toward me as if he didn't expect any pushback, and he studied my face briefly before turning toward the horizon, his expression unidentifiable. Maybe if I knew him better, I could gauge the micro expressions of his face, but he had been a mystery from the moment I met him. He had an unsettling nature that felt both safe and exposing.

"I realized there was more to life than women and whiskey. I decided life had more purpose than only existing."

I softly gasped. It was the first real thing he'd said to me, and those two sentences carried the burden of a lifetime. His eyes bounced between mine.

I reached out to place a hand on his coat-covered forearm, but I stopped myself before making contact. He examined me as though I was a puzzle, and he was searching for a missing piece. I gazed out over the pasture knowing that the time for questions was over. Maybe we had grown up in different worlds, but at that moment, I knew there was something deeper to Soren than met the eye. Maybe he was more than a grump after all.

Chapter Three

Sawyer

IT HAD BEEN TWO hours, and we hadn't seen any evidence of Connor anywhere. I had mentally prepared for the two hours, although I was hopeful that we would have already found him. That I'd be on my way, with him tucked safely in the car.

My heart sank as we hit that two-hour mark. Soren drove us back to the original meeting place on the road, and I briefly contemplated how much of a weirdo this man would think I was if I reached for my chain. Instead, I bit the inside of my cheek, a habit I always resorted to in the presence of someone I didn't know that well. Soren hadn't received a call from Travis or Fulton saying they had found Connor either. When you routinely handle situations where a teen or child has runaway, you don't freak out nearly as much as someone who's never experienced it. You immediately begin working out the logistics and handling the crisis. I felt as if I was on the brink of panicking again. I knew both through training and firsthand experience that when a child's life was in complete chaos, running away was their way of asserting control. They were essentially deciding where they were, the place they lived, and who they surrounded themselves with. What made this situation different was that he had never run in such a rural area, and I worried about the elements, wild animals, and the creeks that crisscrossed the land. None of the creeks I'd seen looked especially deep. We had crossed two with the UTV and my feet had even stayed dry, but that didn't mean the water wasn't deep in other places. I tapped my fingers trying to calm my nerves. Fulton and Travis were waiting for us when we reached the road.

"Any luck?" Travis asked, his dark brows raised in expectation.

"Not a trace," Soren answered solemnly.

"We're gonna need to call in backup. I checked with the deputies patrolling and talking to neighbors, and there's been no lead there either."

Fulton looked toward the sky. "We've got a good three to three-and-a-half hours of daylight left, and that cold front is supposed to be moving in tonight. Was the kid wearing a jacket?" He turned toward me, his eyes permanently crinkled from years of smiling, although he wasn't smiling now.

"No, he left it in the car. I'm worried, he's not used to all this."

I gestured somberly toward the surrounding fields.

"We'll find him. Let's head back to the farm and fuel up again. I'll round up a few more guys and we'll keep searching," Soren said with a determined tilt to his chin, driving toward his house.

"Can I please borrow your phone, or is there somewhere I'll have steady cell service? I need to check in with my team and my friend."

I reached toward my phone that was now fully charged. My toes were cold, and all I wanted was a warm pair of socks.

"Yeah, I'll help you get connected to my Wi-Fi, and I have a landline for emergencies you can use."

Within minutes, we pulled up at his house. Fulton and Travis both went separate ways to tackle their tasks. I unbuckled, and Soren directed me toward the door. I didn't know what I was expecting his house to resemble on the inside, but it wasn't this. You could tell a lot about someone on how they kept the place they lived. It was tidy and masculine, complete with a matching set of intentionally aged leather furniture and a few wall hangings. The decor was homey in a minimal but cozy way. The colors throughout the modern farmhouse were touches of cream, copper, and navy. It appeared freshly remodeled, and everything centered around a large stone fireplace that flanked the middle of the room with a weathered wood beam mantel. The mantel held a scattering of photos and a wooden hand carved horse. A large painting in muted earth tones, depicting a field of cattle and cowboys, rested at the center of the mantel.

"Let me see your phone and I'll input the password." Soren said from my side where he had been as my eyes wandered the space.

I handed over my phone. My screensaver was a floral quote card that simply stated "You are loved." He raised an eyebrow but didn't say anything. I felt embarrassed since no one ever used my phone and saw that.

After a painfully exhausting day a couple of months ago, Talia had snagged my phone and added it, and I had never changed it. At times I needed the reminder that I was not completely alone in this world. Sometimes, loneliness felt like a dark bottomless void.

He perhaps wondered what it meant, but I didn't feel comfortable trauma dumping on someone who would essentially always be a stranger. He was good at deflection, but I was the master of it. You didn't grow up the way I did and not learn how to artfully avoid intrusive questions.

"It's locked." *Oh, good grief.*

"Oh, sorry." Our hands brushed as I typed in the passcode.

He worked quickly connecting the Wi-Fi and handed it back.

"There. That should work." He retrieved a cordless phone and handed it to me.

"Thank you."

"Bathroom is down the hall. First door on the left. I'm going to call a few people and round up some help." He walked to his kitchen counter, pulled out a barstool, and called someone on his cell.

I placed the phone on an end table and immediately headed for the bathroom. I'd needed to go for the last thirty minutes. I caught my reflection in the mirror as I washed my hands and shuddered. My cheeks were wind burned, my hair tangled with flyaways. I was a mess. I sighed at my hopeless reflection and went to call my team and Talia. The call with the team went as expected. My boss took notes, and I promised to text or call depending on the signal once he was found. I would continue to report back as there were updates. I called Talia, and she was ten minutes out. My chin trembled as tears threatened to spill over. I was bone tired. My headache had eased but was still present, and my feet tingled now that they were warming up. I immediately called the Martins, Connor's foster parents, and the Baileys, Connor's respite home for the weekend, and explained the situation. The foster family insisted on returning from their couple's trip, but I talked them into holding off for a couple of hours. I promised to update them as soon as possible. By the time they arranged transportation and arrived, hours would have passed, and hopefully, by that point, Connor would be found. The respite family had offered to come help, but they were an older couple, and between Fulton and Soren, we would have plenty of help.

As I finished the calls, I glanced up. Soren was studying me as he talked to someone on his cell about joining the search. His free hand fidgeted, flipping a coin across his knuckles. He finished his call, pocketed the coin, and he walked toward where I was in the family room.

"Travis is refueling the UTVs. Fulton called in two off-duty deputies and five volunteer first responders, and I have six local guys with their own UTVs headed this way. Everyone will be here within twenty minutes. Then we'll head back out."

He delivered this information while he did that thing, as if he was taking inventory of my exhausted state. His intense hazel eyes appeared more green-gray than amber in the interior lighting. It was unnerving, but there was something about him that told me, on a deeper level, that he approached everything in life with this intensity, like he lived his life with consuming intention.

"Thank you. I'm really sorry. I knew he was upset, I just didn't realize how much. This is my fault," I stated.

I raised my eyes to meet his. I was sure the exhaustion was evident on my face.

"My friend Talia will be here any minute. She's bringing me a change of clothes and boots."

I bit my lip, unsure of what else to say, and willed my tears not to spill over. I never cried, except for when I was tired, and I was beyond tired. He cleared his throat. Of course, I was making him uncomfortable. I was making myself uncomfortable. But exhaustion was exhaustion, and my body was turning on me. I blinked rapidly in an attempt to dispel the tears.

"I don't think you're the type of person that someone would run from." His words were quiet but left me questioning what he truly meant.

A moment later, his phone rang, and the awkwardness lessened. At least for now.

Chapter Four

Soren

WHAT THE HELL WAS wrong with me? You would think I had never talked to a woman in my life. And yeah, it'd been a solid eight years since I'd been on a date, but hell. I ran a hand down my face as I listened to Lane talk while he loaded up his UTV on his trailer.

I certainly wasn't in the market to date, but I wanted to think I still had a little game. Lane would say I suffered from "awkward as hell-ness" for the last few years, and on this one count, I might have to say the bonehead was right. That awkwardness may or may not have made me act like a complete jackass when I was unsure of what was going on. It wasn't every day you walked up from feeding cattle and there was a beautiful stranger sitting on your porch steps. At least not out here in the middle of rural Kansas. Well, there was that one time that made today feel like déjà vu, but I couldn't dredge into the past right now. I'd leave the women to Lane. The last time a woman sat on my porch in exactly the same way, my life was blasted to pieces. She had dropped a bomb that initiated the second hardest day of my life. Deep breath. I needed to focus, but this woman was entirely too attractive. I needed to help her find this child so she could be on her way, and I could go back to my purposefully female-free life. I was pretty sure I'd scared the hell out of her earlier, and I wanted to go back to square one and not act like an asshole. Something about her told me she was used to assholery, and I didn't want to be another jerk she had to deal with. I saw her fingers tapping like I'd seen Jonah do on more than one occasion. I knew I'd screwed up and my gut sank at the thought that I had caused that reaction. I was a safe person, but because of the way I'd acted, she didn't know that. Something about her threw me off-kilter and instead of pausing as I knew to do, I reacted. I made the decision that I'd try to do better. Today was a rough day, but that wasn't her fault. Abruptly, a knock sounded on the door. I walked toward the entrance with Sawyer in tow. Her faint delicate perfume that smelled of strawberries and cream wafting toward me at her nearness. A woman stood on the other side of the door and lit up like a Christmas tree when her eyes landed on Sawyer.

"Hey, darlin'." She made an exaggerated sad face, her bubblegum pink lips turning down as she pulled Sawyer into a fierce embrace. She rocked Sawyer from side to side in an exaggerated hug. Everything about this woman screamed loud. Extra loud. Neon loud.

Sawyer made introductions, and I shut the door once Talia was inside.

I'd never seen a more opposite coupling of friends. Her friend was at least five foot eleven, with black, curly hair and brown eyes that danced with amusement. She was larger than life with her neon pink blouse, black leather skinny jeans, and sunshine yellow hoop earrings and matching shoes. Her nails were painted the same color as her lips. Everything about her screamed loud and bold, while everything about Sawyer whispered quiet and soft.

Sawyer turned around, and a wetness covered her pale blue eyes. I scrubbed a hand across my sternum. I hated tears; I never knew what to say. Thankfully, she took the bag off of Talia's shoulder and quietly padded to the bathroom to change. Talia sashayed deeper into the family room and narrowed her eyes as she gave me a once over. She didn't hide the fact she was sizing me up. Her gaze made me think of my days in Coach Walder's class in school. Coach Walder had a reputation of being able to scare the devil straight out of you. Lane was still terrified of her. I'd witnessed all six feet three inches of the man duck under a booth table at Ronnie's Diner to avoid her. Talia had the appearance of friendliness, but there was no mistaking her protectiveness toward Sawyer.

"You live here?" Talia clarified as she waved one brightly painted nail in a circular pattern. She walked around the family room, scrutinizing an item here and there. She was one of those people that naturally walked into a place with self-possession, as though they owned it. It wasn't pretentious or haughty, but more of a self-assurance she carried. The more I observed her, the more I realized she and Lane would have a lot in common.

"Yes."

"Hmmm . . . " she hummed as she surveyed a photo of me and my best friends, Jonah and Lane, who were more my brothers than friends. We'd known each other since elementary school and played football and baseball together.

"Single?" She raised a brow at me, clearly prepared for an inquisition.

"Uhhh yeah." I wasn't a man that blushed, but her directness caused my neck to heat.

"Sawyer is a single Pringle too."

Her bluntness caused me to chuckle. In what world was someone like Sawyer walking around single? I ran my hand down my five o'clock shadow. Talia lightly ran a finger along the back of a hand-carved wooden horse on my mantel.

"Have you ever met someone who is too good for this world?"

As soon as she spoke the words, his face filled my mind. My throat was dry. My stomach tightened. There was no way she knew. She was only asking a question. I released a pent up breath.

"Yes, I have."

My throat tightened and my voice sounded hoarse to my own ears. She turned and stared me directly in the eyes.

"That's Sawyer."

"What's Sawyer?"

I heard the soft voice to my left. Sawyer had changed into light wash denim jeans, a thick cream sweater, and sable cowgirl boots pulled up over her jeans. A jacket was folded over her arm. She was breathtakingly beautiful. But the thing that stopped my breath was the wavy, hip-length hair the color of wheat harvested in summer flowing over her shoulders. She was more relaxed, and the color of her hair brought out the freckles that dusted her nose and upper cheeks. Her eyes were a striking blend of light blues that resembled shattered sea glass. They were eyes that stopped men cold in their tracks. Eyes that haunted you long after you caught a glimpse of them.

"Only that you're the best friend a gal could ask for," Talia replied cheekily, winking at me as she added, "Let me braid your hair."

Instead of torturing myself thinking about running my fingers through her hair, I texted Lane and Jonah and got an ETA. Within a couple of minutes, Sawyer's hair was in a thick braid down her back, with a few soft wisps that had escaped brushing her cheeks. I had to keep myself busy so I didn't gawk like a high schooler while Talia expertly twisted the golden mass of waves into order. If there was anything I knew, it was that Sawyer was without a doubt the most beautiful woman I'd ever laid eyes on. I also knew it had been over eight years since I'd made that gamble, and I didn't plan on rolling the dice any time soon.

Ten minutes later, we had a crew of about thirty people ready to search for Connor. After a tight hug from Sawyer, Talia left to pick up her daughter. Lane and Jonah brought their UTVs, along with five local farmers. Travis headed to do all the evening chores of feeding cattle, which had to be done regardless of the crisis at hand. Gene began feeding after he'd made it back from town, but, between checking all the pastures, it was a two man job. Particularly because I had stopped partway through chores earlier when I found Sawyer.

Everyone gathered around my front porch steps, Sawyer and Fulton standing partway down the stairs on either side of me. I gave directives of areas we had already covered. The locals nodded, being almost as familiar with the area as I was. Many of them were lifelong residents who had been here for three or four generations. This part of Kansas had a heavy population of German and Irish settlers who had traveled to the area in hopes of worthwhile farming. Many of those farms were still in operation, having been passed down through generations. Some of the older generations still spoke German in addition to English, which caused their English to have a slight Germanic accent.

After assigning areas to search, Fulton set forth a plan to make contact again in two hours if we hadn't found Connor by then. Additional law enforcement agencies would be called in, along with search and rescue dogs. Two officers would continue to patrol sections of land, searching for clues and questioning locals to see if anyone had spotted Connor walking down the road.

I turned to Sawyer at my side and quietly asked, "Anything you want to add?" Her shattered blue eyes met mine, and she gave a small nod.

Once Fulton was done giving instructions, I cut in. "This is Sawyer." I nodded to her. "She knows Connor."

"Hi. I just wanted to add that I really appreciate you coming out to help. Connor is truly a sweet kid, but he's just dealing with some disappointment right now. Also, to reiterate, he's wearing a light blue sweater and khaki dress pants." She expelled a deep breath, turned toward me, and inclined her head.

"All right. Everyone follow me and Fulton, and we'll split up at the marker," I called out, turning to Sawyer.

"You're with me."

I wasn't about to let anyone spend time in her light. Call me selfish, but I wanted her warmth all to myself. There was something about her I couldn't put my finger on, but I didn't have time to wonder. A lost little boy needed to be found, and the temperature drop tonight was becoming more concerning. A small child couldn't survive in twenty-nine degree weather without a jacket, without the risk of injury or more. As we neared the UTV, I gave her back my hoodie in case she needed it. Her brows met.

"In case you get cold, or we need it for Connor."

Because I want my hoodie on you. What was wrong with me? I had barely met this woman and she was already under my skin. I didn't have time for a relationship, and my last not-relationship had nearly cost me everything. The entire town was witness to that destruction, and I blamed myself for my parents leaving soon after that. They had expressed a desire to retire from farming and travel the country in their RV. Although, sometimes I wondered if it was to keep their distance from me and my ruin. Sure, they loved me and encouraged me from a distance, but all I had ever done was cause them grief and shame. I couldn't blame anyone for keeping their distance, because I devastated the things I loved. How could I pursue a woman if it always ended in ruin?

Chapter Five

Sawyer

THE VOLUNTEERS DISPERSED AND were driving into the field toward where Connor had run. We had already covered this area, but maybe with more eyes, we'd see something we had missed. But what if—

"Wait!" I blurted.

Soren turned toward me, his eyebrows raised in surprise.

"What if he doubled back and ran into the fields on the other side of the road?" Soren paused, his eyes scanning the area.

"It's worth checking out."

We headed off in that direction after he radioed the other searchers and gave them a heads-up. The fact that he had accepted my ideas so easily made me pause. It felt good. Growing up, I had learned that speaking up often led to consequences I didn't want to pay. Those ingrained responses often kept me from speaking my mind unless I was truly comfortable with someone. We rode an hour in silence, only making noise to call out Connor's name. The clock ticked away as the threat of darkness got closer and closer. I didn't talk, the tension of concern for Connor weighing heavily on my mind. This was beginning to seem more and more scary by the moment. I ran my hands down my jean-clad thighs. Soren looked toward me at the movement.

"I won't stop until we find him."

His voice was firm and confident, and somehow, I knew with complete certainty he was telling me the truth. He continued driving by a creek bank that twisted and curved like a ribbon. We paused from time to time when he'd lean over the side and scan the muddy bank. He never indicated why but simply continued along the path. We continued to call out, hoping that Connor could hear us over the wind that howled more fiercely as the cold front moved in. I tucked my hands beneath Soren's hoodie that was acting as a blanket over my legs.

Further down the creek, Soren slowed down and extended his long muscular arm, pointing toward a small figure in the distance. Connor was huddled against a tree near the edge of the creek, his legs pulled up to his chin and his head laid across his knees. I took a deep breath for what felt like the first time in hours. The sound of the UTV must have registered, because his head shot up and his red, teary eyes widened. Soren drove us the rest of the distance until we pulled up alongside his huddled body. Connor's stance spoke of defeat and his stormy eyes met mine. Soren killed the engine but didn't move, and I slowly climbed off the UTV, clutching the hoodie in my hands.

"Connor. Would you like to put this hoodie on?"

I held it out as a peace offering, trying to get a read on his mood and anticipate possible movements. Would he come willingly with us, or would this be a struggle? He immediately took the hoodie from my outstretched hand and shimmied into it. It nearly came to his ankles. His own sweater had been pulled down to cover his red fingers from the cold. To my side, I saw Soren texting on his phone, most likely informing the others Connor had been located. My heart finally slowed until it was beating normally. Connor took a choppy gasp. His cheeks were reddened from windburn and the chill in the air. Scanning his body, I didn't see anything out of place other than his eyes that were red from crying, a few mud smears, and minor scratches here and there.

"I shouldn't have run away." The defeat was evident in his shaky voice.

He peered up once more. I paused. I wanted to tell him everything would be okay, but in reality, he took a risk today and could have been injured or worse.

"It wasn't a safe choice because you could have been hurt, but I understand that you were disappointed. I was worried about you," I offered softly.

"I just want my dad back."

His words caught on a sob, and his face crumbled as he buried it in his arm, now covered in the thick, way-too-big hoodie. I heard Soren shift in his seat, clearly uncomfortable about standing back. I could sense his struggle in not helping. In the little time I'd been around him, I could tell he was a 'take charge' kind of man. I edged closer to Connor, hoping to bring comfort. I wanted to wrap him in my arms and tell him everything would be okay, but I knew better than most that sometimes everything wasn't okay. I also knew sometimes physical touch was not the answer—or was even welcomed. I knelt beside him.

"Would you like a hug, Connor?"

"Uh-huh," he mumbled as he dove for me.

I wrapped my arms around his shoulders as his little arms, encased in the hoodie, wrapped around me, and he buried his face in my shoulder.

It was hard to make out his words through the tears, but his next sentence rattled the center of my soul.

"I just want to be like other kids."

I sniffed against the chill and held him close. I knew that feeling. I knew it better than I knew my own name. I still experienced it, except now I was an adult in a world that was built for "other" adults. Adults without the daily modifications from being a kid that fell through the cracks. Adults without bizarre and broken idiosyncrasies like me. I was closely acquainted with the emotions of "other."

They say kids are resilient, but are they really when they grow up to be adults who need therapy to unpack things that happened decades ago? Things that had been swept under the rug of resilience.

"I understand," I said softly.

I wanted to tell Connor I knew exactly how he felt, but the audience of Soren made me hesitant and unsure. I debated how much was too much to share with a nine-year-old. If there was anything I could do to make him feel less alone in this world, I knew I should. I strived daily to be the adult I wished I'd had as a child, and that adult would have helped regardless of who was onlooking. His incredulous eyes found mine.

"When I say I understand, Connor, it's because I really do. I grew up being moved a lot, and it sucked, but you will have better days. I promise." I held out my pinky for a pinky promise, because we had made others before. His small pinky linked with mine.

I would not tell him how few better days I had until I was an adult, but Connor was one of *my* kids. I was determined he'd never set foot into some of the sickening homes I had. I wasn't going to let him see that side of things. The side that destroyed me from the inside out. The side that made me incomplete as an adult.

I could hear Soren shift again in his seat behind me, as if the band that restrained him was about to snap with action. I appreciated that he wanted to do something when he saw that something was wrong. The world needed more people like him. People that would be moved with compassion to do something. Connor wiped at his eyes.

"You were a foster kid?" Connor asked in disbelief. I paused.

"Yes, I was."

The heat of Soren's eyes burned on my back. I usually never vocalized anything personal, because nothing made me recognize my differences more than talking about my hell of a childhood. Connor looked at me before promising, "I'm sorry. I won't run away again."

I patted his shoulder and guided him toward the UTV. Only time would tell if he'd keep his word, but until then, I'd do everything in my power to help him have the best childhood possible.

"Lane will be here in a minute, then we can ride back to my place," Soren instructed.

I couldn't meet his eyes right now. Not when I'd laid my soul excruciatingly bare for someone I'd just met.

Soren stood and gestured to his seat, where I could sit while Connor took mine. Soren pulled a pack of Skittles from his backpack and tossed them to Connor.

"Hey, dude. I'm Soren." Connor's eyes met Soren, and he gave a small smile.

"Thank you!" Connor ripped open the bag and made quick work of the candy.

I scrubbed my hands down my face. Equally tired and relieved. The telltale signs of coming down from an adrenaline rush. Soren grasped his hand on my shoulder and gave it a gentle squeeze. Like Connor, I wished I was normal. Because instead of seeing it as an innocent comforting gesture, it surprised me and made me involuntarily flinch. Embarrassment made my face crimson. Soren removed his hand as gently as he had placed it and leaned down to search my face, meeting my eyes.

I didn't know him well enough to explain. I wanted to tell him that I appreciated the gesture, but that sometimes my body and brain couldn't agree on how to respond to things that startled me. Once I had time to reflect and take a moment for my racing heart to settle, I realized I was pushing away the very things I wanted most. Sometimes being completely wrapped up in a hug by someone I trusted sounded like the best thing that could ever exist in this world. Talia had long since ignored my immediate responses to things like hugs. I hardly ever had those involuntary physical reactions to her anymore, because she made it her business to hug me often and fiercely. It was as if my body and brain had realized that she was safe. She always said I could consider her my personal hug machine. I would always laugh, and she'd always squeeze me tighter. I did something brave and placed my hand on his forearm.

His brow was quizzical, and the heat from his body bled through the thick canvas of his coat.

"Thank you. I couldn't have found him without you."

His mouth tugged at one corner and he nodded. He wasn't quite smiling but his gaze was warm. Swiftly, someone who I was assuming was Lane crested the hill behind us and came riding up. He was oddly familiar as though I'd seen him before but it was potentially from the meeting earlier at Soren's house. He was tall, athletically lean, and could be a cover model, with sandy blond hair and emerald eyes. After introductions, Connor buckled in on Lane's UTV, and we headed back toward Soren's house. The volunteers dispersed after I thanked each one. Medics examined Connor as I made several calls to the office, the Martins, the Baileys, and a quick text to Talia. The Baileys lived twenty minutes away and insisted on coming to pick up Connor to make the transition as easy as possible for him. They were truly some of the kindest people I had ever known. If I had ever had grandparents, I would have wanted someone like them. Mrs. Bailey was an avid gardener and baker, always sending me away with fresh baked goods anytime I transported kids to or from their home. I had even gotten her to share her delicious apple pie recipe. I hugged Connor once more, and he apologized to Soren who was more than gracious, even though I knew that monopolizing his afternoon had messed up his day. I waved at the Baileys and Connor as they pulled away.

Soren stood beside me, and I turned, saying, "I'll be out of your hair now. Thank you again, and I hope the rest of your day is far less eventful." A small smile tugged at my lips.

"Yeah." He drew out the word and rubbed the back of his neck before his hazel eyes found mine. "Sawyer, I live my life with a 'no regrets' approach. I'd kick my own butt if I didn't ask. There's not anyone hurting you right? You're safe?" My breath caught. My eyes widened and my cheeks heated as I realized he was referencing touching my shoulder earlier. I felt like a complete freak, but I was also strangely comforted that he was the type of man that would ask and not turn a blind eye.

"Not anymore." I shared too much but also thought this sincere question deserved a truthful answer.

"Okay." He nodded his head slowly, his eyes locked with mine, assessing and seeing too much.

"I should get going . . . "

I hitched a thumb toward the car, having already collected all of my things. I didn't know why, but part of me wanted to stay. That familiar sensation hit me again as if I'd been here before, but I pushed it aside because the exhaustion was creeping in again.

"Is someone coming to get you? You must be exhausted," he asked.

"No, I live about forty-five minutes away so I'll be home soon."

"You can't drive this tired." His brow lowered, and the hard lines from earlier found his face again.

"I don't have a choice," I rebuffed.

"Let me drive you home. Lane or Jonah can follow and bring me back."

"No," I clipped. My pride prevented me from burdening this man with one more thing today. "No, you've done enough," I reasoned.

His face darkened and something resembling a growl escaped him.

"Give me your phone." He held his hand out expectantly as if I'd simply obey. I furrowed my eyebrows. "Please." That without question was a growl.

"You're not my keeper." My hands found my hips. I normally had a hard time standing up for myself, but there was something about him that made me want to be braver than I typically was.

"Give me the phone or I'm following you all the way home to make sure you get there safely." He tilted his head in challenge.

I squinted my eyes because even in the short time I'd been around him, I knew enough to know he would. Jerk. I handed over my unlocked phone, albeit as slowly as possible. I couldn't see what he was doing, but he scrolled a few seconds then held the phone to his ear. What?! Who was he calling? I reached for my phone and he shifted away.

"Hey!" I shrieked. At this point, I was an ankle-biter dog trying to scale this mountain of a man—avoiding contact but still reaching for my phone.

"Hey, Talia. It's Soren from earlier." Oh, good grief! He paused as if he were listening.

"Oh, yeah. She's fine, but she's being stubborn. Hey, since she won't let me drive her home, do you think you could talk to her on the drive home to make sure she doesn't fall asleep?" Now I growled. Ugh. Double jerk. Soren smiled a deeply satisfied smile as he paused and listened, as if he chatted with my best friend all the time.

He flicked an amused glance at my grabby hands and shifted away. His eyes sparkled with delight. His smile temporarily stunned me into silence. He was entirely handsome.

"Mmm-hmm. She does like her questions," he responded cheekily.

"Yeah, she's looking sorta . . . grumpy," he remarked with a smirk, making a show of looking me up and down like he was assessing my behavior. I crossed my arms across my chest.

Talia must be chatting away because he smiled, nodded, and remarked with affirmatives occasionally.

"Yep. Sounds good. Here she is."

He held out the phone and passed it to me. I swiped it up as fast as possible.

"Here ya go, Pretty Girl. Drive safe."

Soren winked at me, a smirk on his lips as he inclined his head and confidently walked away toward his porch. He watched me connect my phone to the car, buckle, and drive away. He raised a hand like he was the cowboy king of front porches, and he'd done me a favor by contacting my friend. I pushed aside the feeling that I liked how concerned he was about me driving home safely.

Chapter Six

Sawyer

AFTER FALLING INTO BED with my clothes still on, I slept for a solid twelve hours Thursday night. On Friday, I baked while watching multiple YouTube videos on how to stop your toilet from constantly sounding like there was running water in the tank. I still wasn't sure if I had figured that out, and I hated to bother the landlord if it was something I could figure out myself. It was one of those things that I could ask Talia about, but she and her husband Rob already did too much for me. Later in the day, I went for a run and read a few chapters of a middle grade book

I was buddy reading with one of my pre-teens. By Saturday morning, I was a brand new woman, refreshed from having a day that wasn't complete chaos. I had baked dozens of oatmeal butterscotch cookies as a thank you to Soren, Officer Fulton, and the volunteers, along with a chocolate chip cookie dough cheesecake for Talia.

Baking was comforting to me. It forced me to think about something unimportant and allowed my mind to take a break. I liked the certainty of measuring ingredients to produce a desired outcome. Baking was so much easier than people. If only I could apply the same goals to situations and get the desired outcome every time. I planned to deliver the cheesecake to Talia, take some cookies to the sheriff's office, and then drop some off at Soren's house. It was presumptuous, especially since I didn't have his contact information to ask if it was okay. Although, after wrecking almost his entire day on Thursday, I thought cookies were a nice gesture to say thank you for his help. Mrs. Bailey had called on Friday to say that Connor was in better spirits and had been building a wooden birdhouse with Mr. Bailey.

Once the fog of extreme exhaustion had cleared, I couldn't stop thinking about how familiar everything seemed in that part of Rhodes County, especially in the town of Kennedy. I had visited the Bailey's house multiple times to transport children, but never from the direction I drove on Thursday. I had no recollection of having ever visited the picturesque small town of Kennedy, but there was something about it. After I dropped off the cookies and expressed my appreciation, I wanted to drive around and see if any memories surfaced. It was like a splinter in my memory, and I couldn't stop thinking about it because it all struck me as being just out of reach. But first I needed a shower, because after the hot mess I was on Thursday, I wanted to look nice when I dropped those cookies off. By 9 a.m., I was freshly showered, with my hair down in soft waves. I spent entirely too much time on a face of makeup that was purposefully meant to appear as though I wasn't wearing any. According to the videos I watched online, it was the go-to makeup application technique. I completed the outfit with thick black leggings and an oversized chambray shirt rolled up at the elbows that covered my bum. I pulled on light brown knee-high boots and added a pair of small, star-shaped gold studs. My chain always stayed beneath my shirt, so there was never a need to try to match metals. Although, according to my ever-present online research, metals could be mixed. I just didn't understand the rules of when it worked and when it didn't. As with all things I didn't fully understand, I avoided even attempting it.

After I placed the cookies and cheesecake into containers, I drove over to Talia's. She was returning to her porch after a jog, pushing her athletic stroller that held her daughter, Ava. She swiped an arm over her glistening forehead and chugged a few sips of water. Today's ensemble was cobalt blue yoga pants with a cheetah print crewneck that had cobalt blue seams that matched her pants. She smiled brightly, eagerly waving me over.

"I had to get a slog in because I knew you were bringing my weakness over!" She called out with a laugh as I walked up. I smiled at her excitement and her use of the word slog. It was her way of saying slow jog.

"I tweaked the topping a little. Let me know what you think once you have a chance to try it." I peeked in the stroller and saw Ava, her eighteen-month-old, fast asleep. Her thick black lashes rested on her round cheeks.

"Sure thing! Everything you make is always good."

We walked toward the front steps of her light gray, Craftsman-style home, and Talia took the cheesecake inside to the kitchen. I stood with the stroller outside and brushed my finger across Ava's soft forehead as I tucked a stuffed animal frog beside her. Talia would say she had plenty of toys, but I always retorted that this sweet girl could never be spoiled too much. Ava was too young to know it now, but she had seriously lucked out in the parent department. Talia wasn't sunshine, she was the sun, and her husband, Rob, was head over heels in love with her. Talia owned a therapy practice where she worked three days a week, spending the rest of her time with Ava. Rob was the local Assistant District Attorney. Their love was a once-in-a-lifetime kind of love, and I knew whatever they faced, they'd face it together. To say Ava had the best parents in the world was an understatement. She'd never have the childhood worries I had, and no matter what, I'd be there for her. Talia was already trying to teach her to say Auntie Sawyer, which came out as a jumble of too many A's and S's. It was adorable. I'd always be Ava's cheerleader, and she had years of spoiling ahead.

When Talia returned, we settled on the porch steps that were lined with potted plants, and Talia did what Talia does best and read me like a book.

"*Soo* . . . you're going to see that hot cowboy again? You look cute by the way." She winked and nudged my shoulder with hers. Subtlety was not her strong suit. I rolled my eyes.

"I mean, if he's there, but only to say thank you. You remember how I was saying something felt familiar about the area?"

"Yeah." She said while taking another sip of water.

"Well . . . I can't shake that feeling. It's like I lived nearby or something. It's strange but familiar." I tilted my head back. "Ugh. It's so frustrating sometimes piecing my childhood together, but you know how sometimes I'll have bad reactions about places and not be able to explain why?"

She nodded, and I continued.

"There's something about the town of Kennedy and that part of Rhodes County. Something big happened there, but I don't remember what. I don't necessarily have a bad or good vibe, but more like it's something substantial. I don't know." I shook my head. "I'm hoping that something clicks today. Sometimes . . . I wonder if the things I find or remember are things I should be happy I forgot." I rubbed the thumbnail of one hand against the palm of my other. Talia reached out and placed her soft hand on mine to still my fidgeting.

"Your childhood was a battlefield. It's understandable you spent most of it in survival mode, Sawyer. Do you need me to go with you? I'm off today. I'll go if you need me." She was the best friend a girl could ever hope for.

"No, I'll be okay. I'm going to drop off the cookies and drive around the area to see if anything comes to me." I leaned my head on her shoulder, and she rested her cheek on my head.

"Forever friends," she promised, and I echoed the same.

This was something we established our freshman year of college. I was the youngest in my class, having completed college classes while also attending high school. I was completely overwhelmed by the atmosphere of the college life experience. The people were loud, and I was almost always trying to avoid guys. For the first time in my life, I had structure and complete freedom at the same time. Talia found me lost on the first day of classes and quickly deemed that we were destined to be forever friends. She didn't know until almost a year afterward how much those words meant to me. After a hard test one day, I had crumbled, and I couldn't hide my broken childhood from her anymore. I explained my quirks as best as I understood them. My over-the-top organization, my reaction to people touching me, my discomfort in loud places, and the reasons I avoided all men—despite their attractiveness or my desire to have a family. Talia declared that my life story reminded her of a Lifetime movie where you wondered how many bad things could happen repeatedly to one person.

She admitted one night that she had never contemplated how adults that grew up in foster care, or kids from difficult backgrounds, might have lingering effects, or how simply becoming an adult didn't miraculously fix years of trauma. It was then that she had changed her major to become a therapist specializing in childhood trauma. Her parents were furious that she left the path to law school, but she was determined to make a difference in another way. Talia knew that my focus in social work was my way of preventing the childhood I had from happening to more children. A childhood where adults turned a blind eye to the atrocities that happened to me. Where they willingly stood by while I endured unthinkable things. The foster parents always said the right things, and I had appeared fed and was clothed, so they would check the right boxes and let things be. I hit some extremely dark places in my teenage years, but the kindness of a small handful of individuals throughout my childhood provided the light I needed to keep moving forward, one step at a time. I knew the statistics I faced, and I had refused to fall victim to the traumas of my childhood. I would graduate from high school. I would complete college. I would not repeat the patterns of abuse and cruelty I had endured. Everything was going to stop with me. Talia took the time to befriend my misunderstood college self, and I was forever grateful when she became my friend.

We caught up for a few more minutes before I kissed sweet Ava's forehead while Talia sent me off with a laugh about seeing a hot cowboy.

Chapter Seven

Sawyer

AFTER DROPPING OFF THE oatmeal butterscotch cookies at the Rhodes County sheriff's office, I pulled in and parked at Soren's house. I had noticed the tire swing hanging from a nearby tree on Thursday. It twirled in the breeze, a signal of a happy childhood. I had always thought tire swings looked like fun, but it wasn't one of those things you could find at a city park. That familiar sensation washed over me again. I knew I had never lived anywhere as cozy as Soren's house and especially not here. This place was nearly heaven on earth from the wraparound porch and large white barn to the rolling hills surrounding it. The porch swing was painted the perfect shade of sunshine yellow. There were even fluffy white clouds above. It was perfect. I clutched the container of cookies in my hands and walked toward the swing. It was a beacon, and I was a ship lost at sea. I shifted the container in my arms, along with Soren's freshly washed hoodie and reached to touch the rubber tire. I gave it a small push. It swayed, and I backed out of the way to watch it, mesmerized by the motion. If I had a suitable tree in my tiny duplex yard, I would watch a YouTube video on how to build a tire swing. It seemed incredibly fun, and before I knew it, I pushed the tire again, completely lost in this delayed childhood fascination.

"You always make a habit of trespassing on other people's property?" a loud voice called out behind me and I jerked in surprise. I spun around taking an involuntary step back as the tire knocked into my shoulder, and I dropped the container of cookies and hoodie on the ground.

I saw Soren walking from the barn as he slapped a pair of leather gloves against one of his thick thighs, dust flying from the action. He somehow appeared more handsome than I remembered. He wore a long-sleeve chambray shirt tucked into jeans that hugged his solid, muscular body, and a ball cap. I hurriedly reached to scoop up the hoodie and the cookie container (that thankfully had stayed closed) before he reached me. He stopped in front of me with that same intensity that felt borderline too much, and he was wearing that intimidating expression on his face again. I held out the large Tupperware container of cookies as a peace offering. He looked me over and I was unsure about my choice of returning at all. Was this weird? I knew sometimes social cues were lost on me because my brain was constantly assessing my surroundings.

Maybe the cookies were too much. Why didn't Talia tell me the cookies were too much? I shouldn't have come.

"Uhh . . . I brought a 'thank you' for your help, and here's your hoodie back." My hand shook with nerves.

He didn't reach for the cookies, but his eyes roved my face as if searching for something. He was intense again. Not the playful man I left on Thursday. It was as though we were starting from scratch all over again. I shouldn't have come. I was a fool for taking the effort to appear extra nice. After a moment his hand brushed mine as he took the container from me. The hoodie was folded over my arm and I reached to extend that also. He flicked a glance at it as though it would give him germs.

"Keep it." He nodded toward the hoodie.

I swallowed, unsure of what to say. Of course he didn't want the hoodie back after I had worn it, but it was freshly washed so why wouldn't he? I enjoyed the idea of keeping it too much to protest.

"Okay. Well, umm, you can keep the container. I wanted to bring those to say thank you." I gave a small forced smile because the awkwardness was suffocating. I turned to go, making my way to my Jeep when I heard his gravelly voice.

"Sawyer." I turned.

"Thanks for the cookies."

He lifted the container. I nodded and loaded up in my Jeep. He watched me leave, and I was relieved to be out of there. Disappointed didn't begin to describe my thoughts, but I wasn't exactly sure why. There was something interesting about him that intrigued me, but at the same time, I was wary. I didn't expect things to be quite so awkward. He didn't scare me as much as my lack of experience around men made me apprehensive. I was completely ignorant. Ignorant wasn't exactly the right word because I was experienced in a lot of things, but not anything I wanted experience in. As the gravel crunched under my tires, I racked my brain concerning that familiar intuition I kept having. My hand subconsciously pulled my chain out of my shirt, and I ran my left thumb repeatedly over the raised words. I turned on a gravel road that led toward the closest town, Kennedy, Kansas. What was it that felt familiar exactly? At first, I thought maybe it was Soren, but I dismissed that. I remember having the sensation before I ever made it to his house. I drove around for a solid twenty minutes, hoping for an inkling of a memory, and in a town the size of Kennedy, Kansas, I had seen everything twice. The town was a combination of old historic limestone buildings that were untouched and a few that appeared painstakingly restored. You could tell the community took pride in their small town. It had that charming, rustic modern overtone that made it contemporary but cozy. The town centered on a square of land that housed the city park that hosted flower beds and colorful birdhouses. There were shade trees and benches along with a wooden play structure that gave the impression it had been there for at least a couple of decades. A trail for walking or running wove throughout it all. The city block was framed by local shops such as a library, hardware store, diner, bakery and a farm store along with several other local businesses. Around the block were lamp posts with hooks that held overflowing hanging baskets of flowers. This was the kind of small town where people dreamed of living. How could I have forgotten a place like this? I was in the middle of Main Street when it hit me. Abel. I slammed on my brakes without warning and a car honked from behind me.

"Sorry!" I called as if they could hear me as I sped up again.

This had to be where Abel lived. I pulled into a parking spot in front of the coffee shop and bakery that boasted of having the best pie and bierocks this side of the Mississippi, a claim that I would normally be very interested in testing out. "Spill the Tea" was painted on the large glass pane window in front, along with drawings of bakery desserts.

I immediately grabbed my cell, connected to the free Wi-Fi, and searched "Abel Kennedy, KS." It had been years since I'd known him, so I couldn't remember his last name.

When that yielded nothing. I reached for my chain, which, in reality, were military tags around my neck. Abel had given them to me, saying they were his Grandpa's. There was a chance it was his paternal grandpa. The last name on the tags read *Roberts*. I edited the text in the search bar to say "Abel Roberts Kennedy, KS."

I was giddy with excitement at the possibility of reconnecting with my childhood friend. Abel was one of those people that was a light in my childhood.

We had ridden on the bus together, and one day after I was bullied by another student, he had invited me to sit by him. From there on out we were inseparable. I remembered him being a boy that loved sports but had a soft heart toward new kids like me. I was in a particularly horrific foster home at the time. Abel had given me his grandpa's military identification tags because he said they'd make me brave given that he believed they made his grandpa brave. It was his kindness in the end that had helped me tell someone what was happening to me. This became the thing I cherished most after that and was the only sentimental item that made it through my entire childhood, becoming my touchstone when anxiety and panic threatened.

The search engine finally stopped spinning, and I felt every ounce of air evacuate my body at the first result. It was the image of a headstone from a website that helped individuals with genealogy research. What? The sensation of pin pricks rushed down my body as if I was doused in frigid water. This couldn't be right. Tears pricked my eyes and my nose stung. This couldn't be. Not Abel. I clicked the link with a shaking hand, determined to find that it had to be an error. A full photo of the headstone appeared along with the location of where to find it. My heartbeat raced as I worked to slow my intakes of air. There had to be an error. The headstone photo became more blurry as I zoomed in, pixelated to the point I couldn't make out the small oval photo inset on the headstone. I blinked away my tears and input the cemetery address. I had to see it for myself. This couldn't be. The cemetery was about five minutes away back toward the gravel road I had come from. I made it there in record time. There were about three dozen headstones scattered about, and the gate was open. A large oak tree sat in the corner, barely outside the fence, while the grass inside the cemetery was cut short. I clutched my phone as I climbed out of my Jeep, scanning for a headstone that matched the screenshot I had taken since I suspected I might lose cell service again. There were several headstones off to the side near the tree. There was one near the corner that resembled the one in the photo. It was taller and thinner than the others and came to a point at the top. I circled the stone and engraved in a bold font was the name.

Abel Griffin Roberts

The small portrait photo resembled an older version of the kid I had known. According to the dates, he was seventeen when he died. My fingertips traced his name carved in the cold stone.

NO! No, this couldn't be right.

A sob overtook my body as memories and emotions rushed in with the force of a tsunami. How could this be? I crumbled against the headstone, willing memories of my time here to stop. I rested my back against the corner of the cold stone and pulled the chain over my head, cradling it in my hands. Tears flooded down my cheeks and trickled down my jaw. Abel was the only person I had ever considered a real friend growing up. We were seven or eight years old when I lived outside of the town of Kennedy and attended the same school as Abel. Abel's friendship profoundly impacted me, most likely because of my erratic childhood. My mind was working overtime to unscramble the flashes of memories in my head. Sweet memories and horrific ones jumbled together. I think I had been placed in this town for the spring semester of my second-grade year. That summer, I was removed from the foster home I lived in after I confided in a neighbor, an action I never would have been brave enough to do without Abel. I squeezed my eyes shut and patterned each intake and exhale as my therapist had taught me. Abel had been the only thing that kept me going those few months. He was the only light in my life. I had thought of him many times over the years, and every time, I envisioned him living a happy life. Never this. Never cold in a grave. His light dispelled the darkest parts of my soul when I had been with him. I couldn't believe he died when he was seventeen. He was just a kid. They always said the good ones die young, but something about his light leaving earth felt incredibly selfish. Abel's light had lit up some of the darkest parts of my childhood, and I couldn't imagine how I would have survived without it.

Chapter Eight

Sawyer

(Age Eight)

I RECEIVED ONE HUNDRED percent on my spelling test, and Mrs.
Barnes said she was proud of me and that I could do the advanced
word list next time.

I pulled my blue coat tight, but it didn't make me any warmer. The cold wind blew on me as I walked from the school building to the bus. It was missing three buttons. I couldn't wait to see my friend Abel.

Mrs. Thompson brought me to school today, so I didn't get to ride the bus this morning. I liked sitting with Abel because he was nice. He made everything better. I climbed the steps and walked toward our seat. He was already on the bus. As I was walking past the fifth row, a foot shot out and tripped me. I hit the floor with an *oomph*. The weight of my faded blue backpack held my thin body down. Tears stung my eyes, but I wouldn't give Jimmy Johnson the satisfaction of letting him know my knees hurt from the fall. Jimmy was always mean. This wasn't the first time he'd pushed me around. I wasn't sure what I had done to the fifth grader to make him bully me, but I wished I had never met him. But there were a lot of people I wished I had never met. Abel leaned his head out into the aisle and saw me on the ground. His big greenish eyes widened, and he rushed toward me.

"You okay, Sawyer?" His eyebrows were squished together.

"Yeah." He reached for my upper arm to help me up. I gasped. He didn't know there was a bruise on my arm, but I needed his help because the backpack was too heavy.

"Awww . . . Seth, look. Abel has a thing for Bony Baloney."

Jimmy snickered, and I tugged my jacket closer. Seth laughed.

"Bony Baloney?" Seth asked, still laughing.

"Yeah, she's bony, and she smells like baloney!" Jimmy and Seth laughed like it was the best joke they had ever heard. They were mean and dumb.

I wanted to scream that I wouldn't be bony if someone fed me regularly. When you only ate Monday through Friday at school, I guess things like that happened. As far as the smell. I didn't like it either. I hated being dirty. I hated when my fingernails were dirty and my head felt itchy. I hated that there wasn't a lock on the bathroom door. I had tried to figure out how to work the washer and dryer at the Thompson's house, but I wasn't tall enough to reach the knobs. I had to drag a bar stool to the laundry room to climb atop to reach. The last time I tried that, Mr. Thompson had found me in there and by the time he was done, I didn't care what my clothes smelled like. I felt dirtier than my clothes, except it was the kind of feeling that water couldn't wash away.

I hated Mr. Thompson. I hated Dawton. Sometimes I hated Dawton worse than Mr. Thompson. I hated all of them. Dawton was the reason my arm was bruised. He was a bully like Jimmy Johnson half the time, and the other half . . . well, he was a lot like Mr. Thompson.

"Jimmy Johnson, you shut it or I'll tell your dad what a stink face you are!" Abel replied. As if by some miracle, Jimmy quieted. I didn't understand why, because Abel was much smaller than Jimmy. But I didn't care. I just wanted to be safe by the window seat and have Abel sitting beside me. I made my way to the bench seat we always shared.

"Sawyer?"

I turned to look at him and lugged off my backpack. Set it in my lap and wrapped my skinny arms around it. I used it as a pillow sometimes because I could actually sleep on the bus. I didn't know why, but sometimes I wondered if it was because I felt safe enough to sleep.

"I'm sorry Jimmy is so mean." Abel's brown hair fell across his forehead.

"Why'd he leave you alone? I thought for sure he'd beat you into the ground." I wanted to figure out how I could get him to leave me alone, too.

"His dad works for my dad," Abel answered, as if that explained everything, and to him it probably did. I nodded, although I didn't exactly understand.

"I wish I could be brave like you," I said quietly.

"My grandpa wore these when he was a soldier and my grandma said soldiers are the best kind of men there are. When I grow up, I'm gonna be just like him!" Abel declared, pulling out a chain with two metal pieces on the end with words written across them.

I looked closer.

"What are they?" I tipped my head to the side to study the words.

"She says they're dog tags."

"That's a weird name, but how does it work? Is it like magic?"

"Yeah," he said, like they were very special.

"I wish I had dog tags to make me brave." If these things really worked, maybe I wouldn't be scared at home all the time.

"Why do you need to be brave?"

I'd never told Abel what happened when I wasn't at school. I tried to tell my social worker, but she'd mostly sit outside with Mrs. Thompson and they'd talk while they smoked cigarettes. I was scared to tell her with Mrs. Thompson watching. She'd always say I was lying again and pull my hair. I hated when she did that. She always got spit on me when she talked and I hated that too.

"I don't like living with the Thompsons."

"Why?" His forehead wrinkled.

"Sometimes it's scary." I looked out the window as the rolling hills passed by before turning back.

Abel stared at me like he was looking for secrets, and then before I knew it, he took off the dog tags and slipped them over my head.

"You can have them. They can make you brave too." I wrapped my bony arms around Abel and gave him a tight hug.

"What? Really? You're the best friend ever!"

"Awww naww," he mumbled, ducking his head. "Are you going to take a nap, like always? You can lean on me."

Abel's cheeks were pink, and I settled into the seat and laid my head against his shoulder. I held the dog tags in my hand, rubbing my thumb across the words until I fell asleep. The last thing I remember thinking, as the rocking of the bus made me fall asleep, was I wanted to be like Abel one day.

Every time I saw him, he made everything better. It was like he was magic. He was a warm light, and it made things not seem so dark and cold. If I could make people feel that way, I wanted to do that more than anything else in this world.

Chapter Nine

Sawyer

(Present)

A TRUCK DOOR SLAMMED. I flinched, unaware that anyone had driven up, lost in the fog of my memories. I could sense his eyes boring into me before I ever looked up. I clutched the dog tags in my hand for their initial purpose. Bravery. I knew now they weren't magic, but somehow,

I still treated them like they were. His long legs ate up the ground as he stalked toward me. *What was he doing here?*

The scowl on his face sent a shiver through me and reminded me that I didn't completely know him. My past told me to make myself small, even though my logical brain told me that I didn't think I had to fear him. Sure, things were awkward when I dropped off the cookies earlier, but they weren't unsafe. The headstone dug into my back. My arms were still wrapped around my knees. Previous therapy told me to regulate each respiration to calm my nerves before they completely took over. My brain was racing as to why he was here and why he was furious.

"What the hell are you doing here?!"

I wasn't sure what I expected, but that wasn't it. I sank even more into myself if that was even possible. Grief and confusion warred in my mind. I simply wanted to say goodbye to my childhood friend. My throat tightened and the words wouldn't come. Blood roared in my ears, drowning out his voice. My fingertips began to tingle as dark spots danced in my vision.

"You have no right to be here," he gritted out in my silence. His eyes burned a bluish and amber flame. I knew I needed to talk, but I also knew the logical part of my brain was slipping away.

My throat closed. My thoughts raced, and all I could hear was my adrenaline telling me to run. RUN. I had been labeled a runaway my entire childhood. I often ran before even acknowledging the decision.

I didn't remember making the choice to stand, but the next thing I knew, I was standing and backing away. His eyes glinted in anger. His hands fisted by his side. My hand squeezed around the military tags. The metal cutting into my palm. He took a step toward me as larger dark spots clouded my vision. I raised a hand to ward him off. All logical thoughts vacated my mind. My years of experience handling angry people were tossed out the window. My ability to calmly handle disgruntled people had disappeared. Between discovering that Abel was gone and having flashbacks of the horrific abuse I had endured, my mind raced with old memories that I had wanted to forget long ago. I didn't feel like the independent, kick-butt-and-take-names kind of social worker anymore . . . I was that little girl that needed a social worker, one that'd stand up for her. He raked a hand through his thick chestnut hair. His lips that were set in a firm line parted as something unrecognizable passed across his face. I took another step back. His hand came toward me and then everything went black.

Soren

Something wasn't right. Why was she raising her hand toward me? Did she think I was going to hit her? I'd made a lot of mistakes in my life, but I would never cross that line and lay a hand on a woman. Then the sickening thought flashed through my mind. She had indicated she'd been hurt before. I remembered the flinch at the creek when I squeezed her shoulder after we'd found Connor. I had asked her shortly after if anyone was hurting her, and she had said not anymore. Air whooshed out of my body in a rush. My stomach bottomed out when I saw her eyes roll back in her head, and I reached to catch her before her head connected with another gravestone behind her. When I stepped forward a moment ago, I had been trying to stop her from tripping on another gravestone. Her sunshine blonde hair spilled all over me and her as I fumbled to ease her body to the soft green grass. It was difficult catching someone while you were facing them, especially when they fell back instead of forward. Confusion didn't begin to explain my state of mind. Hell. What had I done? Had she just fainted? I pushed the hair away from her face as it puddled around her small body like liquid gold. I was angry with myself for being the world's biggest jackass. What was it about this woman that entangled my thoughts? And why did she keep showing up on the worst days? I had been caught off guard earlier when she stopped by my house and was angry at myself about something else. It wasn't that I didn't want to see her. Her presence had been unexpected both days, and these days were the hardest to face every year. I didn't think I'd see her again, especially here. Why was she leaning against my brother's grave? Her long eyelashes laid against her pale cheeks, and there was no doubt she had been crying. There was a dusting of light freckles across her nose and the tops of her cheeks. Her lips were notably full, and there was a crease in the center of her bottom lip. She was an angel, except for the wet lashes. She'd gotten under my skin in a way that no one ever had before, and it unnerved me. Sawyer made me off-kilter. I once lived for one-night stands and too much whiskey that would drown everything out. I used to be able to walk into a bar and leave with whatever woman I wanted without even trying.

But that was before and this was now. I felt a pit in my stomach when I reflected on my previous behavior. Shame poured over me as I remembered my words to her. Did I scare her to the point that she fainted? Hell. Was there something medically wrong with her? I brushed my thumb across her rose petal soft cheek as I knelt beside her. The soft scent of strawberries clung to her. I wished I could explain why today was so heavy, even though I knew it wouldn't excuse my words or actions. My earlier anger had completely dissipated. I *had* to fix this.

"Wake up, Sawyer. Come back to me." I reached for her hand and placed it in mine. Her heartbeat was strong. That was when I noticed it. Her hand had fallen open and twisted around her wrist and hand was a chain. A chain attached to old military identification tags. As I lifted her hand, I noticed the name. *Henry Abel Roberts.*

What the hell?! Why did she have my grandpa's dog tags? I thought I'd had enough surprises this week. Once she came to, we were going to have a nice long talk about what was going on. I tucked the tags into my pocket and slid my arms under her knees and back. I had jumped out of my truck quickly, and as a result left it running. I didn't want her laying on the cool ground. Maybe the warmer air of the truck would make her wake up, and if she stayed unconscious too long, I could get her to the clinic more quickly. She was small in my arms. I juggled her slightly, hooked my index finger under the handle and opened the passenger door. I settled her in the seat and, for good measure, reached to recline it some so she wouldn't fall forward. Cupping her cheek as gently as my calloused hands could, I rubbed my thumb across her chin. Her skin was like silk.

"Everything is going to be okay, Sawyer. Please wake up."

If I accomplished anything today, I was going to get down to the bottom of what was going on. Her eyelashes fluttered.

"That's it. Pretty Girl. Wake up."

Her shattered, light-wash denim eyes met mine. I saw emotions cross her face in rapid succession. Confusion. Surprise. Awareness of her surroundings. Fear. Then absolute terror overtook her before she began attacking me with as much force as a one hundred and twenty-five pound woman could. Until this moment, I'd never truly appreciated the time spent boxing with Lane and Jonah at the gym. I swiftly blocked the strikes and gently secured her wrists, taking care to not hurt her with too much pressure. Her chest heaved with exertion and, most likely, adrenaline.

"It's okay. You passed out. I brought you to my truck so you wouldn't be on the ground."

"Let go of me!" she spit out, squirming to get loose.

"I am. I'm not going to hurt you. I don't want you to hurt yourself." Her brow lowered in anger but her movements ceased. She breathed in a pattern I was intimately familiar with.

Sawyer's voice was strained and timid when she explained, "I'm not going to be able to calm down until you stop touching me."

Her voice sounded more level. I took a step back and released her hands as if they had burned me and held my hands up in surrender. She sat straight and stared out the windshield, as if to verify she was still at the cemetery. After a moment, her breathing slowed, and she turned to me with accusation in her eyes.

"Why were you yelling at me?"

I ran my hand through my hair in frustration and she flinched again.

"Why do you keep doing that?" I asked, exasperated.

She ignored my question and went to get out of the truck. I held out a hand to stop her. Not touching her, but blocking her path because I didn't want a repeat of her fainting again, especially from the height of my truck.

"Sit down before you pass out again. You're not going anywhere until we talk." I scowled.

I didn't know it, but that was the worst thing I could have said at the moment. Her eyes blazed before she started flailing with everything inside her. That temporarily stunned me, and she fought to get around me again. I stumbled back in surprise.

"Get outta my way!" she screamed, fighting with everything inside her. It was as though she was somewhere else, with someone else.

"Hell, Sawyer! I'm trying to help you," I barked.

She made it around me and turned to face me, as though preparing for a duel. My lip smarted in pain. I tried again, desperate to understand. There was a wildness in her eyes that I'd never seen before.

"Sawyer. I'm sorry I yelled at you. Today was a rough day, and I took it out on the wrong person. I'd really like to understand what you're doing at my brother's grave."

She completely froze. Her shoulders dropped as a wheeze of air left her body.

"Abel is your brother?" Her eyes tracked between mine as if searching for the truth.

"Yes, he was."

"I'll stay, but I can't think when you're touching me." Her hands came up to her face to cover her mouth that had fallen open. Her eyes widened with surprise.

"Oh my gosh! I busted your lip. I'm so sorry!" she gasped. I hadn't even realized it.

I rolled my bottom lip and noticed the copper taste of blood.

"It'll be alright. The guys are going to give me grief for getting taken by such a lightweight. I shouldn't have scared you."

I attempted to lighten the mood. She wrapped her arms around herself and bit her plump lower lip as tears swam in her eyes.

"Have you had lunch?" I asked.

She shook her head, staring intently toward Abel's grave.

"I was headed to the diner when I saw you. Can I buy you lunch?"

Her almost too big eyes made a study of my face. I didn't know her well enough to recognize all her expressions, but I could see she was guarded and guilt burned through me again about being such a jackass. After a thorough inspection, she must have decided it was okay.

"Okay. But I'll meet you there."

I didn't blame her. I had given her a shitty impression of me. The worst. I couldn't remember the last time I'd raised my voice at anyone, much less a woman.

"Okay. Just follow me. Ronnie's Diner is on Main Street," I explained.

She turned to walk away, but abruptly stopped.

"Where is my necklace?" She frantically clutched at her neck while scanning the ground, searching.

"These were my grandfather's." I held them up as they dangled from my index finger. Tears puddled her eyes again and her head dropped.

"Abel gave them to me," she whispered, defeated.

As much as I valued sentimental things, there was something in her face that told me she needed them more than I did. I walked toward her and grasped her small hand, placed them in her palm, and closed her fingers over them. A lone tear rolled down her cheek, and I itched to brush it away, but I knew she'd shy away from my touch.

"These mean more to me than anything else I own," she whispered, clutching them to her chest.

"Let me buy you lunch and we'll talk, okay?" She nodded, and we both walked to our vehicles.

My mind wandered as I led the way to the diner.

Ronnie's had been a staple of the community for over fifty years. The red and white awning was dated, but Ronnie made the best greasy cheeseburger around—one that left oil stains on brown paper bags. The milkshakes and homemade onion rings were what drew people in, though. Abel had loved the strawberry milkshake the best. He'd convince Mom and Dad that it was a serving of fruit and, therefore, it was okay to have them as often as possible. Mom would always laugh and tell him to "stop acting like your dad," and dad would tousle his hair with a chuckle. I was desperate to know how Sawyer knew Abel—especially since I didn't have any memories of her *at all*.

The Grand Canyon sized hole his loss had left in our family was evident every single day. Today would have been his twenty-seventh birthday. Abel would have insisted on eating an ice cream cake while drinking an ice cream shake, spouting off about how his birthday was only once a year and it should practically be considered a national holiday. The thing about him though, was that he made the same fuss about other people's birthdays too. Once, for my birthday, he paid for me to have a hot shave at a fancy barbershop in Kansas City before we went to a Royals game. He was fifteen and the tickets and shave must have cost him most of his lawn mowing money that summer, but he didn't care. He lived big, but he loved bigger. If you were in his orbit, you felt the warmth of his light. Many people would grumble about having a little brother, but not me. There was a seven-year age difference, but Abel and I had been best friends. He'd hung out with me and my high school friends while we practiced baseball and football. He tagged along with us everywhere. Lane and Jonah had even claimed him, and after we graduated, we still went to as many of his baseball games as possible. Occasionally, only one of us could make it to the game, so we'd update each other on the plays afterward.

I parked at the diner and hopped out, but Sawyer sat in her Jeep, not moving. I tapped on her window and seemed to pull her from a trance. She opened her door but stayed buckled. Damn. I should have never let her drive in this state. *What had I been thinking?*

"Sawyer, are you okay?" Her eyes became watery again.

"I don't think I can talk about Abel around other people. I didn't even know he was gone." Her voice trailed off at the end.

Grief. I knew it excruciatingly well inside and out, but I knew regret better. She hadn't even known he had died, and it'd been ten years. Her somber voice held me. I placed a hand on her steering wheel and leaned closer to meet her shining eyes that had been staring at my shoulder.

"I'm going to pick up our food, but I want you to ride with me back to my house and we'll eat and talk. Okay?" She nodded, knowing the underlying thing I was thinking. It was not safe for her to be driving in this state.

"What's your favorite kind of ice cream?"

"Strawberry," she whispered. Of course it was.

"Okay. Let's get your car locked up. Grab whatever you need. We'll get you in my truck and then I'll grab lunch." I texted Tina—a waitress at the diner who was friends with my mom—our food order while I helped get Sawyer settled in my truck.

Her whole countenance reflected deep sorrow, and if anyone knew heartbreak, it was me.

Chapter Ten

Soren

I TOOK A SIP of my chocolate milkshake as we turned into my drive. Sawyer hadn't spoken a word the entire time. I didn't know what to do. I wanted to hold her hand or offer a hug. My mom was the biggest hugger I knew, and I guess being her son must have rubbed it off on me. But how did you comfort someone when touch was taken out of the equation? I contemplated the right words as I grabbed my milkshake and the grease stained bag of burgers in one hand and rounded the hood to help her out. Sawyer sat, holding her milkshake in one hand, as she stared ahead. I was certain she hadn't even taken a sip. I nudged her cup with mine.

"Abel liked strawberry too." She studied the cup as if seeing it for the first time and took a sip, followed by another.

"This is good," she replied softly, turning toward me.

"Ronnie makes a great milkshake. His burgers are solid too," I commented, holding up the brown paper bag.

We made our way up the porch steps and since it was such a mild day, we decided to eat on the porch swing. I separated the food between us. Setting our cups in the cup holders built into the armrests, we dug into the burgers and homemade, seasoned onion rings between us. After Sawyer finished eating, she pulled her knees to her chest and rested her chin atop her knees. It was as if she were curling in on herself. She had remained quiet throughout the meal, but she ate as if she were genuinely hungry. She was so small all wrapped up that I had that instinct to hug her again. Her face was that of complete vulnerability as she took a shaky breath.

"Abel was my best friend during a difficult time in my childhood."

I shifted my body toward her to absorb every word she spoke. When you lived with grief daily, you learned that it resembled tides in the ocean. There were times where it was a flood, and then there were other times where it was less, but it was always still there. For a season, I couldn't talk about Abel. The pain ate at me, but as the years had created some distance between the event that ended his life and the memories of our childhood, I craved every moment. I wanted to remember all the things that made my best friend, my brother, exactly who he was. To know these previously unknown parts of his life was like standing in a field on the verge of drought, praying for rain and there were storm clouds brewing in the distance. They were pieces of him I had never seen.

"When was that?" I asked, desperately wanting to know more.

"We were seven or eight years old, I think. I'd been moved once again to a new foster home. My childhood is a jumble of memories. It's hard to map it out sometimes or remember the sequence of houses I lived in. Partially because I moved frequently and partially because my brain was in survival mode, which made it difficult to retain information." She paused, clearing her throat, and continued, "I always excelled and felt safe at school, though. Abel and I were in the same class. We always sat together at lunch and on the school bus."

I rubbed my sternum against the ache there. I couldn't imagine her childhood.

"I'm sorry. I can't imagine." My throat was thick. "Do you remember how long you lived here, or where you lived?"

"I think maybe five or six months. I have a memory of a Christmas party with Abel at school and another of us making a flower craft for May Day. I don't remember the foster family's name, but I think the dad went to jail after I left. He was arrested the night I left . . . the neighbor's name was Sally, I think." I noted that she didn't finish the sentence.

"Could have been Sally Thomas. She was a retired teacher. She was in her late seventies when she passed away about two years ago. Her house would be on the same bus route, or at least it used to be. A few new houses have popped up in the last decade." She tilted her head to the side as if she were thinking, her hair spilling over her shoulder.

"That would be about the right age, I think . . . everyone feels older when you're seven or eight years old."

"Why did the foster dad get arrested?" I hesitated to ask, but I knew I wouldn't sleep tonight. Did he still live nearby, or had he moved back to the area?

She rubbed her chin on her knee, appearing even smaller.

"He and their teenage foster son were abusing me."

I almost missed her soft whisper. A white hot rage filled my body so rapidly as my heart hammered in my chest, but I forced myself to appear calm. How anyone could hurt this woman I couldn't comprehend. My fists tightened, but I uncurled them, not wanting to do anything that made her uncomfortable. I already knew I was going to have to spend some time with a boxing bag tonight.

"Abel gave me the military tags because he said they'd make me brave. He'd asked about my home life, and I told him I didn't like living there."

Of course Abel was trying to fix things in his little kid logic way. That's who he was. There was no way Abel hadn't talked about Sawyer after school, and my mom's memory was a steel trap. I'd bet she remembered Sawyer. I would have had my farm permit then and drove myself to school during those years because of high school sports practice in the afternoons.

"That sounds like Abel. Did things get better after you moved?" I had to hope.

"I moved into another bad placement, but it wasn't the same type of abuse."

Hell.

It was a punch in the stomach. Had her entire childhood been this way? Trading one abusive hell for another? She studied a spot on the cuff of her sweater sleeve, as if shock was still slowly leaching from her body.

"Is that why you flinch when I touch you?" Her wide eyes met mine.

"Yes. But it's not you, it's me." She laughed awkwardly at her word usage. My heart ached for her and for the way I had treated her.

"A therapist told me that my body has memories that my brain can't remember, or doesn't want to remember. It's as if my brain is trying to protect me in a selective amnesia sort of way. There's plenty I can remember too, but it's not something I want to do. Certain kinds of touch are sometimes linked to old memories or buried memories." Her voice quieted near the end.

I didn't know what to say. What could you say? *"I'm sorry your life has been hell."* Where could I even start? I knew one thing I unquestionably wanted to do, and that was to thoroughly apologize. Shame wasn't a heavy enough word for the emotion I had for the way I'd spoken to her at the cemetery.

"Sawyer, I want to apologize for how I treated you earlier. I was an asshole. It's been almost a decade since I've lost my temper like that. It's not an excuse, but I'd like to tell you why. I was up late last night with a tough situation, and it wasn't until lunch time that I realized it was Abel's birthday. I've never forgotten his birthday. He always made such a big deal about mine, and I was angry at myself for forgetting. Not to mention, I received another phone call about another issue, and when I saw you, I was confused and took it out on you. It had nothing to do with you. Thursday was the anniversary of Abel's death. It won't happen again. I know right now that sounds like a line, but I can guarantee it'll never happen again."

I had eight years' worth of putting money, time, and effort into making choices that helped people, but she knew none of that. She had seen me on two of my worst days and after everything she'd revealed, I hated that.

Her eyes softened.

"It's okay."

"No, it's not," I spoke firmly. "Even though you don't know me well, I want you to know that I'd never lay a hand on you in anger. Ever." Her eyes searched my face, and she nodded as if she saw the truth.

"I can't believe I just told you all this," she whispered, tucking a strand of hair behind her ear, her cheeks pinkening. "It's been a while since I've had such a severe C-PTSD episode. Thinking of Abel and finding out he was gone triggered those old buried memories, and it felt suffocating."

"And then I yelled at you," I stated as I rubbed my hand down my face. I felt like dirt. Lower than dirt. Manure. Crap. Shit.

"When I was out here on Thursday, I kept having these moments as if something was familiar. I had a hard time placing it. Then, when I was driving down Main Street in Kennedy, I remembered that this was where I met Abel. I was so excited that he may still live here that when I saw he had passed, I was blindsided. Abel was a remarkable person," she finished softly.

"He was the best little brother." I blinked away the moisture in my eyes.

"Can you tell me how he passed?" she asked hesitantly as her eyes soberly searched my face.

"Car wreck." I still hated saying the words.

"Oh. Soren."

She tentatively placed her hand on my forearm closest to her. The gentle touch pressed through my sleeve. Her compassion was appreciated, but it was somewhere I was not comfortable camping out. I had put in the hard work with George, but I could never shake the regret that Abel would be here if it wasn't for me.

"He would have been twenty-seven today."

"I saw the dates on the headstone, but I didn't make the connection. I only knew Abel for a short period, but his friendship forever impacted my life. He was the only person I considered a childhood friend."

Her words hit me squarely in the chest. She'd only known him for a few months, years ago. As someone who was still best friends with two of my childhood friends, I couldn't imagine. My friends saved my life after Abel died. Jonah was the deep thinker in our trio, but I usually took time to think things over before I made a decision. I determined at that moment I wanted to get to know this woman better.

I didn't have a lot of experience with women outside the bedroom, because I'd avoided them for years. This was going to be a journey, but knowing she had known Abel made me want to get to know her even more than I already did. The pull to know her was unlike anything I had ever experienced. As if there was no way my life could go forward without staying in contact with her somehow. I didn't know exactly what I wanted other than getting to know her more, but it was one of those "no regrets" moments, and I wasn't going to let it pass me by.

"I want to get to know you." Her eyes widened, and I laughed awkwardly at my blunt statement. Heat crept up my neck.

"Uh okay." She paused, having the appearance that she didn't know what to say, and as always, my awkwardness was batting at a thousand. Maybe I could learn a thing or two from Lane.

Chapter Eleven

Sawyer

"WHAT DO YOU ENJOY doing in your free time?" Soren asked.

I paused. My mind raced through the last hour that led to me sitting on Soren's porch swing. He was Abel's brother, and he wanted to get to know me. His blunt words made me think of Talia. A smile tugged at my lips.

"Hmmm, I work a lot, but I love baking. I dropped off a chocolate chip cookie dough cheesecake for Talia before I came over here. I run almost every day, which is a good thing since I enjoy baking so much.

I enjoy watching baseball and football. I don't understand all the rules, but sometimes I simply turn on a game for background noise. I listen to games like some people listen to coffee shop music. It makes me feel calm. I tried basketball, but the sound of their shoes on the floor . . ." I cringed. A small smile tipped his mouth. "It didn't have the same effect." I surprised myself with how much I had shared. There was something about him that was comfortable. It was a sentiment I was unfamiliar with experiencing this quickly with people, and sometimes I never felt it at all, regardless of how long I knew someone.

His hazel eyes up close were a work of art with speckles of blue, green, and copper. They made me think of a stained glass art project I did in high school. All the pieces of broken glass were blues and greens overlapped in a box, creating something beautiful even before they were assembled. Broken stained glass always made me think of my life. There were innumerable pieces, but I wasn't sure how to piece them together. Who was I kidding? The pieces of my life weren't big enough to be shards of glass. My life resembled debris that floated in the air after a bomb exploded on my favorite TV show about a group of Texas rangers. My life was like shattered dust. I didn't have anything to offer this man. I could barely manage to maintain the one friendship I had. It wasn't that I didn't want to try. Relationships of any kind were challenging for me. I smiled, I made people feel comfortable, all the while, my mind raced, trying to catch up because it was so preoccupied logging every potential threat around me. I was self-aware enough to know I was different. My mind was in a constant state of overworking to fit in. YouTube was bookmarked on my laptop to watch how-to videos, which was something I did regularly. I had been diagnosed by a psychologist with attachment disorders along with C-PTSD. I understood the gist of it all because Talia had answered endless questions. Sometimes I felt as though I was broken beyond repair because in the end, how can you build anything from dust?

"Sawyer?"

I jolted.

"I'm sorry. I missed what you said." His too observant eyes roved my face, making me feel exposed but not uncomfortable.

"I played baseball and football in high school. I could teach you the rules if you're interested?"

He stood, gathering our trash and placing it back in the brown paper bag.

"Thank you. I'd like that. Do you still play?" I asked, although I have no intention of ever seeking him out. People say all kinds of things they'd never do out of courtesy. We walked toward the door and he turned back to answer while halfway in the door.

"From time to time, we'll have baseball tournaments for fundraisers. The week of the county fair we put together an adult rec league to play. I mostly stay busy with—" He cut off when his cell phone rang. He checked the screen and frowned.

"I'm sorry I need to take this."

He walked inside toward the kitchen to toss the trash, putting the phone to his ear.

He answered with a simple, "Yeah."

It was beyond clear he was not excited to take this call. I briefly contemplated why he answered if he obviously didn't want to talk, but I reminded myself that it was none of my business. I stayed in the family room, unsure if I should follow. I noted again how tidy his house was, and it gave me a sense of peace similar to my duplex. I could hear his voice occasionally, but not his exact words. A small, wallet-size framed photo on the mantel caught my eye and I walked closer, not having noticed it on Thursday. It was a photo of Abel and Soren. Abel was about fifteen or sixteen with a ball cap flipped backward, and Soren had an arm resting over his shoulders in a man version of a side hug. Both were smiling as if they were having the best day ever. My heart warmed knowing Abel had been completely adored.

"Sawyer?" I jumped and turned toward Soren. His face softened as he saw what I was studying.

"That was on his sixteenth birthday." He walked closer. "I have a situation I have to handle. I'm sorry, but I have to leave. I'll drop you off at your Jeep." There was a line of concern on his forehead, clearly not happy with whatever he had to deal with. Within fifteen minutes, we were back to my car, and I waved a quick goodbye and thanks for lunch as I jumped out.

"Wait," he called. I turned back.

"Can I have your number?" he asked hesitantly.

"Sure."

He pulled out his phone and typed in my number as I called it out. My phone vibrated immediately from a text. He waved as I loaded up in my Jeep. I swiped open my phone and saw the text from him.

Soren

> **Thanks, Pretty Girl. I'll see you around.**

I smiled when I read "Pretty Girl." It was as though there were a thousand butterflies in my belly taking flight. I didn't know what it was about Soren, but I had this immediate connection with him similar to the one I had with Abel. A sense of instant safety that simultaneously made me want to run. The safe feeling made me feel unsafe. I was such a mess.

Chapter Twelve

Soren

SWEAT TRICKLED DOWN MY brow as I darted left to miss the swift right jab Lane threw. It was almost nine and Jonah's gym was nearly empty except for Jonah, who was pumping iron outside the boxing ring.

"You're moving slow, Roberts," Lane tossed out, working to throw me off my game, but he wasn't wrong. Ever since my conversation with Sawyer yesterday, everything felt unbearably heavy. Like I was buried in sand and couldn't move at my typical pace. How could anyone have survived her childhood?

I had heard stories of childhood abuse, like everyone had, but nothing as heartbreaking as when it happened to someone I now knew. Her story . . . at least the pieces she shared, were similar to something you'd hear about on the nightly news. I had this insane urge to protect her, to wrap her in my arms and shield her from everything. Her light was too special to be broken. I shook my head, trying to clear it. I'd never had similar thoughts for a woman I barely knew. Lane's fist connected with my left cheek. My head snapped back, and Lane dropped his fighter stance as Jonah stopped and watched.

"Man, what is up? This doesn't seem like a good fight because something obviously has you distracted," Jonah remarked in his deep voice.

Jonah's dark eyes were concerned, and I grabbed a towel to swipe over my face. How did I explain Sawyer without sharing her personal story? Lane squirted a stream of water into his mouth as he toweled off his sweat.

"Yeah, man. You called us here to spar, but honestly, you've been fighting like a rookie since you stepped into the ring. What gives?" Lane remarked, his green eyes shifting to Jonah with a knowing look. This was the problem with having lifelong friends. I couldn't keep anything from them, even the things I wanted to.

"I wanted to punch something. I needed to blow off some steam," I disclosed. Jonah quirked a black brow.

"Sure, man, but you're distracted. I don't feel right beating up on you." Lane smirked. "Besides, it looks like you've already been beat up with that busted lip." He gestured to my lip.

"You wish," I shot as I grabbed my water bottle and took a swig. There wasn't any point in continuing; I took off the wrap on my hands.

"We're not leaving till you talk," Lane threatened.

I walked to an empty weight bench as Lane climbed out of the ring after me. I raked my hand through my wet hair. Where did I even begin?

"Remember Sawyer from the search the other day?"

Both of the guys wore shocked expressions as they glanced at each other. It had been at least eight years since I'd brought up a woman to them.

"Uh yeah, man. She's not the kind of girl you forget," Lane, the constant flirt, broadcasted.

I briefly wished I would have connected my fist to his pretty boy face a few more times while boxing.

"She used to live here," I explained.

"There's no way, man. I wouldn't forget her," Lane scoffed. I clearly should have let my fist connect more with his face.

"Really? I don't remember her." Jonah ran his thumb under his bottom lip in thought. His tattoo sleeve was on full display in his cut t-shirt.

"She's six or seven years younger than us; I doubt we ever would have crossed paths, but she knew Abel." At that, Lane's knee, which he'd been absentmindedly bouncing, stopped. The air was sucked from the room.

"What?" Jonah wheezed out.

Abel wasn't only my little brother. He was a little brother to all of us. We all lost someone that day, and the gut reaction of loss would never leave. You couldn't fill the space of Abel in our lives, because no person or thing could occupy the space where his light used to be. His memory resembled a prism of light. It couldn't be captured or contained because every recollection we had, he was a part of that too. His light made me think of Sawyer. Something told me I'd do whatever I could to stay in the warmth of her light, too.

"Yeah, she was only here for a semester, I think, but Abel gave her our grandpa's military tags."

"My man laying claim even as a young grasshopper." Lane gave a watery laugh. He used humor to cover the things he kept buried. George would have a field day with him.

"Did she know who you were?" Jonah asked. I spent the next ten minutes explaining my day yesterday, hopefully without sharing too much. The abuse Sawyer suffered was her own story and not mine to tell.

"Why'd she leave?" Lane asked.

"She went to live in another foster home," I answered.

"Man," Lane drew out.

"I think that might have been for the better," I hedged, as I took another sip from my water bottle.

"Now that I think about it, something does seem slightly familiar about her," Lane considered, then continued, "You gonna ask her out?"

Lane, ever the flirt.

"I told her I wanted to get to know her as a friend."

That brought a hyena laugh from Lane, and even Jonah's mouth tugged into a smile. I was sure to get razzed for that.

"My dude. Let me give you some tips for the ladies." Lane threw an arm over my shoulders, leaning in as if he was going to share a secret. I shrugged his sweaty arm off and grabbed my wraps, water bottle, and towel.

"I don't need your pretty playboy tips. It's been awhile, but I know women. I'm not sure Sawyer is looking for anything, and I'm not sure I am either. Who knows? She might already have someone," I stated, even though I knew it wasn't true according to her friend Talia.

"You think I'm pretty?" Lane batted his eyelashes, his hand under his chin as if he was trying to show his best angles. Jonah and I rolled our eyes, familiar with his antics.

"But you're interested?" Lane asked, bobbing his head, mirroring a doggy on a dashboard.

"I'm not *not* interested, I don't know. She seems . . . "

"Beautiful. Drop dead gorgeous. Sexy as hell," Lane quipped. Jackass. Jonah rolled his eyes again.

"Hey! Keep your slimy eyeballs off her." I tossed my sweaty towel in the bucket.

"No worries, Roberts. I won't steal your girl," Lane boasted.

"She's not my girl." Even though I could get used to the way that sounded. *My girl.*

"She most definitely is your girl. She just doesn't know it yet." Lane howled in laughter at his own joke. "Let me know when you need my wooing skills. They're available for the low, low price of $19.99 a month, but if you act now, I'll plan a date that'll sweep her off her feet." Lane used his best infomercial voice. His utter insanity shined brightly. He was a lunatic sometimes.

I looked at Jonah and he shook his head.

"Dude. If you have such amazing wooing skills, then why're you still single?" I laughed.

"Why settle for one when you can have some variety?" Lane's eyebrows bounced as his arms slung wide. I scoffed because I knew all about variety, and the high cost of it all.

"Jokes aside. She seems like a girl worth getting to know," Jonah affirmed in his quiet way. Without a doubt, she was.

"I'm out. I've gotta fly to Atlanta tomorrow for some meetings, but I'll be back Tuesday if you guys want to fight?" Lane said, glancing down at his phone.

Lane had retired from the MLB last year but was still involved in numerous business pursuits, especially his organization that provided a safe space for kids after school. There were only a handful of people in the world that knew how many things he funded. All jokes aside, Lane was one of the best people I knew. He was straightforward with his hookups, but I couldn't live that life anymore. I'd been burned too badly, and now, I wanted more than something casual. It wasn't enough. Lane grabbed his gear and headed out, tossing out a quick, "Call if you need anything."

Jonah was the quietest of our trio. He intimidated most people he met, but underneath the tattoos, muscles, beast size stature, and pensive assessing focus, he had a heart of gold. The dude had a library with a rolling ladder and everything. The classic example of why it was never okay to judge a book by its cover.

"What are you going to do?" His deep, even voice asked. His muscled arms crossed over his chest.

"I don't know, man." I ran my hand through my hair. "This might sound crazy, but it's like I feel this pull . . . I have to get to know her better, but I've screwed around so much before, and I don't want to treat her like that. I can't play games with her." Jonah was my go-to when I needed sound advice.

"Then don't," he simply replied.

A puff of air blew past my lips.

"Okay. Well, thanks for nothing," I drew out.

"No. It's that simple, Sor. If you want something different, you have to do something different."

His dark eyes watched me closely. He was right. If I wanted some-thing different from the chaos I had before, I'd have to do something different. I'd have to be different. The thing was that I was different. I wasn't the reckless, grieving brother anymore that used alcohol and sex to try to fill a void. A void that only increased in size regardless of how often I had tried to fill it.

"Since high school, I've never not had the end goal of getting some, but with her it's different." I studied the large American flag on the gym wall. "Man. I don't know. She's different. I'm not sure I'm ready for a relationship, but something tells me I'd be a fool to let her get away."

"Take the time to get to know her," Jonah advised.

For a man who rarely talked about his own dating life, Jonah had a point. All I had to do was get to know her and simply see how it went. The question was whether I had the ability to date like that without screwing things up. After all, I had a track record of ruining the things I loved.

Chapter Thirteen

Soren

"Hey, sweetheart!" my mom crooned in my ear as though I was a kid coming home from the first day of kindergarten. She had good intentions. Abel's death had affected us all differently, and it had made her more affectionate than she had already been, and sometimes it was downright embarrassing. It sounded like she was taking a fitness class because I could hear instructions in the background and eighties music. She sounded slightly out of breath, and someone yelled, "Raise your left leg higher!"

To which she mumbled, "Lucinda, I've had two nine-pound toddlers walk outta this body. It doesn't raise like that anymore!" I rubbed my hand across my eyes, trying to resist awkward laughter.

"Hey, I have a question for you," I say.

"Oh good! Because I have answers." She quipped with a laugh. There was a song from the sixties pumping in the background now while someone continued to yell out instructions.

"Do you remember Abel having a friend named Sawyer?"

"Hmmmm . . . do you know when?" she asked with a puff.

"In elementary school. She was a foster child. She may have lived near Sally Thomas."

"Ohhhh, yes! I remember her. Such a tiny little angel. Poor thing was placed with that crazy Thompson family. I always thought they did foster care for the wrong reasons. Bill barely held down a job. Why do you ask?"

I knew she'd remember.

"Well, I met her the other day, but I think because of the age difference, I didn't remember her," I said, pouring myself a glass of water, the phone wedged between my ear and my shoulder.

"Hmmm. I think I only saw her a handful of times when I helped in Abel's class. I remember her having incredibly striking eyes . . . I think they were maybe blue, or was it green? Either way, I remember them being bright and beautiful. She wasn't around for too long, and I remember Bill getting arrested after she left. I never heard exactly why, but I always thought it might have been connected. How is she doing now?"

I heard someone giving instructions for another exercise. I settled on a barstool in my kitchen and gave her the rundown of helping search for Connor.

"Wow. Good for her! Making such a difference in children's lives." She was always looking for the bright side.

We ended the call a few minutes later as Mom had to do something involving jump roping and wasn't sure if she'd be able to continue to talk. I knew she'd remember Sawyer, because she was sharp as a tack with details. It was what had made her successful. She worked remotely as a part-time insurance saleswoman while my dad enjoyed his retirement, experimenting with new hobbies. According to my mom, his latest hobby was birdwatching, which fit his quiet and reflective personality. My mom and dad were good, decent people, and someday I hoped I'd have the ability to make them proud, especially since I'd spent so many years doing the opposite.

Soren:

Hey, Pretty Girl.

Sawyer:

Hi.

Soren:

Would you be interested in coming over next Sunday? I'm grilling and having a couple of my friends over.

Sawyer:

Sorry, but I can't.

Two Days Later

Soren:

Hey, Pretty Girl. I have a meeting in Lewis City tomorrow. Want to grab ice cream afterward?

Sawyer:

I can't. Maybe another time.

Chapter Fourteen

Sawyer

"Sawyer!"

I turned toward the person shouting across the parking lot. Inwardly, I cringed because it was Friday and I was scheduled off for
the rest of the day. I'd already maxed out my hours due to a 3 a.m.
emergency placement situation. Thankfully, I was able to contact a
sweet family about thirty minutes away who had been fostering for
a few years and had an available opening.

Greg, my least favorite coworker, came striding toward me. I knew he was going to ask me to do something for him before he even opened his mouth. If you searched for "slacker" in the dictionary, there would be a photo of Greg—most likely sitting in an office chair with his feet propped up, slacking. He tried to flirt sometimes, but I couldn't think of anyone on the planet I was less interested in. He reminded me of a social worker from my childhood who was always doing the bare minimum. His hair was slicked back with gel similar to cringy used car salesmen on tv ads, and he gave off that same nauseating vibe. He always brought candy or donuts to the office so that no one was clued in on how little work he truly completed. He was nearly everyone's favorite, except mine. Maybe he was too likable, if that was a thing, and it felt completely insincere. Either way, he wasn't someone I enjoyed being around, and I tried to minimize interactions whenever possible.

"Can you take Brooke to the Bailey family for respite? I'm transporting Kenna to Hays."

The Baileys were the same family that had done respite for Connor last week. I always enjoyed seeing them. Brooke was such a sweet kid that loved playing dress up, but this was the kind of thing that Greg tried to pull all the time. Most likely he was supposed to transport Brooke this morning and Kenna this afternoon, but somehow appeared to be busy all morning while Brooke waited.

"I'm off the clock. Is transport not available?" I asked. His unnatural blond hair reflected in the sunlight.

"No, everyone is booked, and it'll be after 7 p.m. before anyone else can take her."

Seven hours for a five-year-old to sit in an office after probably waiting all morning. I couldn't let her do that. I didn't have anything planned other than grocery shopping and trying a new strawberry streusel recipe, but groceries could wait because I always put my kids first.

"I can take her."

The transportation and drop off for Brooke went smoothly, as expected. Mrs. Bailey had even shared a slice of freshly baked banana bread with me as she shared about her summer garden plans. Technically, I was off the clock after Brooke had arrived, but I stayed and chatted for a few minutes. Mrs. Bailey was one of the most inviting and kind people I'd ever met. She had a slight southern lilt to her voice that made it seem as though you were tucked into a homemade quilt, listening to a cozy audiobook.

Five-year-old Brooke was a round-faced brunette with an unshakable affinity for mermaids. She insisted on calling me Princess Mermaid Sawyer, which I indulged by talking to her as if I was underwater. She giggled uncontrollably, and I loved it.

After running around all week, I found that the drive in rural Rhodes County was relaxing. The Flint Hills rolled past, and the sky was a bright blue with white fluffy clouds. The weather was perfect. There was a gentle breeze, and the fresh air was invigorating. I wondered briefly what Soren was doing.

He'd tried meeting up with me twice, but I couldn't. I mean, I *could*, but it was such a battle in my mind. I wanted to get to know him better, but getting to know people deeper than surface level was extremely difficult for me. I thrived on surface level conversations, even though I hated talking about things that didn't really matter. There was something about him that made me think I couldn't keep things surface-level with him—like he'd see through my carefully built walls. And that made me feel even more vulnerable than the things I had already shared with him.

I'd told him things I never told anyone, and I didn't understand why. How did I explain that my fragmented childhood still affects me, even at twenty-six years old? How did I not freak the hell out when he touched me? How did he not see I wasn't worth pursuing? I mean, that was what he was trying to do, right?

I wasn't even sure. Talia would curse my train of thought while using her therapist's voice to remind me of my value.

I knew I had value for the work that I did, but sometimes I still questioned the value of me. Not the me who could be charming and calm down intense situations, but the me who became extremely overwhelmed. The me that sat in dark rooms because even the light was too loud. Was I worth knowing? And more importantly than that, if I was valuable, then why was I never wanted? Why was I never chosen? Why had no one ever stayed? Why couldn't I have been one of those kids that someone cared enough about to adopt?

I had years where I could have been, and it never happened. They'd posted my photo on the adoption website, and no one had inquired to adopt me. I never met potential families, like many of my foster siblings had over the years. I imagined parents scrolling through the website like they were shopping for the perfect child, and somehow I was never what anyone wanted. It all made me sick to my stomach. I'd never had anyone truly choose me first. Sure, Talia was the best friend anyone could ever have, but she had Rob and Ava. I'd never had anyone that was mine. I wondered what it'd feel like to belong to someone. Belonging scared me, but the thought of somehow belonging to someone and then possibly losing them terrified me even more. Walls would keep me safe—they always had.

I once had a foster mom who was convinced something was wrong with me. She had me tested dozens of times when I lived with her. What I knew now was that most likely my trauma responses made her uncomfortable. I'd gotten better at hiding things with age, but, at the time, she had chalked them up to demons, muttering that I needed more prayer. Walking down the long aisle at her church with her clutching my wrist was mortifying, but I went to a happier place in my head and blocked it all out. When we got to the altar, she spilled all of my personal story to a complete stranger while they looked as horrified as I felt. I can still remember the bewildered compassion in their eyes, and that maybe they thought she was acting as peculiar as I did.

Teenage girls should be having crushes on boys, learning makeup, and dancing, but I had been the opposite of all of those things. I avoided men at all costs. I never dated. It wasn't until I met Talia that she taught me the finer points of skillfully applied makeup. What I hadn't learned from her, I'd learned online. And I wasn't coordinated enough for dancing. I was me, and they were them. I didn't have anything in common with the average woman. If anything depraved or evil could have been done to me, it had been. These were only a few of the reasons I couldn't be friends with Soren. He was everything that was wholesome, and I was everything that was not.

I was simply a social worker trying to prevent children from experiencing the hell that was my childhood. Maybe if people had second lives, I'd try to get to know him better, but in this life, I was all wrong for a good man such as him. I didn't particularly enjoy how he saw too much because when he saw all of me, he'd want to leave like everyone else had. Instead of giving him the choice to choose me or not, I made the decision for him. It was a harsh truth to accept that you weren't worth staying for, but it was simply the fact of my existence. I didn't have heightened emotions about it. I knew it with certainty like I knew that the sky was blue and the grass was green. It was just another fact of my life.

Without warning, I heard a loud pop and hiss. I hit the brakes, fearing the worst. My Jeep came to a sliding stop as the gravel skidded beneath the tires. Gravel dust flew in the air. Dang!

Chapter Fifteen

Sawyer

WHAT WAS IT WITH having issues on the gravel roads of Rhodes County? It was as if they had all united against me. I blew a strand of hair out of my face as I mentally went through the list of people that could help. I'd love to say I knew how to change my own tire, but I didn't. I had never had anyone teach me. Talia and Rob were gone on a day trip to Kansas City, and my coworkers were already maxed out. And that was the end of my painfully short list. I waited for the gravel dust to settle, unbuckled, and climbed out, already knowing what I would find.

Flat tire on the driver's rear side. I could call roadside assistance, but who knew how long that would take? My phone remarkably had two cell bars so I could attempt to call for help. I kicked the tire in frustration. A noisy, old gray pickup rumbled down the road, and a gangly looking, thin man rolled down the window. I gripped my cell phone tighter in my hand. Of course, in a small town like this, people would stop to offer to help. Panic gripped my lungs as I took in my surroundings. I was miles away from anyone. My heart picked up speed at the recognition of how alone I was.

"Need any help, darlin'?" the man called out. He smiled kindly, but I knew immediately I couldn't do this.

"Uh, I have a friend coming!" I called rather loudly, trying to make the lie sound true.

"Alrighty then, didn't want to leave you stuck out here without stopping to ask."

He was harmless, but what if the next passerby wasn't? The only person I knew in the area was Soren. Ugh. Surely, he'd have a suggestion for a mechanic or tow company, even though I despised the idea of asking him for help. I pulled up his number as the man drove away, raising his hand out the window. I locked myself back in my Jeep to text Soren.

Sawyer:

Hi. Is there a mechanic you recommend in the area?

Three dots appeared and disappeared, and then my phone was ringing. Of course he simply wouldn't respond by text. I took a deep breath and answered.

"Hello."

"Hey, Sawyer. What do you need a mechanic for?" Straight to the point. What did I expect?

"Something mechanic-y." *Ugh. I was such a freak. Why did I text him?*

That tall, thin man was clearly perfectly harmless. He could have helped me, and I wouldn't have had to call Soren. He gave a small laugh, and chill bumps skated across my skin.

"Mechanic-y?" You could hear the laughter in his voice.

"Yeah."

"Are you nearby?" he asked, as if he was looking around.

"Maybe, but I don't want to bother you. Can you just tell me who to call?" I reasoned.

"You could never bother me. Tell me where you are." His voice was serious, mirroring the first time I met him.

"I had a little incident . . . with a rock, and I have a flat tire. I'm sure a mechanic can fix it."

"Where are you?" His voice brooked no argument.

"I liked it better when you were talking nicely to me," I replied.

"Well. I'll like it better when I know that you're safe." I hated being a burden.

I didn't know what to say. I desperately needed help, but I was hesitant to be around him again. I had turned down his two previous offers to get together, and I honestly didn't know why. He made me feel safe even when he was grumpy, but it was the way he saw all of me that came across as unnerving.

"Drop me a pin of your location. Please." He ground out that 'please' like it killed him to say it.

"Uh. Okay. I'm sorry." I blew out a breath and sent the location pin.

"There's no reason to be sorry, Pretty Girl. I'm on my way." *Click.*

I spent the next ten minutes spiraling about how much I hated being a burden to people and lamenting the fact I didn't know how to change a tire. How does one learn that as an adult if you never had someone teach you? I'd search for some YouTube videos tonight before bed. I heard the crunch of gravel and glanced in my rearview mirror to see Soren's forest green mammoth of a truck pull in behind me. Well, here we go.

I unlocked my door and slid out. Soren's long-legged denim-clad stride ate up the gravel between us, his eyes pinning me down. Concern was evident on his face.

"Are you okay?"

He wrapped me in a hug, and my body went ramrod straight. It wasn't that I didn't want a hug. It had completely shocked me. Sometimes I had to sit in a moment before I could make my body and brain get on the same page. He quickly pulled away, and I swore I saw hurt as one of the many emotions that rapidly crossed his face before he turned.

"Yeah, I'm so sorry. I didn't mean for you to stop what you're doing to help me," I supplied.

"I will always stop for you," he stated matter-of-factly.

My fingers had already found my chain, and my thumb brushed against the raised words, processing his statement. "I've never learned how to change a tire, and I don't know what to do."

"Roll your sleeves up, Pretty Girl. I'm putting you to work." My eyes jumped to his, and his eyes crinkled in the corners in a smile.

Over the next twenty minutes, Soren walked me through every step and answered every question as if it was the best question he'd ever heard. He even let me twist this metal tool that I now knew was a lug wrench. We put the replacement tire on before he went around one more time, pulling strenuously and making his biceps flex. I had changed my first tire! And this was way better than learning through an instructional online video. I would certainly be noting this in my journal tonight. Look out tires, Sawyer was here to save the day! I felt so independent and strong because he had taken the time to teach me, and he had a way of doing it where I didn't feel dumb or small. I snapped a few photos as reminders throughout the various stages, in case I had to employ this newly learned skill again.

"You really lucked out with having a real spare tire and not just a donut. What are you doing for the rest of the day?" Soren asked while wiping his hands on a rag.

"Grocery shopping and then some baking."

"What do you think about seeing some baby calves?" he asked with a grin.

Chapter Sixteen

Sawyer

SERIOUSLY, WHO CAN'T TURN down adorable baby animals? Me, apparently. I followed Soren back to his house, and we loaded up on his UTV with the promise of seeing multiple baby calves.

"How many will there be?" I asked as I sat on the UTV.

"It's near the end of calving season. I'm checking on them to make sure everyone is good, but as of yesterday, there were fifty-three in this pasture."

"Fifty-three babies!" I squeaked in excitement.

He laughed as he reached around me, and I involuntarily stiffened, unsure of what he was doing. He paused, searching my eyes as he grasped the seat belt strap.

"Oh, I was going to get it," I wheezed out. His nearness made me feel like I couldn't take a full breath.

My hand brushed his, and a zing ran through my body. What was that? I fastened the buckle into place and found my chain again to settle my nerves.

"Always wear a seatbelt, Pretty Girl." The weight of his words stopped me.

"I always do," I responded.

He nodded. I wished I could read him better. His face wasn't expressive in big ways, but there were micro expressions, like a slight lift of an eyebrow, that could be missed if you weren't watching closely.

Soren was all square jawline and stubble.

He turned on the key in the ignition and some archaic version of wailing country music began playing from the speakers on the dash.

"What is this? Do you listen to old people's country music?" That was surprising. He coughed out a laugh.

"Old people country music?" he finally snorted out in mock offense, one of his perfect eyebrows quirking.

"Yeah . . . " There was something about being in this place that made me feel free and more lighthearted.

"These are the classics," he spoke with exaggerated reverence and then turned to smile at me while he made a turn.

"Wow. I never figured you for old people's music . . . " I tipped my head, biting back a smile.

"You don't even know my age. Maybe I am old," he reasoned, still smiling. His hazel eyes danced with mirth.

"According to your taste in music?" I tapped my finger on my chin and tipped my head. "Ninety-eight?" I guessed. He scoffed, grinning.

"Thirty-three." His hands flexed on the steering wheel.

"See! Too young for old people's music." I reasoned with a smile.

"Alright, for this blasphemy I'm going to teach you all about the classics!" he declared.

For the next twenty minutes, we talked about all things music. I told him that I enjoyed the newer country style, which he asserted wasn't even country, it was pop. I enjoyed our back and forth teasing because it made me relax before I even realized it. The stress of the week melted away. He made me stop over-analyzing everything and completely be in the moment. All the muscles that were tight from stress relaxed, and I enjoyed seeing glimpses of his world.

We entered a field with dozens of cows and calves. The smile on my face was somewhat ridiculous, but I couldn't stop it. The calves were fuzzy and adorable. There was a calf that was freshly born. It was still stumbling around, learning to walk on wobbly legs. The cows mostly ignored us as we drove except for a few that raised their large heads to see what we were up to. I brought my hands together under my chin in excitement.

"Do they have names?"

"They have ear tags. There's too many to name." He gestured toward a particularly cute calf.

"Everyone deserves a name!"

"Have at it, but good luck trying to remember them all." He smiled and gestured toward the herd. He did have a point.

"Hmmm . . . maybe I can name one cow and one calf?" I observed them for a moment, deciding which pair I should choose.

"That would be easier to keep track of." He pulled out an iPad from the glove box and began noting information on the herd.

"Hmmm. Which one has the best personality?" I asked.

His laugh made my insides all tingly.

"*Wellllll . . . ,*" he drawled, as though he'd never considered it in those terms. "That one is a decent mama cow. She always raises good calves." He pointed the stylus from his iPad toward a beautiful red and white cow with what resembled freckles of white on her face.

"She certainly deserves a name. What about Freckles?"

"That fits."

"Is the calf a boy or girl?" I asked, tipping my head to the side as if I'd know what I was looking at.

"We're gonna have to teach you some ranch terms. A female cow that hasn't had any calves yet is a heifer. That calf is a heifer."

"After she has a baby, she's a cow?"

"Yep," he confirmed, continuing to make notes next to a list of numbers that matched the bright orange ear tags.

"What about Freckles and Delta?" He studied the cow and calf, dipping his chin in a nod.

"Sounds good, Pretty Girl." A smile tugged at his lips.

I wasn't used to having someone call me terms of endearment, and this man used them as though he was tossing candy in a parade. He must be this way with everyone. I had a coworker named Sharon that was always calling everyone sweetheart, darling, and honey. I craved his easy way of existing. He welcomed people easily, and it seemed as if once he knew someone, they simply belonged. I envied the people that knew him well. The good, wholesome people that belonged to him, and he belonged to them. A jolt from the UTV brought me back to the present.

"Hey." I must have missed him calling my name.

"Uh. Sorry, my mind was wandering." My cheeks heated.

"Can I ask you something?" The sudden seriousness of his tone made me question if I wanted to say yes.

"Uh, okay."

"Is there a reason you've been avoiding me?" His voice was gentle. I couldn't lie, not when his eyes peered into my soul. I looked down at my hands and reached for my chain.

"Soren. I'm not like other people." Why did he have this ability to make me say things I never spoke to anyone?

I blew out a deep breath and continued fidgeting with the tags, my eyes watching my fingers. It was best to lay things out in the open, even if it was embarrassing.

"Maybe that's why I want to get to know you." His quiet confidence nearly undid me.

"I don't do well with new people," I pushed back.

"What if I don't want to be a 'new person' anymore?" His voice sounded low.

I peeked up and the soft sincerity in his eyes caught me by surprise.

"What do you mean?"

"What if I want to get to know you so thoroughly that I'm not a new person to you anymore?"

I ducked my head again and a heated blush painted my cheeks. My fingers rubbed a familiar pattern over the dog tags. His straightforward directness was something I wasn't accustomed with.

"Why?" I studied his face as he watched me in return.

"Because you're someone I want to know." How could he know that?

I wasn't sure if I completely understood why, but what would it hurt? I was used to people being in my life for short periods of time. I had hundreds of foster siblings float in and out of my life over the years. This wouldn't be any different. We would get to know each other, and then he'd move on because everyone always does. I simply had to make sure that I kept my expectations where they should be.

"Okay. But only if I convince you to listen to some newer country music," I quipped because everything was too heavy, and avoiding experiencing real emotions was my specialty.

He laughed, most likely seeing the moment for what it was but being thoughtful enough to let it be.

"Alright. Who should I listen to?"

Chapter Seventeen

Soren

THERE WAS SOMETHING ABOUT being with Sawyer that was addicting, and if anyone understood addiction, it was me. I wanted to weigh the pros and cons of giving into the addiction. My fingers itched to text George and schedule a time to meet. I would as soon as Sawyer left, but for now, I indulged and held fast to any moment she would talk to me. I had never experienced these feelings about a woman, especially one I barely knew. Any moment spent with her was as if a delicate butterfly had landed on my finger, and I didn't want to do anything that would make her fly away. The fragile balance of making sure she felt safe and not overwhelming her with my intense hope to know her was crucial. To be around her. To spend moments of time in her light. I was a plant desperate for warmth from the sun. This fierce desire to make her feel safe was something I couldn't escape. I had acted impulsively when I hugged her earlier, but the panic that shot through me was staggering. When she said she was stranded with a flat tire, my heart raced full speed ahead until I laid eyes on her beautiful face and knew everything was okay. It scared me how much I wanted to know her. Yes, she was incredibly beautiful, but it was more than that. I could listen to her soft voice for days. Her gentleness pulled at a protective streak in me that wanted to run wild. I wanted to capture her fidgeting hands in mine, but I knew she wasn't comfortable with me reaching for her. She was adorable in ways she would never understand. The light in her eyes when she'd been able to quickly run her hand over the coat of a calf was like Christmas morning and fireworks on the fourth of July wrapped into one. I memorized that smile because I didn't want to forget it. We were on our way back to my house, but I didn't want the afternoon to end. After we parked, I unbuckled and turned toward her.

"What can I do to make you feel safe so that you'll come to my house on Sunday for dinner with a couple of my friends?" I would do anything.

"You would do that for me?" Her forehead scrunched as if she were confused.

"Sawyer, I'm finding that I would do anything for you." Her cheeks blushed because my mouth and my brain had run off with themselves where she was concerned. She bit her lip and dipped her head.

"W-Would it be okay if Talia and her husband, Rob, came with me?" Her voice was quiet when she asked.

"Of course, Talia and I go *wayyy* back." She laughed, and I added, "It'll be me and my friends, Lane and Jonah. They helped during the search."

"Okay. What should I bring?" She bit the inside of her cheek.

"What about that cheesecake Talia was bragging about?"

That tugged another smile out of her. I could tell she was overthinking, so I made a specific request that would ease some of the anxiety for her.

"I think I could do that. Chocolate chip cookie dough or a classic cheesecake?" she asked.

"What type of question is that? If chocolate is involved, it's always the answer."

"Then chocolate you shall have." She tipped her head.

Her shy, playful smile made my chest tight, and I realized in that moment I'd do whatever it took to keep a smile on her face. Talia was right the first time I met her. There was something special about Sawyer, but as certain as I knew this, I also knew she didn't realize it. Her light was something I never wanted to be without, but I had also felt that way about Abel, and I had ruined that.

Chapter Eighteen

Sawyer

I HAD OVERANALYZED GOING to Soren's on Sunday until I couldn't dissect it anymore. I wanted to get to know him better but my curiosity battled my anxiety. I knew I needed to call Talia to talk me down before I sent a text to cancel. I was twenty-six years old. I needed to woman-up and just go. I unloaded my work bag with my laptop and drudged everything inside. Once I had traded my work clothes for a set of oatmeal-colored, cozy loungewear and settled into my nest of weighted blankets in my overstuffed chair, I called Talia. She answered right away.

"Hey, what's up?" Her voice was vibrant and cheery.

"I think I made a mistake."

I put the phone on speaker, tugging my weighted blankets up to cover my shoulders.

"Oh. How so?"

"I saw Soren today, and he invited me to his house for dinner on Sunday, but I told him I couldn't come without you. Puh-lease tell me you're available."

Talia laughed.

"How'd you run into Soren?" She asked.

I caught her up on how I'd seen him today and what had happened with my tire.

"Ooooh. So you've been getting sexy tire changing lessons?" Talia teased in a saucy voice. I was so deep in my panic, I couldn't even laugh at her teasing tone.

"Tal. I'm such a freak. Why can't I just go to dinner like a normal person?"

"Would you let someone call me that?" Her question caught me off guard.

"What?" I asked, my brow scrunched.

"Would you let someone call me a freak?" Her calm therapist voice was out on full display.

"No, of course not." Talia was the best human I knew.

"Why would I let my best friend who is brave and fierce and kind and smart and funny call herself a freak?" My heart momentarily stopped in my chest and tears filled my eyes as she gently added, "You deserve good things Sawyer Brannan. The best things, and it's time that you saw that."

146

I sniffed, trying to keep my tears at bay even as one slid down my cheek.

"Okay," I finally said, unsure of what to say.

"Ava is due for some grandparent time with Gigi. Rob and I can go, but I'm not tolerating any of this freak talk about my best friend okay?"

"Okay," I answered. I wished I could see myself the way she saw me. "Thank you, Tal. I panicked, and then I was debating sending a text to cancel." I rubbed my thumb over the inscription on the tags.

"You better not cancel on that hot cowboy!" she chastised. "Besides, going will give me a better chance to investigate him, since I can't find him online and Rob won't do any of my dirty work. What's the point of being married to an ADA if they won't be nosy for you?"

She laughed since we both knew she had FBI-level social media stalking skills and that she was as obsessed with Rob as he was with her.

"Oh, good grief!" I laughed, knowing I had the best friend in the world.

Soren:

Photo of Freckles and Delta

Your friends say "Hi."

Sawyer:

five heart eye emojis

Tell them "Hey" back! Delta is already so much bigger!

Chapter Nineteen

Sawyer

SUNDAY CAME AROUND FASTER than I anticipated, but I did some soul searching over the last couple of days and was determined to relax and have fun. Rob drove while Talia and I chatted most of the way to Soren's house and I tried to relax. Rob had remained quiet for the first part of the trip, however when Talia and I had reached a lull, he asked, "Am I supposed to play the tough big brother, or am I playing more of a wingman?" Talia and I both laughed.

"Neither!" I retorted between laughs. His sense of humor was one of my favorite things about him.

"I didn't bring a shotgun and I feel less effective pulling the tough guy act without one." His voice took on a twang as he added, "You wantin' to go sparkin' with my little sister, son? I'm going to need your date of birth, social security number, and credit score."

He glanced back in the rearview mirror, his eyes sparkling with humor.

"No shotgun needed, babe," Talia advised, patting his forearm. "Besides, your courtroom stare-down is intimidating enough."

Talia and I both knew that was true. I wouldn't want to be on the opposing side in a courtroom when it came to Rob Sharpe. He was intimidating enough at six foot five, but his dark green eyes could cut like a knife. Talia and I sat in on a significant trial he had a couple of years ago where Rob prosecuted a man that had killed his own neighbor. Talia had wanted to support him and didn't want to be alone. I would have confessed right away if I was on the receiving end of his persuasive presentation skills and intense stare.

"I'm not sure he wants to 'spark' me!" I could barely hold back my laughter at the antiquated term.

"Let me be the judge of that, li'l sister," he quipped in his twang again. It was undoubtedly the most exaggerated twang I had ever heard. I laughed again at his ridiculousness. I was beyond thankful for my friendship with Talia and Rob. They both knew me better than anyone, and their teasing helped to distract me. I was a fish out of water when it came to dating or even being around a man. I'd never dated, and although this wasn't a date, it felt new and different and dating adjacent. After everything I'd been through, the idea of unnecessarily engaging in an interaction with a man had not been high on my list of things to do. In all honesty, I avoided it whenever I could.

"Thank you both for coming." My eyes watered at how much they meant to me and how they had sacrificed their time to come with me.

"All kidding aside, Sawyer. You deserve all the good things in life, and I hope Mr. Soren Montgomery Roberts realizes that." My mouth dropped open at the same time Talia swatted at Rob's arm.

"Hey, hey!" He raised his arm to shield himself, his smile taking over his whole face.

"You investigated him and didn't tell me!" Talia squealed.

"I'm going to an unknown man's house with two of my favorite ladies. Of course, I looked him up! You'll be glad to know he's got a good credit score."

I knew he was kidding about his credit score, but it cracked me up all the same.

"Oh my word!" I exclaimed.

Talia laughed, her eyes dancing with amusement. I loved these moments of seeing a healthy relationship like theirs up close. They were best friends, but there was no mistaking the way they were attracted to each other. Talia and Rob were lucky to love each other so fiercely. If I ever were to fall in love, I'd want a relationship like theirs where I could be fully myself and be loved, flaws and all.

Chapter Twenty

Soren

I CARRIED OUT A baking sheet laden with seasoned ribs and tin-foil-wrapped asparagus with lemon, parmesan cheese, and butter, along with a shake of creole seasoning. It was always a crowd favorite, and Lane specifically asked me if I was making it. I lifted the grill lid and transferred the items to the racks. The smell of Applewood was in the air. Sawyer would be here soon and I had nerves of anticipation. I had slept with more women than I cared to admit, but I hadn't truly dated that much, which left me feeling unbalanced and awkward. I'd never been this nervous before, and it wasn't even a date. There was something inside me that wanted to be around Sawyer. It was more than getting a piece of Abel back, it was more than attraction. There was a spark in her that made me feel like a moth chasing after the warmth of light.

Outside of the two years where I walked through hell and then ultimately hit rock bottom, I'd had a good life. I still remembered the second worst day of my life in vivid detail, and it made me gun shy where women were concerned. I had rolled up from the pasture to a blonde sitting on my front porch steps, just as Sawyer had, except the difference had been night and day. A devil and an angel. Their differences couldn't be cataloged, there were too many. I swallowed past the acidic bile that rose in my throat. Sawyer wasn't anything like her, but the experience made me cautious to put myself in that vulnerable place ever again. I had a lot more to lose now. I heard the sound of tires on gravel and looked up to see a black BMW SUV pull in. That had to be Sawyer and her friends, Talia and Rob. They parked alongside my dark green pickup. I glanced down at the grill temp, closed the lid, wiped my already clean hands on the hand towel over my shoulder, and walked down the side steps. Sawyer stepped out wearing a pair of light wash distressed jeans cuffed at the ankle, a white shirt that was trimmed in lace, and white sneakers. Her waist length blonde hair was a cascade of loose curls over her shoulders and back. Everything about her was soft. Her eyes met mine as I realized I'd walked up to her without even realizing I was moving.

"Hey," I rasped, the nerves evident in my voice. Hell, I was acting like some punk kid. What was wrong with me? At least Lane wasn't here yet to witness this because I knew he wouldn't let it go.

The corners of her full lips kicked up.

"I brought cheesecake." She held up a food container.

"Good girl."

Double what the hell. I had told her "good girl" like . . . I raked a hand through my hair. Her eyes widened and danced with amusement, and that's when I heard a man clear his throat. I couldn't even tear my eyes away from her to glance at where the sound came from.

"Can I try again?" I asked despite the heat crawling up my neck.

I blew out a breath and scrubbed a hand down my face. Why was I so awkward with her?

She nodded, biting her lip to contain her smile as light danced across her bright blue eyes.

"Hey, Pretty Girl. I'm glad you're here."

A smile lit up her face.

"Me too," she agreed as she bit the inside of her cheek.

She turned to the couple that were now watching us as if we were a science experiment. I recognized Talia right away, and she was wearing another neon outfit that fit her personality. Today, she was mostly sunshine yellow. Next to her was a man who was almost as tall as Jonah, with thick black hair and intense dark green eyes.

"You've met Talia, and this is her husband, Rob."

I stretched out my hand and Rob gave me a handshake that might have been more firm than necessary.

Talia was bubbly which I suspected was her typical nature. Rob was outgoing albeit a lot more reserved than his wife. His staredown was intimidating, but I couldn't blame him for being protective of this girl. She was worth protecting.

"Come on in. I'll carry that."

I reached to take the container Sawyer was holding as Rob carried a casserole container for Talia. She passed it over, and I asked them about their drive over. After getting everything settled, I offered them glass bottle sodas and we gathered around the side porch by the grill. The conversation was stiff at first, but after a few minutes, things relaxed. Talia was excellent at keeping things flowing with small talk, and Jonah drove up in his matte black truck not long after.

"Hey, man." He greeted me by smacking my shoulder after he had carried in a bowl of homemade guacamole and chips to the refrigerator. I made the introductions, and although Jonah was not a talker, I could see that he was trying to be welcoming. Rob was still watching me intensely and my neck burned in embarrassment at my earlier fumble. My mom would have slapped me upside the head. *I* wanted to slap me upside the head.

"Did you see the text from Lane?" Jonah asked, getting settled with a glass bottle of root beer.

"No. What'd it say?" I asked as I rotated the ribs on the grill.

"He's running late but said he's still going to make it. Something about a meeting running late."

"That figures," I replied as I nodded, because it wasn't unusual. Lane ran an empire, although nobody here in Kennedy knew that. Regardless of his smart mouth and ability to joke his way through life, I knew that he could be serious when needed. He had done a lot of good after his MLB retirement. I had never realized how complex his life was until a few months ago when he felt overwhelmed and spilled the beans during a boxing session. He had been having these moments of feeling maxed out, but he still wouldn't stop, and sometimes you could tell he hadn't been sleeping enough. I certainly wasn't the best influence either because I ran non-stop too. I had pressure pushing in on me from all directions, but not nearly as much as he did. You couldn't manage everything I did without sensing the weight of responsibility. These times when I'd have the guys over were when I intentionally made the time to take a break. Partly because I needed one, but also because I saw that they did too. If I presented it as my idea, then it didn't feel like they were taking a break, it was them showing up for a friend. When things seriously counted, Lane and Jonah had always shown up for me.

Chapter Twenty-One

Soren

THE WEATHER WAS PERFECT for a cook out and after everything was off the grill, we settled around the large wooden table on the west side of the house. Everyone settled in, eating and carrying on conversation as if we'd known each other for years. I found out that Rob and Talia had been married for three years and that they had a daughter named Ava. Talia and Sawyer met in college during basics, and after graduation, Talia met Rob while assisting him on a case.

Lane had texted with apologies a couple times saying he was running even later than expected, but was still stopping by. I went ahead and made a plate and set it aside for him. Sawyer commented sparingly throughout the meal, but she seemed to be enjoying herself. She was extremely close with the Sharpes, and I was glad that she had people in her corner like Talia and Rob. Although I didn't know them well, I could tell that they genuinely cared about her; their presence alone spoke of that. She nearly glowed when she talked about their daughter, Ava, pulling out her phone to show me a photo. I pulled up a photo of Hope, Jonah's toddler niece, who I had claimed as my own.

Sawyer and I cleared the last of the dishes while Jonah was talking about his gym with Rob and Talia in the family room. I knew that was a stretch for him since he preferred solitude. Rob had expressed an interest in boxing and Jonah was telling him what classes and programs were available. Gaines, Jonah's gym, was known throughout the region as the premier place to be trained. It was a drive for most people, being located in Kennedy, but one they were willing to make to have top-notch instructors.

Lane entered the house with a bravado that only he could muster. I heard him long before I saw him, as he had let himself in and called out a welcome. From the tidbits I could hear from the kitchen, Lane was certainly shaking hands and making apologies for being late. Sawyer slid up her white lacy sleeves as she faced the sink.

"What are you doing?" I asked, bringing the washcloth I had used to wipe down the counter back to the sink.

"Washing the dishes," She answered matter-of-factly, twisting her hair around and swinging the silky rope behind her back. I walked up behind her, placing my hands on the counter on either side of her as she faced the sink. The front of my body was a hair's breadth away from hers.

"No way. I'll do this later. It's time for you to relax," I pointed out, leaning to see her face. I wasn't touching any part of her body, but I smelled the soft scent of strawberries as the wisps of hair near her ear and neck fluttered from my exhale.

"I can help," she offered, a bit breathless. I watched in fascination as pale pink spread across the smattering of freckles on her cheeks.

"Nope."

She turned toward me, leaning against the farmhouse-style sink, and I stepped back, dropping my arms to give her space.

"Okay."

She looked like she wanted to push, but paused, then added, "Thank you for dinner and letting me bring Talia and Rob."

"I'm glad you came." I'd do whatever I needed to see her.

Her shattered blue eyes met mine in a gentle smile that made the freckles on her face resemble gold confetti.

"Me too," she replied softly.

She pushed off the counter and walked toward the family room, turning back as if waiting for me to join her. She didn't realize that I'd follow her wherever she went. I pulled the hand towel off my shoulder and draped it on the sink basin to join her. Instantaneously, I saw it all happen in slow motion. Lane rounded the corner from the family room to the kitchen as Sawyer was facing away from him. His goofy smile stretched across his face as he dropped both of his large hands onto Sawyer's shoulders while loudly exclaiming, "*Well.* If it isn't the little lady that caught my buddy's eye!"

Sawyer froze, eyes huge, and immediately dropped to the ground shielding herself. The whimper that emitted from her throat ripped my heart from my chest. Her hands covered her head as her knees were tucked by her face. Lane stood paralyzed, a thousand questions in his eyes that were as wide as Sawyer's had been. He held his hands up in surrender and most likely surprise. I rushed toward Sawyer but clasped a hand on Lane's shoulder, hastily meeting his stunned green eyes. Lane and I had a conversation that you can only have with someone you know, where words are not needed—just a look. The regret and self-condemnation on his face was palpable.

"Go save Jonah. I've got this."

I squeezed his shoulder as he nodded, backing away slowly. I knew Jonah had to be reaching the end of his word usage for the day. I had no doubt Lane could pull out his class clown act that made him a crowd favorite and keep the room thoroughly entertained. It'd give Sawyer a moment of privacy as I tried to navigate what had just happened. I sat beside her, legs outstretched making sure not to touch her.

"Sawyer?" I softened my voice, afraid to startle her further.

She didn't move. Could she hear me in this state?

"Pretty Girl. It's me, Soren. Is it okay if I hold your hand?"

I stretched out a hand beside her palm up, allowing her to make the first move. I wanted it to be her choice.

After a moment, I saw a slight movement of her head that resembled a nod. Her forehead rested on her knees. She was repeating a breathing pattern that I was sure was something she used to cope when these moments happened.

"Here's my hand. Can you hold it?"

With some hesitation, her small trembling hand slid from covering her head and found mine. Her hand was soft and delicate against my larger calloused one. I threaded her fingers through mine. She rested her temple on her knees as she turned toward me and regarded me with glassy red-rimmed eyes.

"It's going to be okay, Pretty Girl." I would have asked if she was okay, but it was as if she needed to be assured that everything was fine.

My thumb stroked the silky skin on the back of her hand. She took in a choppy deep breath.

"I'm sorry. Was that Lane? Please tell him I'm sorry. He's going to think I'm crazy."

"You have nothing to be sorry about. Don't worry about Lane. I'll talk to him. He's a loud bonehead sometimes."

This brought out a small watery laugh, and my heart began to slow from the breakneck rhythm it had been beating at. I would do whatever I could to keep a smile on her face. I didn't fully understand C-PTSD, but I was going to change that. I wanted to be someone she could count on, and how could I do that without knowing more about something that affected her this deeply?

We sat for a few minutes before she was comfortable enough to stand. I made her a glass of iced water and after a couple of sips, we walked into the family room as if nothing had happened. Lane's eyes met mine, and I knew we'd be talking tonight. Rob had connected the dots to who Lane was, but other than saying he had one hell of a career, no one made a big deal. We talked for another thirty minutes or so, and then everyone made their leave. I walked Sawyer out and hoped with everything inside me that we could try this again.

Gym at 10 p.m.?

There.

Yeah.

Chapter Twenty-Two

Soren

I KNEW I'D BE getting the third degree, but I also knew I had to explain. I changed into navy joggers and a white t-shirt and headed to the gym. After parking, I pulled the keys from the ignition and flipped a coin down my knuckles as I collected my thoughts. I wasn't nervous, but this thing with Sawyer felt massive, even as I fought the voice that said I should stay away from her. She had enough going on without my regrets. I wasn't sure how to encompass what it was about her that felt like she had a string tied to my heart, even though I barely knew her. Lane and Jonah both knew I hadn't had a woman in my life in years, ever since my life blew up and the metaphorical shrapnel nearly annihilated everyone around me. I also was thoroughly aware of how foreign this was for them to see me with someone. I was protective of Sawyer and wanted to make sure they understood that, without sharing too much. I made my way to the glass doors, ran my key fob over the sensor, and went inside. The sound system blared rock music, which was most undeniably Lane's choice. Jonah was jumping rope while Lane obliterated a punching bag. Sweat trickled down from his dirty blond hair and soaked his gray, vintage concert shirt with cut-off sleeves.

They both paused when they saw me. Jonah cut off the roar of music from his phone.

"Damn. I'm so sorry, man." Lane's face was overtaken with anguish. No doubt he had been beating himself up over what had happened. I raised a hand to cut him off because he didn't know the whole story, and I felt partially responsible that I hadn't said anything. I wasn't sure what I would have said anyway. I didn't know all the ways in which she had been impacted by trauma.

Jonah nodded toward the table with chairs in the far corner by the water cooler. "Let's grab some water," he said.

We all took a seat and I began.

"It wasn't you so much as what you did that surprised her. Sawyer has C-PTSD." Jonah's expression barely shifted, but an understanding lit his eyes. He knew firsthand the effects of Post-Traumatic Stress Disorder. Lane scrubbed a hand over his mouth. "She was upset and asked me to apologize to you, which I told her wasn't necessary. The messed up thing is she couldn't help her reaction any more than you could have known you'd cause a reaction."

Lane wasn't a stranger to mental health struggles either, but at his core he had a tender heart, like a tagalong puppy, that he covered with his class clown routine.

"What does the C stand for? I've heard of PTSD, but not the C part," Lane asked, rubbing his towel across his forehead.

"Complex. It means she's had multiple traumatic events in her life that caused Post-Traumatic Stress Disorder."

"Dammit, man. I'm sorry. I know you don't just bring women around. I know she's special. I hate what happened. I won't ever make that mistake again. I should have chilled the hell out." It didn't matter what I responded with, Lane would beat himself up over what happened.

"I should have said something, but I wanted to protect her privacy. I want to get to know her better, and I haven't felt that way about a woman in a long time," I stated as I rested my forearms on my knees. Admitting that out loud was terrifying, but they were the truest words I'd ever spoken.

"What can we do to help Sawyer be comfortable when she's around us?" Jonah asked.

He was one of those people that didn't talk a lot but when he did, it was worth genuinely listening to. He not only was concerned for Sawyer, but he was also giving Lane something else to focus his attention on besides guilt for something that was out of his control.

"Well. I don't know all of her triggers, but I know one is unexpected touch, and another is loud sounds or anger."

I went on to briefly explain what happened at the graveside. I could tell Lane all day everyday he wasn't at fault, but I'd never forgive myself for the way I treated her that day. Both of them nodded where it was appropriate and asked clarifying questions from time to time. Shame was a rock in my stomach as I talked about my behavior, but they deserved to know I hadn't been my best self either.

"Hell. I feel even worse," Lane commented.

"Yeah." I rubbed a hand down my face.

"Unless there's something else, I think I might be up for a run." I needed to burn off the tension of watching her hit the floor earlier. I rubbed my sternum to relieve the sensation that someone was squeezing my heart in a vise.

"Nah, I'm good," Lane noted quietly.

"You're going to take care of her, right?" Jonah asked in his deep voice. Ever the caretaker. His onyx eyes met mine.

"Yeah." I nodded.

I rubbed at the tightness in my chest again. Why did I feel like I would do whatever it took to take care of her? I wanted to believe it was her connection to Abel that made me feel this tie between us, but I knew that couldn't be it. It'd been this way before I knew about the past. Sawyer had a pull on me unlike anything I had ever experienced before.

"All right, let's run," Jonah announced. There was no way I'd last as long as him. No one else in town could. We grabbed what we needed, found parallel treadmills, and I ran seven miles before I called it quits and Jonah and Lane waved me on as I walked out the door.

Chapter
Twenty-Three

Sawyer

GREG WAS THE LITERAL worst. Worst coworker. Worst employee. Worst lunch eater, if that was even a thing.

I couldn't prove it, but I was convinced he was stealing my lunch from the office fridge. I had made a series of check-ins around lunchtime. I would run to monitor the status of my lunchbox in the fridge as coworkers trickled in and out of the break room and narrowed it down to him. Sure, if he needed my lunch, I would share, but I knew that wasn't the case, especially when he most likely made a higher salary than I did.

What caused a man to steal his coworker's lunch? Laziness? Boredom? Did he seriously like my leftovers from dinner the night before that much? The whole thing was bizarre, but now that I had narrowed it down to him, I wasn't sure how to confront it.

Did I blaze a trail and say, "Greg, why are you stealing my lunch?" That made me want to vomit.

Should I casually say in a conversation around him, "Hmmmm . . . I wonder who ate my lunch?"

But who was going to fess up to being the lunch thief? The *leftover* lunch thief at that.

I blew out a huff as I perused the fridge, the cold air doing little to combat my hangry temper. As I debated the hassle of going out to lunch after I had packed a perfectly good lunch, I glanced at the screen of my phone to check the time. I had an hour before I needed to be back, but what caught my attention was an unread text that came in four minutes ago. I hadn't noticed it because my phone had been silenced from court that morning.

Soren

In Lewis City unexpectedly. Can I buy you lunch?

Lunch sounded amazing. Maybe then I'd stop thinking about how I was going to force a confession out of the leftover lunch thief, Greg. *The jerk!* The idea of seeing Soren made me feel giddy, and I'd never experienced anything similar before. Weird. I was also anxious after what had happened the last time I'd seen him. At some point, he would stop wanting to spend time with me, but what could it hurt to spend a little time with him until he decided to move on?

> It just so happens that the lunch thief struck again and I'm lunchless.

My phone rang a minute later.

"Hello."

"Hey, who do I need to set straight about taking my Pretty Girl's lunch? Send me your location and I'll be there ASAP." My Pretty Girl. My belly fluttered again at his words, and I sent him my location as I gathered my sweater and purse.

"Apparently someone that enjoys leftover lasagna," I whined.

"Did you make it?" I could hear his blinker in the background.

"Yes . . . " I drew it out. Why did that matter?

"Can't blame 'em! It had to be last meal worthy," he exclaimed.

"Last meal?" I asked, making my way back to my desk.

"Ya know, like the last meal on death row," he explained as if he had considered this *many* times.

"Okay. Why do I get the feeling you've spent a lot of time contemplating this and know exactly what you'd want?" I could hear his blinker again in the background.

"You haven't?!" His outrage made me smile.

"Uh, no. I don't plan on being on death row."

"Chicken fried steak, homemade mashed potatoes and gravy, peach iced tea, those little pieces of cake in the refrigerator section at gas stations, and a piece of your cheesecake," he stated matter-of-factly.

"Should I be concerned that you listed my cheesecake in the same sentence as gas station cake? I'm not even sure I know what you're talking about."

"Prettttty girlllllll." He drew out his name for me as though it was the saddest news he'd ever heard. "We need to fix that," he added, and I smiled at his exasperated tone.

"I suppose I could be persuaded," I conceded.

"I'm here to persuade. Pulling into the parking lot now." His confidence was incredibly hot.

"I'll be right out." I ended the call and made my way out the doors.

Soren was in his signature dark jeans and brown, square-toe boots with a slate blue flannel shirt that had a Carhartt light brown vest over the top. If "masculine" had a photo in the dictionary, it'd be him. His long legs ate up the asphalt as we met in the parking lot. He smiled that soft smile that was fully him, and I resisted the urge to touch him. There was something about him that made me want to be near him. It was foreign and strange and warm all at the same time.

"Ready?" he asked, tipping his head toward his truck. I almost wished he'd hug me again, but after that awkward exchange with the flat tire I thought that was unlikely. It was the weighty elephant in the room. But I smiled and shoved the elephant back under the rug, where I preferred to keep all of my elephants.

"Yep." He waved an arm toward his truck, as if it was a chariot, and opened my door. I climbed in, which was always a feat because of the height. He grabbed my seat belt strap as he had on the first day we met and buckled it. His body never touched mine, but heat flushed through my body like a wildfire. His eyes caught mine and conveyed things I didn't understand, but I wanted to as he leaned back to close the door. He rounded the hood, and I took the opportunity to take a deep breath to steady my heart that raced anytime he was near.

We settled on a local café that sold specialty sandwiches because apparently down the street was a gas station that held the "last meal" refrigerator sliced cake. Soren insisted we go there after lunch. I ordered a sandwich labeled a Memphis Club while Soren chose a spicy sandwich labeled The New Orleans Club. The teenager at the counter with the side swept bangs mumbled he'd bring us our meals once they were prepared. Soren guided me through the tables. He never touched me, but I could sense the heat from his body when we walked closely together. I sat on one side of a tan leather booth while Soren sat on the other.

"Do you really have a lunch thief?" Soren asked.

"Yes! I know who it is, but I don't know why." I pondered it still.

"If your cheesecake and cookies are any indication of how great your lasagna is, then I pity the poor soul who has to work with you knowing what's in your lunch box." He slowly shook his head from side to side.

"Pity the soul? What about my hungry soul when I see that my lunch is gone?!" Soren let out a laugh, and I had to roll my lips together not to beam at our lighthearted exchange. He made me relaxed simply with his presence. The darkness that usually crept in as a thick fog when I tried, and often failed, to connect with new people felt distant now. It was as if being in his light fought off my darkness, and I felt less alone. My ability to connect with him reminded me of Abel. There was something about these Roberts boys that made them extra special. They starved the darkness away, and only left me with remembrances of light.

Chapter Twenty-Four

Soren

WAS IT POSSIBLE TO get drunk off a person? I was quickly becoming addicted to being in the presence of Sawyer Brannan. Sure, she was breathtakingly beautiful, but it wasn't simply her beauty that drew me in. She had this almost fragile softness that made me want to protect her, but she also held a strength unlike anyone I had ever met. I wanted to be her safe place so that she could shine.

When I met her, I didn't know her story, but ever since that talk on my front porch, this fierce protectiveness made me feel like a damn fool when it came to her. She wasn't even mine. I barely knew her, and somehow I knew deep in my core I'd do whatever it took to protect her at all costs. There was a string connected to me, and she held the other end. I was but a fool under the magic of her spell, and I never wanted to be anywhere else. After we ate our sandwiches, we loaded up in my truck to hit up the Mason's across the street. The gas station chain always carried Mama Kathy's slices of cold cake, and I had to correct the disservice of her having never tasted one. We went in, and she giggled as we collected three types of cake to taste, along with two bottles of water to cleanse our palettes in between each taste test. We loaded back up in the truck, and I ceremoniously opened the waxed butcher paper that contained the first slice of cake. Her eyes sparkled as I exaggerated the process.

"First up, we have the delectable white chocolate raspberry." I broke off a small piece and held it to her mouth. Her eyes widened and after briefly and shyly meeting my eyes, she opened her mouth. I wasn't prepared for the fire that shot through my body as her plump, soft bottom lip grazed my thumb. Her face lit up as she tasted the cake, as if she hadn't been struck by the same lighting I had. She nodded her head as she finished chewing and swallowed.

"Okay, okay. Not bad, Cowboy."

"Cowboy, huh? Next, we have a milk chocolate fudge cake with white frosting." I held out a piece, questioning my sanity as I repeated the process. This time, her lip didn't touch me. My erratic heartbeat couldn't take that again if we were only going to be friends. Although, I knew I was pushing the boundaries of friends every moment I could. Her eyes lit up as she chewed this bite.

"Oooohhh. That might be my favorite!" She took a sip of water as I unwrapped the third slice of cake.

"Last, we have a delicious strawberry cake with cream cheese frosting." I repeated the process, and she clapped her hands animatedly. Her eyes danced with delight as she savored the flavor.

"THIS! This is my favorite, favorite!" I chuckled at her enthusiasm.

"Mine too." Why did the two words feel so intimate? So right. Why did the territorial caveman part of me want to say I wanted her to be mine because she was my favorite too? But instead, we shared the cake, and I tried to think of anything else other than being her friend, because that might be the death of me. The first thing that came to mind was something that happened during lunch that I couldn't forget.

"So . . . if you know who is taking your lunch, why haven't you talked to them to see what's going on?" Her dappled blue eyes grew to the size of half dollars. Her hands instinctively reached to rub her thumb on the military tags that were tucked inside her shirt.

"Uhh . . . I'm not the best with confrontation and . . ." She looked away, as if she was embarrassed.

I hooked my index finger under her chin and turned her toward me.

"Tell me." Her teeth caught her bottom lip.

"I don't like conflict . . . " She glanced down at her phone. She had ten minutes before she needed to be back at work.

"What do you do when you disagree with something?"

She glanced at her phone again, avoiding telling me, which told me she always made herself agreeable.

"Um, I think I need to go back to work. I really appreciate you taking me to lunch. You're right about the cake. It's fantastic." She smiled as if I'd forget my question.

"You're welcome." I reached my hand toward her, then stopped. "May I hold your hand?"

She nodded, biting her lower lip. I engulfed her small hand in mine to ground her while I talked to her.

"Sawyer, you matter too." She ducked her head, and I knew that if I weren't holding her hand, she'd bolt from the truck. Her other hand was still rubbing a pattern on the tags.

"If you disagree with something or dislike something, it's okay to say that. You weren't okay with the mix-up on your sandwich at lunch, were you?" During lunch the cafe had mistakenly given her mayo instead of honey mustard. She had replied that it didn't matter, but I thought I'd caught her grimacing a couple of times while chewing.

She shook her head the smallest amount.

"Can you tell me?" I asked as gently as I could.

Her eyes found mine, and she took a steadying breath.

"I don't like mayo. It makes me want to puke. Someone made me eat old mayo once, and I've had a hard time eating it since. The café didn't know that and I didn't want to upset anyone."

My throat was tight and I burned with anger that anyone that could treat her badly, and with compassion for the beautiful woman at war with wanting to be herself. How anyone could cause pain to this woman was beyond me. She was gentle and kind. I had seen the way she handled Connor, even after the situation had derailed her day and she still had patience. She exhibited genuine kindness in a way that gave the impression that warmth seeped from her skin.

"I'm sorry that happened to you. Can we make a deal?" My thumb skimmed the back of her soft hand.

Her eyes searched mine and then another slight nod.

"If this happens again, will you tell me? I'll buy you another sandwich."

She shook her head and tugged at her hand to create distance. I let go, knowing that her controlling her space was more important than my desire to hold her hand.

"We'll treat it like a game. Every time I see you, I want you to disagree with me about something. You can practice on me."

Her eyes searched mine again, her forehead furrowed.

"Why?" It was almost a whisper.

"Because you should have a place to be authentically you and I want to be that place."

"And you won't get angry at me?" she asked as though she was having a hard time believing it.

"Nope."

"Okay," she responded. Although I wasn't sure if that was a full agreement, I was prepared to move forward and give her that space to be herself. Now that I knew her go-to was to make herself small to accommodate others, I'd watch more closely and make sure she knew she could be herself with me.

"Deal. But here's the thing—you can't say no for another five minutes." I should have gotten her to say yes before this whole empowering "no" talk. Apparently, I had become a rookie after not dating for so long.

"This feels like a trick," she said as a smile tugged at her lips.

"I have tickets to the Cal Austin concert next Friday. I thought I'd try out some of this pop country music if you want to come with me?" I knew Cal Austin was one of her favorites because she had played me two of his songs while we checked on the calves. When I saw they were coming to a nearby town, I had talked to Lane, and he had worked his charm and acquired me a pair of tickets.

"Really? Yes!" A smile stretched across her face like it was Christmas. I had never looked forward to a concert that was sure to make my ears bleed more in my life.

Chapter Twenty-Five

Sawyer

I SNUGGLED DOWN IN my comfy chair with my weighted blanket. Today was emotionally exhausting and my dang toilet was still making that trickling water sound. I needed to fix it before I lost my mind. Talia would be over shortly, but I wasn't sure if I could even convey everything that happened today. Soren intrigued me on a level that I'd never experienced before. I was still perplexed about disagreeing with him. It didn't seem a desirable trait to have in someone you wanted to be around, and yet, somehow I already knew Talia was going to love it. Knowing her, she would.

A ridiculous patterned knocking sounded at the door—one that she'd later claim sounded exactly like a hit boy band song—before Talia announced herself and used her key to unlock it. She even knocked in a happy way.

She came in as a burst of sunshine. She was wearing a bubblegum pink romper, matching lipstick, and thick, key lime-colored plastic hoops. Her black hair curled into corkscrews every which way around her head.

"Honey." She drew the word out and placed the bag of what I knew to be shrimp tacos on the coffee table. Her eyes were assessing. My hair was in a messy bun. I was makeup-less and wearing Soren's hoodie that had quickly become my favorite. "Talk or tacos?"

"Tacos."

She grabbed two cans of soda from my fridge and a couple of plates.

"Drink." She handed me the can and began making our plates.

I drank a fizzy sip and readjusted, pulling my blankets down to better free my hands.

She passed me a plate, and we ate in comfortable silence. The kind of silence that two longtime friends can have and not feel awkward. Within fifteen minutes, we had finished our food, and I was less overwhelmed.

"Thank you." Talia placed our plates on the coffee table and turned to me, concern etched in her brow.

"How are you feeling now?" she asked softly.

"I think you're going to be happy, but I'm a jumble of emotions."

"What emotion are you experiencing the most?" she inquired.

"Soren took me to lunch today," I said because I wasn't sure which emotion was the loudest.

Talia's face broke into a huge smile, as I knew it would. She knew I didn't date. Not because I didn't get asked regularly, but because I didn't see the need. Sure, a relationship sounds nice from the outside, until you've seen relationships unravel. I'd seen people pushed to the brink and being single sounded so much better than experiencing the hellish conditions I had again. The yelling, the screaming, the fighting. Sure, sometimes I was lonely, but my job kept me busy, and I wasn't one of those people that easily built relationships with others. I was broken beyond repair. The only person that'd made it past my walls of keeping my heart safe was Talia. Although, lately, my walls didn't feel thick enough against the intensity of one Soren Roberts. What was it about this man that made me feel things that didn't normally make it through my fortress walls? I wasn't even exactly sure what I was feeling.

I preferred my perfectly organized existence. I liked things being predictable. After a lifetime of instability, I craved sameness. I didn't like these new emotions Soren stirred within me, but at the same time, his kindness was disarming. I wanted to spend time with him. I wanted to know him. *Truly* know him. But doing that was daunting.

"Earth to Sawyer." Talia was waving a hand in front of my face. I blinked, lost in my head.

"Sorry, what did you ask?" I asked as I squirmed in my blanket nest.

"I asked how it went."

"It was unexpected, but not terrible." Talia laughed.

"Not terrible. That's always good," she remarked, her eyes dancing.

"I tried this gas station cake he likes. It was amazing!" I would certainly be making that a treat going forward.

"Oh yeah?"

"He wants me to disagree with him," I stated.

"Oooohhhh. Tell me more." Talia's psychology degree took over.

"Soren said every time I'm with him, I have to disagree about one thing. But he said he wouldn't get angry at me."

"Why do you think he wants to do that?" she asked as if she already knew the answer.

"He said I should have space to be 'authentically me.'" I raised my fingers in air quotes.

"Sounds like maybe he noticed how you always put others first. How does that make you feel?" Therapist Talia asked.

"I guess it makes me feel too many things. He wants to be more than friends, but he doesn't know how messed up I am . . . "

Talia pulled my blanket burrito body into her arms.

"You listen to me, Sawyer Brannan. You've been through more hell than anyone I know, but you aren't 'messed up.' You deserve to be happy, and if being around Soren makes you happy, then I want that for you."

I leaned into her embrace. Talia was the only human that I allowed to hug me. She was the best friend anyone could ask for, but sometimes I wondered what I'd eventually do to push her away. When she'd see through me for who I truly was. I fought the fear that she'd leave—because everyone always did—but it didn't stop me from sinking into her hug. A fierce squeeze that melted away the edge of all the day's big emotions. She had those miraculous hugs that made problems look smaller and less daunting.

"He's taking me to a concert," I said as my face was smashed against Talia's shoulder.

She pulled back, her body nearly vibrating with energy.

"What? Way to bury the lede! Tell me everything!" she exclaimed excitedly.

"It's the Cal Austin concert." I wanted to scream with excitement, but the anxiety of something new ate at me.

"Girl. We gotta find you a smokin' outfit!"

"Tal, it isn't a date. It's. . . like friends," I explained.

With an exaggerated eye roll and a smile still on her face, she declared, "Friends to lovers is my favorite trope! What do you think about watching a rom-com and doing some online shopping with quick shipping, so you can look extra hot?" She cackled at herself as she reached for the remote.

"Talia, what if I have another panic attack? You know I don't do things like this," I asked, reaching for my chain. Talia stilled and turned toward me. Her serious, warm brown eyes met mine.

"Soren helped you before, right?" she asked softly.

"Yeah." He had. He'd been my anchor that settled everything around me.

"Then let him help you again," she reasoned as she gave me another quick squeeze. It wasn't lost on me that she said "let," as if it was just as much my choice to get help as it was for someone to offer it.

She was right. He had held my hand when I was triggered the other night. Soren was the type of person that would help those in need around him. But I still wanted to be more than a pity case to him. And once he realized how fractured I was, he'd leave.

"Ready to find something sexy?" Talia quipped as she snagged my laptop. Her grin was a smidge short of maniacal.

And so it went. We turned on the latest rom-com and let it play in the background while Talia showed me outfits much too bright and revealing for my librarian-style taste in clothing. I finally settled on a light blue dress that Talia claimed would make my eyes pop. We laughed until we couldn't breathe, tears streaming down our faces until we saw stars. It was exactly the evening I needed.

Chapter Twenty-Six

Soren

I TOSSED A ROLL of nine gauge wire onto the bed of my UTV and surveyed the fence I had just repaired. A massive limb had broken off an old tree in the wind last night and it had fallen on the fence. Thankfully, I had noticed the issue before the cattle in this pasture noticed and made a run for it. I could imagine them now, eating on the rows of prairie grass hay bales, while I'd have to round up Gene and Travis to corral them back in. Of course, then they'd be resistant because cows were always stubborn when it came to eating, especially when it was on the opposite side of the fence where they belonged. Travis would come out later and cut the limb into firewood for his and Gene's cabin fireplaces.

As part of their salary for working full-time for me, they were each housed on the property in cabins. It helped to have some of the ranch hands nearby, because farming and ranching wasn't a nine-to-five job. Sure, I'd tried to accommodate typical work hours, but unexpected things happened, like storms popping up or cattle getting out, and those were things that needed immediate attention. Gene had worked for my dad, and I'd asked him to stay on, which he did happily.

I had met Travis at an Alcoholics Anonymous meeting. He had broken down, saying he needed accountability and more distance from his current living situation. He drank for some of the same reasons I had. Where I'd been sober for almost eight years, he'd just reached his six-month mark. I worked to be sober because Lane and Jonah pulled me from the depths of my hellish regret, and Travis had his own reasons.

I hadn't considered AA in a new light until lately. When Sawyer pulled that slip of paper from my hoodie pocket, I had forgotten it was there. Every morning I wrote down how many days I'd been sober with a greater-than sign followed by the number one. Reminding myself that one sip could undo all the days I had worked diligently to achieve. I didn't have the same desire to turn to liquor as I had in the past, but I wasn't foolish enough to think that I couldn't break my sobriety. I never wanted to be the person I was when I used alcohol to cope and live another day. Drunk Soren made so many shitty mistakes, which led to the second worst day of my life.

My life had fractured at the seams, and Lane and Jonah had given me a lesson in tough love. They had locked me in Jonah's house for a solid two weeks while the effects of alcohol addiction racked my body. Lane had hired a private doctor to be at my side. Lane and Jonah sat with me while I broke down repeatedly, experiencing the grief I had ignored by way of an amber-colored liquid. They waited until after the two weeks to say anything to my parents, knowing they couldn't handle seeing their only living son at his lowest. After those hellish two weeks, I went to a rehab facility. After rehab, I met George and he became my sponsor. George was a retired school teacher and coach with over thirty years of sobriety under his belt. He believed in tough love and hard work, in that order. When reality hit, I was shell-shocked by the disaster I had created in my life. I had destroyed the goodwill that most people had toward me, and sometimes, I still heard the small town whispers about me—most of which weren't even true.

Chet Hagan, a frequent coffee drinker at Ronnie's Diner, had always claimed that if you hadn't heard a good rumor by noon, then you should just make something up. Even in a small town, there were those who made stirring the rumor mill their full-time job. It was unorthodox, but George had pretty much adopted me as a nephew, and we'd get together for lunch whenever I was in Lewis City. This was a part of my life that I hadn't talked to Sawyer about. Not because I was necessarily ashamed of it. I know I did the right thing, and I'm deeply grateful for those who walked by my side through it all. But telling her made me nervous and unsettled. It was foolish to think that alcohol was no longer an issue for me, but I had bone deep knowledge that I'd never touch it again. Not because I'd lost the taste for it, but because it obliterated my life before, and I'd never do that again. I had too much to lose. I had people that depended on me for their livelihoods to feed their families. I was in a good place and I wanted to move forward, but the possibility of losing someone else weighed heavily on my chest. My phone rang, and I reached for it. Travis.

"Hey."

"Man . . . " His voice didn't sound right.

"Travis, where are you at?" I tossed things in the bed of the UTV.

"The cabin."

I didn't know Travis as well as Jonah and Lane, but I knew he didn't make unnecessary phone calls. My gut rolled, knowing something wasn't right. I was determined to be the person in his corner, the same as Lane and Jonah had been for me. He had no support, and he had more at stake than I ever did.

Clouds of dust flew as I raced to his cabin, down the gravel roads. When I arrived, he was sitting on the steps, dark hair disheveled but still knotted behind his head, and holding a bottle of unopened whiskey. I paused, watching him. He tossed the bottle between his hands. Left. Right. Left. Whiskey used to be my poison of choice too. I sat beside him. He was about the same size as me, but leaner and more heavily tattooed than Jonah. His calloused hands tossed the bottle back and forth. Back and forth.

"What's going on, man?" I asked calmly.

"I haven't had any, if that's what you're wondering." His voice was husky.

"I can see it's sealed and that you're sober," I acknowledged.

"My mom brought this by." *Damn.*

"Why do you think she did that?" I asked, even as I wanted to swear at the audacity.

"Because it's the only way she knows how to cope," he sounded resigned.

"Travis, you are not her. You have tools," I reminded him.

"I know. It's just that today was so damn hard, and then she came by and I knew I couldn't be trusted to be alone." Reaching the point of acknowledging your weaknesses was such a notable step in this journey.

"Why is today hard?" I studied his face. I didn't know his whole story and I didn't push.

"Today is a year." Grief. Nothing ached quite like the anniversaries of before and after. The day that marked the moment that ripped your life to shreds.

"Hell. I'm sorry, man," I replied, but it didn't feel like enough.

Travis blew out a breath and scrubbed the back of a thumb across his forehead.

"Watch me pour it out?" he asked after a pause.

"Sure, thing," I agreed.

We made our way into the cabin and he poured it down the drain. These days were the most challenging, but I knew that Travis had that same fight in him to make it that I did. That fight in his eyes is what made me hire him six months ago. He'd make it, but it was going to be a hell of a fight along the way. I made a note to include him in more things whenever possible because a good support system made all the difference. We talked a little longer, and I reminded him to reach out again if he needed to. Not long after, we loaded up and went to work on the fence together. He was in good shape again by the time his daughter got home from preschool.

Chapter Twenty-Seven

Sawyer

WHEN WE ARRIVED AT the historic, luxury-style theater on the main street of Wilson, there were groups of people trickling in through the large wooden doors. Men wore starched, pearl-snap dress shirts, cowboy hats, and blazers over denim pants. Soren wore dark denim jeans that molded to his thick thighs with freshly shined cowboy boots. His cream-colored shirt, with a few buttons at the neck, clung to his muscular body in all the right places. He was handsome in a way that made my stomach feel funny. Women were in skin tight denim jeans, cut-off shorts, summer dresses, and cowgirl boots. The light blue summer dress that Talia declared would "make my eyes pop" was what I ended up wearing after sending her multiple selfies to make sure it looked okay. I had curled my hair in waves and left it down. It hung almost to my waist.

I had debated taking off the military tags and carrying them in my clutch, but they were my touchstone in stress. Nerves had me rethinking, and I simply tucked the chain under the neckline of my dress. Out of all the things we had done, this was the most date-like, but we weren't dating. We were friends, although even as I considered this, I wondered what it would be like to belong to someone as good as Soren Roberts. I was such a hot mess when it came to relationships, but not from a lack of wanting to do well. It was embarrassing when I acknowledged that I was twenty-six years old and had never been on a date. The idea of having a string of failed relationships made my stomach clench with anxiety. Relationships like that meant getting close to people. That alone was terrifying, and ultimately, they'd simply be another person that walked away in the revolving door of my life.

Soren walked slightly behind me, but I felt the heat of his body near mine in the crush of people. He had re-routed us multiple times, making sure I had plenty of room to walk. His consideration of me was even hotter than his current purposeful five o'clock shadow that my fingers itched to touch.

"Soren? Is that you?" a high-pitched voice asked. I thought I heard Soren make a disgruntled sound.

A tall, gorgeous woman with unnaturally red hair strode up with a shorter man attached to her arm, who appeared to be trying to catch up.

"Golly, I can't believe it's you! What have you been up to?" she asked in a voice that was much louder than it needed to be.

"The usual. Taking care of the ranch. Felicity, this is Sawyer," Soren introduced, lightly touching my back as a way of acknowledging my presence. I noticed that he didn't use any term to describe me, but I couldn't blame him. The title of friend didn't fit quite right.

She turned to me, towering over me in her heels, and raised one manicured eyebrow.

"Oh my word. I didn't realize you had a daughter, Soren," she squawked, drawing out each word.

Soren sucked in air at such a sharp intake that he began coughing hysterically. He pounded a fist on his chest in an effort to clear his throat.

I knew the game she was playing, but I patted Soren's firm back. He stopped choking after a second, and I did the bravest thing I had done all day—I reached out and placed my hand in his. His hands were large and calloused from hard work, but there wasn't any other hand I wanted to hold.

"I'm his date," I asserted, his eyes burning into the side of my head. The redhead squinted at me as if she hadn't expected me to speak.

Soren cleared his throat and then said, "Good to see you, Felicity, but we need to find our seats." Felicity raised both brows and turned suddenly, pulling along the man without taking the time to introduce him.

Soren led me toward the crowded auditorium and we found our seats, which were way closer to the stage than I had anticipated. We sat down because we were early, and I realized my hand was still in his.

"Date, huh?"

He turned toward me and a smile pulled at his beautiful mouth.

I want to brush my fingertips across his lips.

Where'd that come from? Sure. He was handsome as sin, as Talia would say, but I didn't normally have these kinds of thoughts. I'm not sure I ever had.

"I certainly don't look young enough to be your daughter," I huffed out.

"No, you don't. You look like a beautiful woman on a date." My cheeks immediately proceeded to flush, and the smirk of his lips suggested he had a secret.

We were two songs into the concert and I couldn't do it. The music blared from the speakers. I beat myself up because I should have known. I'd seen videos of concerts online, but I'd never been to one in person. Talia and I had planned to attend one in college, but for some reason or another, we hadn't been able to. I hated that I was a twenty-six-year-old woman with almost no normal life experiences.

Most people didn't understand that when you grew up in a normal loving family, you did normal family things. But when you were bounced around to over one hundred foster homes like me, you didn't have those same moments. You still grew up . . . you simply didn't have any life experiences in common with most people. It was having more traumatic experiences than everyone in the room combined, but not having any typical American life experiences. I'll never forget the time I told Talia I had never had a manicure, and she deemed we had to remedy that immediately. Talia had taken me to see Shelly at Lovely Nails, and I spent entirely too much time deciding which shade of pink I wanted.

I had started to panic partway through the first song, but reminded myself that Soren had bought the tickets. I needed to tough it out, but the volume of the music was like road rash on my ears. I wanted to crawl out of my skin. My body hummed from the intensity of the sound.

"Here."

Soren's breath whispered across my ear, sending chill bumps racing down my body as he extended a pair of expensive earplugs. My eyes watered at his thoughtfulness as I thanked him and swiftly placed them in my ears. They made all the difference. My nervous system began to calm. I could still hear the music perfectly, but at a much lower decibel. His kindness made my nose sting, and I reached down between us, linking our hands together for the remainder of the concert. His touch calmed me and I wanted to hold his hand. The desire to touch anyone was completely foreign, but I decided I would ignore the questions of why *him* and enjoy the concert, because holding his hand felt achingly perfect.

Chapter Twenty-Eight

Sawyer

WE WERE WALKING OUT of the theater after the best first concert of my life when I couldn't wait any longer.

"How did you know I'd need earplugs?" I blurted out.

"I didn't, but I wanted to make sure you had the best time and sometimes it gets loud in there," he answered nonchalantly, but it wasn't a small thing to me. He had spent time considering my needs. These were not cheap ear plugs. I noticed the brand when I took them out and put them in the case. He would have had to order these online for me, they weren't ones you could simply grab at the store. He had thought about me. I'm not sure where my body disconnected from my brain, but I flew into Soren's body. Wrapping my arms tightly around his waist and burying my face in his solid warm chest, I squeezed tight. I heard the "umph" of me slamming into him. What I wasn't prepared for was his body going completely rigid. I didn't expect that, but I also didn't anticipate my reaction to his thoughtfulness. I was overwhelmed with gratitude and felt like I was floating, but I faked my best smile and backed away, hoping to play it off as best I could, though deep down, all I felt was burned. Maybe he didn't feel the same way I did, but I could have sworn he had been flirting with me. I made a mental note to search for videos online about how to recognize if a man was flirting with you.

I glanced up, and the intense expression on his face took me even further aback and the smile died on my lips. I had made a mistake. The sensation of icy cold pinpricks of shame cascaded down my body. His eyes bore into mine as if he was searching for the answer to world hunger or global peace. The vulnerability of knowing that he'd seen too much of me caused my stomach to tighten while my fingers tingled. I had to apologize. I had to fix this.

"I-I'm sorry. I shouldn't have touched you without asking. Thank you. That was extremely thoughtful," I gushed. My voice didn't sound right even to my own ears. Immediately reaching for my chain, my trembling fingers ran their familiar pattern over the raised words. I broke away from our locked eyes and looked down at my chain that I had subconsciously freed from my dress. I felt so dumb for making things awkward because somewhere along the line, I had clearly mis-read a social cue. I should have known he didn't want me. No one ever had.

"Sawyer." His voice was hoarse. I couldn't look at him. I didn't know what was going on, but I couldn't control my body, and I was going to cry and I didn't know why. I never cried. I couldn't even remember the last time I had.

"Look at me." I took a deep breath and willed my body to obey, but it wouldn't listen. His hand flexed at his side like he wanted to reach for me.

"Sawyer, you never have to ask or apologize for touching me." His words surprised me and I found his eyes.

"Okay."

I turned to walk toward the truck, because vulnerable conversations were torture for me. My flight response was pushing me to create distance, and before I knew it, I was running toward the truck. I heard his boots stalking behind me. I was such a freak. My throat burned as I suppressed my tears. Precisely as I reached the truck, his large, tanned hand slammed down, holding the door shut. I was now effectively caged between him and the truck. He wasn't touching me, but his body was centimeters away from mine. My heart raced, but not because I didn't like it. I was confused and wished Talia was here to wrap me in one of her warm hugs. If I were at home, I'd be buried in my comfy chair with several blankets to burrow in. I turned around, his left palm splayed by my face on the door. I stared at his chest, unwilling to meet his eyes.

"Sawyer." His voice was deeper than normal.

The calloused index finger on his right hand hooked under my chin, tilting my head to meet his eyes.

"I'm not going to let you run. I care too much about you to not talk about what just happened." My eyes searched his. He cared about me? Everything was muddled, and I knew he wasn't going to drop this.

"I feel like such a freak." His eyes tracked between mine.

"You are not a freak," he proclaimed fiercely.

"I thought you didn't want me touching you." I bit my lip, and Soren emitted a strangled laugh.

"Sawyer. I'd be a fool to not want your beautiful body touching mine. It just surprised me. Try again?"

He stretched both arms out by his sides in invitation but didn't move. His words surprised me, and I slowly reached around his waist because of our height difference. His warm, muscular arms wrapped around me. Tucking me in and holding me close. My body relaxed after a minute. I wouldn't tell Talia this, but Soren Roberts was a world-class hugger. He bent slightly, rested his chin on my head, and I was completely surrounded by him. I could hear his heart thumping as I rested my cheek on his firm chest. Being cocooned in his embrace seemed like the safest place in the world.

"Pretty Girl?"

"Umm-hmm," I hummed, reluctant to move a single muscle.

"I want to say something, but I want to make sure you really hear me."

"Okay."

"I want to touch you, but I've been waiting because I didn't want to scare you. I don't want to remind you-" he paused and then continued "of someone that has hurt you." His consideration of me was my undoing.

"You don't scare me." And it was true.

"I want you to know something, too. If you ever want to stop, or you don't like how I touch you, it doesn't matter what we're doing, where we are, or how you think I'll feel about it. You can always tell me no. Always." His determined voice rumbled through his chest as he spoke.

I nodded against his chest, and I swore his lips ghosted the top of my head.

"You're a really good hugger." I blushed admitting that.

"I really like what I'm holding." His voice sounded husky before he swallowed. We stood wrapped around each other for what felt like an eternity. At last, I loosened my arms and Soren opened the door for me, buckled me in, and we left, heading back to the ranch.

Chapter Twenty-Nine

Soren

WE DISSECTED ALL OUR favorite moments from the concert and laughed about the older couple sitting a couple seats ahead of us, who were handsy all night. Seeing a seventy-something-year-old man get a butt grab was something I personally would like to unsee, but lucky for him I guess.

The evening was perfect. Sawyer let me hold her hand the whole way home, which reminded me that we needed to have a conversation about our intentions. I wanted to date Sawyer, a significant step—especially considering I hadn't glanced at a woman in over eight years. I'd been head down, working my ass off, day in and day out. Maybe this was a conversation we could have now, after that hug in the parking lot.

I parked the truck, but instead of getting out, we unbuckled and I shifted toward her, resting my back against the door. She mirrored me in her seat.

"Can we talk?" I started

"Uh, yeah." Her brows met.

"You remember earlier, when you told that girl from high school that you were my date?" I grinned because I loved that she had been feisty.

She nodded and bit her lip. I seriously wished she wouldn't do that.

"What if we did date?" I asked, simply watching her face to take in her reaction.

Hazel met blue. Her hand reached for her dog tags.

"You want to date me?" she asked with a hitch in her breath.

"Yes, but only if you want to." *Please want to.*

"What if you decide you don't like me?" she whispered.

There was not a planet in the galaxy where I could be that I would not like Sawyer Brannan. There wasn't a possibility under the heavens that I didn't want every piece of her with me, always, where I could hold her soft hand in mine. I wanted to shield her, protect her, beat my chest, and declare like a proverbial caveman that Sawyer was mine.

"I will always like you." She needed to wipe that concern completely from her mind.

"But how can you know that?" she continued.

"Some things you just know." Her eyes searched mine, doubtful.

"I like having you as a friend, and I'm not sure I want to lose that. Soren, I'm different from the other women you've dated. I have all these gaps of life experiences. I entered the system at two years old after my parents died in a boating accident, and then I aged out at eighteen years old. I know about the darkest parts of life, but I'm twenty-six years old and this was my first time going to a concert. You need a sweet, small-town woman who doesn't have all these broken pieces." She laughed but there was no humor in it as she stared out the front windshield and continued.

"I'm not even broken pieces . . . it's as if my life has been shattered to dust and there are particles of me floating around out there. No matter how hard I try to piece them all together, I can't remember exactly where they belong. I've lived so much of my life in survival mode, it's like I was sleepwalking for so much of it . . . and the things I remember . . . I don't want to." Her voice broke off at that, and I knew I'd have to spar with the heavy bag before bed.

My heart broke at her words. This was her first concert? I knew her childhood was a thing of horror movies, but maybe I didn't account for how much she had missed out on. I wanted to wipe the memories from her mind. I wanted to shelter her in a way that wasn't humanly possible. This was going to be harder than I thought, but one thing I didn't lack was the self-confidence to go after what I wanted. I wanted to never be without the warmth of Sawyer Brannan's light. I was not letting her slip through my fingers. I wanted to give Sawyer the life she'd never dreamed of, a life with me, and that thought scared the hell out of me.

"What if I don't want a sweet, small-town woman? What if I want you?" She shook her head as though it was the craziest notion she'd ever heard, and I leaned across the cab and caught her face in my hands. She stilled, her lips parting.

"Pretty Girl, don't tell me what I want." Her eyes widened.

I went on. "If you don't want me, tell me to stop, but if it's because you think I don't want you, you're dead wrong." She bit her lip, and I used my thumb to tug on her chin so it popped out.

"Okay," she rasped. "I'm scared to lose our friendship. Soren, I've had so many people walk in and out of my life, and I can't lose this, too. Can we just go slow?"

"Yes, ma'am!" She needed a break from this weighty conversation.

I dropped my hands from her face before I could kiss her and saluted, knowing it'd make her laugh. She didn't understand how slow I'd been going. She didn't understand that I'd been under her spell since the moment I met her. She was it. She was the one I was willing to risk my fears of loss and ruin for.

"You said tonight was your first concert?" I settled back against the door, an idea coming to mind.

"Yes."

"Was it what you thought it'd be?" I asked.

"It was wonderful. Thank you again for the ear plugs. I didn't realize it would be so loud," she said with a small smile.

"You're welcome. What do you think of us making a list of things you haven't done, and we'll do those things on dates?" I tossed out my idea.

"Like a bucket list?"

"Yes, but hopefully without kicking the bucket," I teased.

"Yes, that would make it more enjoyable," she quietly joked back, and I couldn't help the ridiculous smile on my face. She had just agreed to be mine.

"I'll make a list on my phone. Tell me something you'd like to do." I pulled out my cell and started a note.

"Hmmm . . . I've never been to the circus," she considered, tipping her head in thought.

I willed my heart to keep beating, and then I immediately vowed to make everything on the list happen. I wanted Sawyer to have these moments more than anything, and I wanted to be there for every single one.

I typed "Take Sawyer to the circus."

"What else?" If she wanted to go to the moon, I'd figure out how to rent a shuttle. My girl was getting everything on this list.

"Hmm . . . I never went to my high school dances, but I'm not sure I want to do that as an adult. Let me think . . . " She laughed.

I typed "Dance with Sawyer" on the list. I was a goner. I'd do whatever this girl said. She named a handful of things that I took notes on.

"This one is kinda dumb . . . but I've always wanted to swing on a tire swing," she said in a wistful tone.

It felt like a kick in the gut when she said it. The day she came by to bring cookies, I had startled her while she gently pushed my childhood tire swing with her hand. I pocketed my phone and called over my shoulder as I opened the door.

"It's not dumb. Let's do it." I jumped from the truck, walked to her side, and flung open her door. She had slid off her shoes as I scooped her up bridal style, because I was on a mission.

"What are you doing?" she shrieked, a smile on her face.

"I'm pushing my girl on a tire swing."

She leaned her head against my chest and I could almost feel her smile through my shirt. The moonlight guided me to the swing as I put her legs through the middle and she grabbed hold of the rope.

"Hang on."

I pulled her back and let go as she sailed through the starlit night sky. She tilted back while holding the rope to get a better view of the sky. Her long hair trailed behind her like a wave of golden silk underneath the light of a billion stars. The rope creaked when it rocked back and forth as she swayed, a smile never leaving her face. After several minutes, she said she was done, and I helped her out, a smile fixed on her face. Once she was on the ground, she partially sat back in the center of the swing, leaning her head back to see the stars.

"It's so beautiful here," she exclaimed reverently.

"It is," I agreed, never taking my eyes off her.

She hopped down and wrapped her arms around my waist, and I wrapped my arms around the most precious woman alive.

"Thank you for sharing this with me," she whispered softly.

And somehow, as the stars shone down on us, I thought of Abel and how he must have made a deal with God to bring this girl into my life. There wasn't anything I could have done to be this lucky.

Chapter Thirty

Sawyer

Pretty Girl, what do you think about me making you lunch and watching a baseball game on Sunday? Lane and Jonah are threatening bodily harm if I don't bring you around more.

> That sounds fun! Tell them I look forward to see-
> ing them again.

Soren:

See ya at 11 a.m.

It had been a week since the not-date that turned into a date. Soren and I had communicated by text and calls throughout the week, but both of us had been too busy to see each other again. When his text came through, I couldn't wait to see him again. I spent entirely too long contemplating what I was going to wear to Soren's, and Talia came over and offered all her opinions on every outfit I tried on. Talia assured me that my distressed light wash jeans, white front-tucked t-shirt, and light pink sneakers were a good choice. Although, she would have loved to see me in something the color of a neon highlighter. My hair was in soft curls and I decided to leave it down. The day before, I had baked an angel food cake with strawberries and homemade whipped cream on top. I didn't make homemade angel food cake often, but it was far superior to anything that could be bought at the grocery store. I also brought along two-dozen chocolate chip cookies because baking calmed my anxiety. The idea of dating for the first time in my life, and the stress of work lately had me baking almost daily, but now, I contemplated if I went overboard. I hated how a simple thing like dating made me feel inadequate, but I refused to allow that to steal my enjoyment of seeing Soren today. I turned into his driveway and parked alongside Soren's truck. I barely had the ignition off before I saw him coming down the steps. He was dressed in dark jeans and a forest-green henley with the sleeves pushed up. I had never felt the way I had when I looked at him. A part of me that I didn't know existed came to life around him. He was handsome. There was no denying that, but when he looked at me, he saw more than I wanted him to see. As though he saw all of me. The me that I tried so diligently to shield from the world. I didn't have any more time to dig into those thoughts before he reached to open my door. I wasn't sure I could unpack that right now, anyway. It simply made me feel too much, and I was supposed to be here to have fun and learn about baseball.

"Pretty Girl. Are you trying to seduce me?" he asked, glancing at the containers of desserts in my front seat. I wasn't prepared for flirty Soren, and the tug of his lips made my stomach do somersaults. A giddy smile stole across my lips.

"I bake when I'm stressed," I answered and handed him the container of cookies.

"Why are you stressed?" His brow lowered, hazel eyes serious, ready to fight on my behalf. Little did he know, he was part of the stress—or rather, my response to him was.

"It's just work stuff and . . ." I trailed off as I got out.

"Tell me." His hand gently wrapped around my shoulder.

"What if I screw this up? I don't want to lose you as a friend."

Wouldn't it be better to ignore the attraction and simply stay friends? That way he wouldn't leave.

"Can I hug you?" he asked as he placed the containers I had passed him on the roof of the Jeep. I nodded.

His warmth engulfed me as his strong arms wrapped me against his firm chest, and I slid my arms around his waist. Soren, I was realizing, was a tactile person in almost every way, and there was something about being wrapped in his arms that made everything quiet.

"Let's make a deal. You keep communicating with me this openly, and we'll talk through any concerns you have. I'm not going anywhere." I wanted to believe him. I wanted to believe that we could build something that would last, but there was my persistent concern that everyone always left because they always had. But I did as I always had and swept those concerns under the rug. I was determined to make the most of this relationship and our time together until everything inevitably fell apart.

I nodded against his chest.

"Soren, you can hug me without asking," I said as I pulled away.

"Don't tempt me with a good time, Pretty Girl," Soren replied, with a wink that made my face flood with heat. I liked this unexpected flirty side of him even if it made my stomach whoosh as if I were driving through the Flint Hills as I did on the way here.

Three hours later, I sat between Soren and Lane on the couch. The baseball game was tied in the ninth inning. They had both been teasing each other about who could teach me better, but it had all been in good humor. I had been anxious about seeing Lane because of the panic attack he had witnessed, but I found out right away that Lane was as extroverted as Talia. He made a quick apology that ended with him kissing the back of my hand in a grand gesture to which Soren threatened, "Keep your slimy lips off my girl!"

That made me laugh, and all the nerves disappeared. My heart felt like it skipped a beat at his use of "my girl". The trio immediately made me feel like I was in their group, and I loved their easy-going familiarity with each other. Despite being famous for his time as a baseball pitcher, Lane was as down to earth as Soren and Jonah. Jonah was much more of an observer and had taken up the oversized chair to sit. He wasn't grumpy per se, but he was not one to be the center of attention. Lane had that covered in spades. Between his size and tattoos, I bet Jonah could be extremely intimidating if he tried, but something told me that beneath the giant of a man was a quiet soul.

"Runnnnn, Gibson!" Lane yelled, pumping his fist as he jumped up. The player rounded third base, headed for home in a game that had me on the edge of my seat.

Soren's leg brushed against mine as he leaned over to whisper with amusement in his voice.

"I'm not sure if Gibson would know to run without Lane's couch coaching."

I laughed, but I was distracted when his breath skated across the skin by my ear, sending tingles across my body. Just then, Gibson made it across home plate.

"YEAH, baby!" Lane yelled again. His enthusiasm was contagious and green eyes sparkled with excitement. I smiled, letting out a pent-up breath, nervous about the outcome.

"Whew. I was worried since the score was so close." I turned to Soren, and he smiled at me. His hazel eyes scanned my face.

"It was a good game. I'm glad you came."

"I'm glad you invited me," I replied quietly. I couldn't stop the ridiculous smile that stretched across my heated face. Soren's eyes tracked across my cheeks, and he smiled.

"We might be looking at a World Series if they keep playing like that," Lane remarked, bringing a water bottle to his lips, his eyebrows bouncing.

"That'd be something. It's been too long," Soren remarked.

"Nearly thirty years," Jonah stated quietly, standing and stretching, the muscular tattooed full sleeve on his left arm rippling with the movement.

"Thanks for lunch, man. I need to head out. I've gotta tackle some emails this evening. Tell Travis I said hey. Hopefully he can hang next time," Lane said, slapping Soren's shoulder in the way that men did.

Travis, Soren's foreman, had been planning to join us with his daughter, Sadie, but she'd caught a stomach bug from preschool. Jonah and Lane left shortly after both snagging a couple of my cookies before walking out the door. Soren threw scowls at them while Lane's eyes danced, knowing he was purposefully riling Soren. I didn't know Lane or Jonah very well, but I knew Soren was lucky to have them. In innumerable ways, they acted as close as brothers, and I knew losing Abel had been painfully impactful to them all. Maybe it was that loss that had caused their bond to be as deep as it was.

Chapter Thirty-One

Soren

JONAH AND LANE LEFT after grabbing a handful of Sawyer's chocolate chip cookies. I threw scowls at the jackasses. Lane's eyes danced with glee, knowing he was intentionally poking the bear. I couldn't blame them though—they were dang good cookies. I collected the snack tray and carried it to the kitchen. Sawyer refolded a throw blanket that had gotten disheveled during the game and draped it across the couch. I liked how she looked in my house. Jonah's little sister, Landry, had helped decorate my house and was responsible for said throw blanket. I loved that I lived in the house I grew up in, but when my parents decided to be retired RV travelers, I renovated and updated almost everything over time.

Landry declared that the blanket made me appear more "normal" and less like a psycho who's paranoid about having a clean house. She was, by far, substantially cooler than all three of us put together. She enjoyed home decor and it helped her pay the bills as a single mom while in college. I listened to her advice because she was one of my best friend's little sisters, which also made her my sister. She was also the mom to one of my favorite people, Hope, an eight-month-old butterball that had dimples that turned me into complete Jello. Had I already installed a playground in Landry's backyard, even though Hope wasn't old enough to play with it? Yeah, and mostly because I wanted to surpass Lane at being her favorite uncle. Jonah was a given, but I was going to be next in line.

Sawyer gathered up the remaining dishes and walked them into the kitchen.

"I thought of something I could disagree with you about," she announced, setting the dishes in the sink.

I raised a brow, aware this was coming out of left field, but also proud that she had been contemplating what I had said.

I leaned a hip against the counter. "Okay, let's hear it."

"Your continued terrible taste in music. I saw what your radio was set to," she quipped, tilting her head to the side toward the radio mounted under my cabinets, making her sunshine hair spill over her shoulder.

I laughed at her spunky statement. She bit her lip, smiling as her bright blue eyes shined.

This was an excellent first disagreement because in the end it really didn't matter, and I was proud of her for remembering our agreement.

"Terrible taste in music, huh?" I bit back my smile as I turned on the water to wash the handful of dishes from earlier.

"Yeah, it's . . . old, and there are so many amazing new songs out there. You liked Cal Austin right, and he's newer."

"Well, Miss Brannan, I didn't realize you hated the elderly," I alleged in mock outrage.

"What?" she shrieked.

"I guess I'll have to remember that before I introduce you to anyone that qualifies for the senior discount at Ronnie's Diner." I turned toward the sink to hide my growing smile as I rolled up my sleeves, knowing that wasn't her intention but having too much fun teasing her.

"That's not what I meant, Soren Roberts, and you know it! I love older people. I'm hanging out with you, after all." I spun to the side as she clapped a hand over her mouth, trying to decide whether her joke was too saucy. Her large eyes darted to my forearms, where I had rolled up my sleeves before finding my face again.

"You think I'm elderly?" I asked, not being able to hold back my grin.

I cupped one hand, scooping a small amount of water and bubbles in my palm, walking toward her on the other side of the island.

She eyed my hand and shook her head. Her eyes were as big as saucers.

"I didn't mean it like that," she tried as she backed away.

"I find that hard to believe." I continued to stalk toward her, but she stopped and tossed a hand on her hip.

"I mean that girl at the concert thought you were my dad," she sassed, knowing full well that Felicity was one of those girls that never matured past high school, and I clearly didn't look that old.

"Well, then come to daddy," I hurled as I lunged for her, flicking the handful of water in her direction. She swiftly veered the other direction before circling the island. She made a run for the sink, scooping up a handful of water and bubbles.

"Soren Roberts, I'm gonna get you!" She launched her hand full of sudsy water at me and I wiped at the drips running down my face. I loved the uninhibited happiness on her face as we spent the next couple of minutes tossing water on each other. We chased each other around the kitchen until I called surrender only so she would get close enough for me to catch her. I slung an arm around her waist and tugged her close.

"Soren!" she squealed as I rubbed my wet cheek against hers, her breath catching at the contact.

"You don't play fair," she accused. Her eyes met mine. This close I could see all the blues of her eyes and the crease in her bottom lip because of the fullness.

"Nope, I play to win." At least where she was concerned. Winning the heart of Sawyer Brannan was something I didn't plan to lose at. I loosened my arm because if I didn't, I would have slid my hands in her hair and kissed her breathless.

"Wash or dry?" I asked, attempting to get my brain back on track and needing something to do besides running my hands across her curves. An indiscernible expression flickered across her face before she responded.

"Wash. I don't trust you with the water." Her lips tipped in a smile that made me wonder if I trusted her with the water. Maybe we should give up and put the dishes in the dishwasher, to stay on the safe side.

Chapter Thirty-Two

Sawyer

AFTER BARELY SLEEPING LAST night due to the incessant sound of running water from my toilet, I found myself at a big-box hardware store after work, staring at toilet parts—or at least what I assumed were toilet parts. Why didn't I simply contact the landlord? This was his responsibility, after all. I already knew the answer to my question, though. One, I didn't want to bother him, and two, I didn't want unnecessary people in my safe space.

"Hon, is there something I can assist you with?"

I jolted at the question, completely lost in my thoughts of what to buy and how to know which pieces to get. Beside me stood a middle-aged man with a worker's vest that indicated he worked for the store.

"Uh, no. I'm good. Thanks though," I said, turning back to the items, willing him to move on and let me continue to stare at the shelves.

"All right. Holler if you need any help," He called as he made his way further down the aisle. I should have asked him for help, but I realized as I studied the packaging that I didn't even know what brand of toilet I had. I studied the packs and tried internet searches on my phone, only to further realize I didn't know what the heck I was doing.

Defeated, I trudged back home, mad at myself for not being able to make a simple call and report that something was broken. I knew it was my imagination, but the water sounded even louder and more annoying as I tried to distract myself by putting away the groceries I'd bought while out. It was Wednesday, and I'd already had a long day and the noise was about to push me over the edge. I opened the pantry door with a little too much force as I lugged my bag over to put away a stack of canned veggies. My pantry had enough food to feed a family of five, exactly the way I wanted it. This was one of my rooted idiosyncrasies. I didn't want Soren to see the parts that made me feel broken and hopeless beyond repair. These parts of me that years of therapy hadn't fixed, albeit had been awhile since I'd had an appointment. I resigned myself to my unconventional pantry closet of secrets and let out a painfully exhausted exhale. If he saw this, he'd know everyth—

My phone rang on the counter. I saw his name before I even picked it up. Soren.

"Hello."

"Hey, I'm in Lewis City and since it's not too late, I thought I might drop by to see you if that's okay? I'll bring dinner." One sentence and my heart raced in my chest. I rapidly scanned my already perfectly clean duplex and shut the pantry door.

"Uh, okay." I didn't know what to say. This was what "normal" dating people did, right? I folded my grocery bag and stowed it away as if I was in a race to hide—what? I didn't know.

"Are you okay?" Soren asked.

"Yeah, I'll text you my address," I replied, putting him on speaker to text as I also hoped he wasn't nearby. After sending the address, he said it would be about thirty minutes because he would swing by to pick up Chinese food. After asking my favorites, we hung up and I fought everything inside me not to panic. I paced throughout my tiny space, making sure it was tidy even though I knew it was. I changed to a matching loungewear set and folded the blankets in my comfy chair that often sat there swaddled in a nest. As I skimmed over my space once more, there was a knock at my door. On the other side was a smiling Soren holding a bag of Chinese food and a bouquet of beautiful multicolored mixed flowers. His hair was tousled in a way that made me want to run my fingers through it. I'd never wanted to run my hand through someone's hair before.

"Hey," I greeted, shy and maybe a little nervous at this new experience.

"Hey," he responded as his eyes skated across my outfit.

"You look beautiful and cozy," he said, standing still. I bit my lip, sensing my cheeks heating.

"I brought you flowers," he offered, holding out the bouquet and lifting up the bag. "And dinner." The flowers were stunning. I carefully took them from his hand as if they were crown jewels. I had never been given flowers before. There was a mixture of all different kinds of flowers in shades of pink, yellow, and blue. The thoughtfulness of the gesture made my nose sting.

"Thank you," I whispered as I lifted the flowers to my nose to smell, hoping my tears would stay put.

"Sawyer, are you okay?" I lifted my nose from the flowers to Soren's concerned face.

"Why?" I asked.

"Why what?" he asked, tilting his head to the side as if he missed something.

"Why did you bring me flowers?" I asked, holding up the bouquet.

"Because you deserve flowers," he answered matter-of-factly, and I couldn't help the smile that overtook my face. I stepped back, letting him in, and walked toward the kitchen, intent on taking care of my flowers. I made it to the kitchen before I realized Soren hadn't followed. He had pulled his cowboy boots off at the door and was letting his eyes take everything in.

"I like your place. It's cozy," he observed as he walked toward me and placed the bag on the counter. I smiled, setting to work putting the flowers in a glass pitcher I had retrieved from an upper cabinet. Soren unpacked the bags as I arranged the flowers in water at the kitchen sink.

"Where's the trash can?" Soren asked as he pulled our food from the bag and laid it out on the counter. My kitchen was fairly small so having him in my space was different, and I liked it.

"Right inside the door." I nodded toward a lower cabinet across the kitchen, turning back toward the sink arranging the flowers just so.

"You must really like green beans." I froze, knowing he'd opened the wrong door.

Chapter Thirty-Three

Soren

Sawyer stood frozen at the sink, water running but not an inch of her moved. Her pantry was stocked as if she were a prepper concerned about food shortages. Everything was in perfect order, all the way down to the cans of veggies with the labels all turned the same way. I was organized and tidy, but this put my pantry to shame. I called her name, but she didn't move. The flowers sat in the container, but she hadn't turned the water off. Slowly, I walked toward her, unsure of what was happening. At her side, I leaned to see her face as a single silent tear slid down her cheek. I reached to turn off the water and gently grasped her shoulders to turn her toward me. Her eyes were fixed on a button on my shirt.

"Did I tell you that my dad and mom used to dance in the kitchen when Abel and I were kids?" I asked, pulling her trembling body toward mine in the middle of the tiny kitchen. I wrapped her in a hug, cradling her body to mine, and slowly rocked side to side. After a minute, her arms found their way around my waist.

"We used to think it was gross as kids, but I think maybe I've changed my mind," I continued. She'd talk when she wanted to. We continued gently rocking back and forth. I ran my hand down her silken hair as her body molded to mine. A tiny hiccup emitted from her body before she spoke.

"I never want to be hungry again," she explained in a quiet, raspy voice. *Damn.* I willed my heart to continue to beat normally. I hadn't planned on going to the gym tonight, but those seven words changed that. I wanted to beat the hell out of everyone that had ever treated her as less than the angel of light that she was. I would never let her want for anything as long as there was air in my lungs.

"Never again," I vowed as I pressed my lips to the top of her head.

After a few more minutes, we loaded our plates with Chinese food and settled at her small round dining table and talked about our days. I had even earned one of her beautiful smiles. She was telling me about babysitting Ava, Rob and Talia's daughter, when I heard it. It sounded like running water. I tilted my head to the side to listen better. I could see the kitchen sink from where I sat, and the water was off.

"Is there water running?" Her cheeks pinkened at my question.

"Yeah, the toilet is making that noise," she answered. "I don't know how to fix it."

"Is this a rental?" I asked. I thought she had mentioned she lived in a rental.

"Yeah, but I don't want to bother the landlord." Every single thing in me wanted to make the case that this was his responsibility, but deep down I knew there was more to it than that.

"After we finish eating, I'll take a look at it," I offer, tipping my fork, wrapped in lo mein noodles, at her.

"Oh, you don't have to do that," she protested.

"Pretty Girl, let me show you my sexy plumber skills." At that, I was rewarded with a laugh at my ridiculousness, and that was exactly why I stopped by. I needed to see my girl happy, and I was willing to do whatever it took to make that happen.

Soren:

How's the toilet holding up?

Sawyer:

About as well as the three other times you've asked? :)

Soren:

Okay. Just making sure you don't need another sexy plumber demonstration. ;)

Chapter Thirty-Four

Soren

IT'D BEEN TWO WEEKS since the first time Sawyer came to my house to watch baseball. We had unofficially deemed Sundays as our day to spend together because we both had jobs that required a high level of commitment. She sat on the countertop, scrolling through her phone, searching for another song to make a case for. Her heavily distressed jeans encased her legs, except where her smooth skin shone through. Her oversized cream sweatshirt hung off one shoulder. My thumb itched to brush across her collarbone. Her chunky blonde braid had loosened to the point that a few waves brushed her slender neck and cheek. It made me think about what it'd be like to kiss a path down the smooth skin of her neck to her pulse point and taste her there. I finished putting our plates in the dishwasher, trying to ignore my increasing attraction.

"Oooohhhh. I found a good one!" Her eyes lit up as she tapped the screen. A country song about dirt roads filtered through her phone speaker. It had a nice beat, I'd give it that, but it wasn't Johnny Cash.

"I'm gonna win you over," she declared.

She didn't realize it, but she already had. I'd sell my soul to keep her light near me. She didn't know how beautiful she was, not only physically, but deep down she was the most beautiful person I knew. If anyone else told me this, I'd poke at them teasingly, but even her soul was beautiful. I was afraid that if she knew how I truly felt, she'd run. I'd continue to play this part of holding her on my finger like a delicate butterfly until she caught up to where I was.

I crossed my arms over my chest, tipped my head to the side, and leaned back against the opposite counter, pretending to evaluate the song. I was three feet away from her smooth tan legs that I could see through the patchwork distress of her loose jeans. I wouldn't be able to remember a single lyric to this song under the threat of death. The song ended and her eyes found mine, her eyebrows raised expectantly.

"So . . . what'd you think?" *You're beautiful.*

I pushed off the counter and went to her. I placed my palms on the counter on either side of her legs. Her eyes widened as I leaned closer. The side of my rogue thumb brushed her bare skin close to her knee. I heard her breath hitch as my nose brushed her left ear.

"It's not Johnny, but I guess the beat is kind of sexy."

An involuntary shiver ran through her body and I bit back a grin. It'd been awhile since I'd flirted with a woman, but this was a game I was good at. The thing was, this time it wasn't a game for me. Not with her.

I pulled back to see her eyes, examining her reaction. Her eyes were dilated, and I loved seeing them this close. All the different shades of blue all pieced together like a watercolor painting of the sky.

"See! There are some good songs made this decade."

Her breath was uneven and her eyes dropped to my mouth before bouncing back up to meet my eyes. I ran my tongue over my lower lip. Her eyes dropped again. I could see her heart racing at the base of her throat. With Sawyer's history, I wanted her to be the one calling the shots and being in control. I wanted it to be her choice, because it always would be. As much as I wanted to claim her mouth and sink my hands in her thick waves of golden silk, I knew it was not the right time. The fact she hadn't moved closer was a sign that she wasn't ready yet.

"I think I like disagreeing with you," she whispered while her eyes bounced between mine.

The amount of restraint I had by not wrapping her in my arms and showing her how beautiful she was, was unbearable.

"It's time for you to head home, Pretty Girl, before it gets too late."

Something unrecognizable passed across her eyes, and she nodded.

I hated the words more than I should, but I knew that if I didn't create some distance between us, I'd do something that she may not be ready for. I'd rather cut off my own arm than do anything that made her feel unsafe. I backed away, helped her round up her dishes and bag, slid on my boots, and walked her to her car.

Sawyer

I didn't have any firsthand experience with romantic relationships, which is embarrassing enough to admit, but I was certain I had almost been kissed. The thing that surprised me was the sensation deep in my core that felt disappointed when it didn't happen. There wasn't a doubt in my mind that kissing Soren would be mind-altering, but the part that felt as though I would never measure up plagued the back of my mind. I slipped off the counter and gathered my things. Ever the gentleman, Soren walked me to the car under the light of the moon.

I wanted to ask him. I wanted to know more than anything why he was going to kiss me and why he didn't. His hand leaned against the roof of my Jeep as I stood by the door, feeling uncertain for the first time on how to say goodbye.

"Thank you for dinner."

I smiled softly. My heart was full and happy regardless of the prior maybe-almost-kiss situation. He smiled and pulled me into a hug. His chin rested on my head, and a part of me never wanted to leave. He was the first man who had ever made me feel safe on this level, and I wanted to burrow into his warmth. I shifted closer, resting my face against his heart to hear the beat. Closing my eyes, I listened until he pulled back. His eyes darkened, and I had that sensation that I was going to be kissed.

He abruptly knocked on the roof of the Jeep twice and said, "Drive safe. Text me when you get home to let me know you made it safe."

I spent half of the car ride home wondering why Soren hadn't kissed me and the other half wondering why I hadn't been brave enough to kiss him first.

Chapter Thirty-Five

Soren

I WATCHED LANE AND Jonah go for a round in the ring. Lane was all talk, which thankfully he could back up most of the time, but Jonah fought as he lived. Jonah was like watching a panther. He was quiet, intense, and dodged hits with an unmatched fluidity while also intimidating his opponent with his intensity. I fought against him regularly, but often lost. He was a black belt in karate, trained in Krav Maga, and was a Veteran Marine. Both men were shirtless and sweating from exertion. I stood to the side, having completed a five-mile run on the treadmill. Unexpectedly, Jonah threw a right hook that connected with Lane's face, and the timer on Jonah's phone went off. I reached to silence it as they returned to their corners and toweled off their faces and chests.

"Man, you've been practicing without me?" Lane asked, working to catch his breath.

"You know he's always practicing," I stated, and we both knew it to be true. Lane had upped his gym time to help with the anxiety he'd been having lately, but Jonah was still a beast to fight against. He'd never said why he felt the need to push so hard, but if I had to guess, it was because of the hell he'd been through as a kid. My demons were playthings compared to the things he and Landry had been through. They fought tooth and nail for everything they had and were two of the best humans I knew.

We made our way to the water bottle station and refilled our bottles.

"Anybody in a rush tonight?" Lane asked.

Jonah met my eyes, and we both gave a negative response and headed for the table unsure of what Lane was about to say.

"I have an idea, and I want to run it by both of you," Lane laid out.

"I've been thinking of ways to help the kids in Kennedy and other small towns similar to ours. Ever since I began coaching at the high school last year, I've been seeing up close how some of the families in town are living. I want to help but not make it seem like a handout, because the people that seriously need help won't go for that. I ran some ideas by one of my baseball buddies that has a few organizations in inner city Detroit. Obviously, it'd have to be adapted to accommodate a rural town, but I was thinking of a resource center. There'd be tutoring, therapy, financial classes, and maybe we can partner with the gym for self-defense. Something that maybe people can volunteer at to give the impression they are giving back. Maybe a perk could be gift cards to the grocery store to help make ends meet, or therapy for kids having issues in school. Sure, there's a school counselor, but it's not enough," he reasoned, rubbing the towel down his neck again. Lane was always searching for ways to give back, and I had partnered with him multiple times over the last eight years.

"I like it. I might have a space you can use. The old Flanagan building is almost done with renovations," Jonah offered.

Most people didn't know it, but Jonah had a business sense that was awe-inspiring. After serving six years as a Marine, he started flipping real estate until he had amassed more properties than anyone in our small town even knew about. Most people simply thought of him as the guy in town that owned the gym, but there was a lot more to Jonah Gaines than met the eye. He used the money he made off his properties to buy more properties and to take care of Landry and Hope while Landry finished her college degree as a single mom.

"Both things sound solid to me. If you decided to add a small food pantry, I could donate fresh beef and volunteer time in my slower seasons. And of course I'd back it with Abel's foundation. Maybe we could use the building for weekly AA meetings, too. The Flanagan building is only two blocks from school, so kids could walk down after class. The library is next door. Maybe they could provide a tutor," I suggested.

We talked out the logistics. Lane had a plan to move forward, and we decided we'd meet tomorrow to walk through the Flanagan building and see if the current floor plan would work.

Chapter Thirty-Six

Sawyer

Today wasn't my day *again*. Greg had eaten my lunch again. Sharon had conveniently overscheduled herself, and I was picking up the slack again.

The "agains" were beginning to add up. I was hungry and tired. I had hit forty hours this morning. Regardless of how much we told upper management we needed two more social workers to make this doable, we got the same response every time.

"We have the jobs listed on multiple employment websites."

That was all well and good, but what ended up happening was those of us that were here for the children picked up the slack for those that assumed this would be a normal nine-to-five job. Social work, especially in the foster care system, was everything but a nine-to-five. It was more of a six in the morning to midnight and then sometimes there was a two in the morning call. We had staff for late nights and emergency calls, but the kids weren't bonded to these employees. They didn't know them and I couldn't say no.

I was angry. Talia and Soren were right. I had a problem saying no. They'd both gently said as much in the last few weeks and months, and they thought I was overdoing it. However, I related too profoundly to the children in my care, and I wanted things to go as smoothly as possible. I wanted to fix everything and I couldn't. I didn't possess that power and it made me sad and angry. I knew what it was to be scared and angry and sick and tired of being shuffled around.

Sometimes I wondered if doing this job was good for my mental health, but I'd always push away that voice because it felt selfish . . . and maybe too honest. I shoved those thoughts under the rug along with everything else. Afterward I'd go home and obsessively organize my pantry, dust my floorboards, and not be able to sleep anywhere other than my nest of blankets in my cozy chair. When I was stressed, all of those things escalated in intensity.

Currently, I was sitting outside a grocery store waiting for a foster mom to come pick up the child I was transporting because Sharon had said I would.

"Ms. Sawyer. Do you know the Brooks?" Nichole asked, clutching her favorite stuffed animal she carried everywhere. I turned toward the seven-year-old.

"Yep, they have two little girls around your age." I smiled hoping to reassure her.

"Do you think they'll like me?" Her concern was etched into her forehead. This I could answer confidently. I knew Matilda and Mandy fairly well. They were giggling balls of sunshiny friendliness and maybe a tad too much brutal honesty. I smiled thinking of the time Matilda told me twenty-six was "super old."

"You bet! They have a pet turtle named John Wayne and two fainting goats." I smiled.

"Fainting goats?" Excitement lit her face as I scanned the parking lot for the car that was meeting us.

"Yep. Oh look, there they are. You'll have to ask them about their goats, Tom and Jerry!"

Nichole loaded up with the Brooks family and her nerves had dissipated. She smiled and waved bye at me as they drove away. I got back in my SUV and took a deep breath. Part of me wanted to rage at the foster care system in general because of the dumpster fire it was most days. Simultaneously, the other part reminded me that there was always a way to be light and light always mattered, regardless of how dark it was. I wanted to make a bigger difference, to see the changes happen faster than they were. I didn't want to meet up with people to exchange children as if it were some black market deal at a grocery store. I was tired and hungry and wanted to punch something. Soren came to mind because I'd heard him talking about boxing before, and I did something I never do. I impulsively texted him first. I was done for the day after dropping off Nichole, and being wrapped in one of his warm hugs felt like it would make everything better.

Sawyer:

Do you have anything I can punch?

Soren:

Rough day?

Sawyer:

Yeah . . . maybe I'm just hangry.

Soren:

Can you meet me here?

A pin drop of a location came through. I didn't expect that response but I input the address.

Sawyer:

It's forty-five minutes from here. Leaving now.

"Extend your arm all the way."

Soren demonstrated throwing a punch and hitting the bag in slow motion. I didn't know what Soren had in mind when I showed up to a mostly empty gym. He gave me a tight hug before feeding me the best bierock I'd ever eaten. After I ate, he showed me the correct form to throw a punch. I tried again, but something was off.

"Here, let me stand behind you."

Soren walked behind me, his warm, solid body against my back. His hands gripped my hips, adjusting them slightly before he grasped my wrists. Fire ignited in the places he touched and spread throughout my whole body. His breath on my neck made the wisps of hair there flutter. He guided my arm through the motion three times before stepping back, and I immediately missed his touch.

"Okay, try again. Since you're wearing gloves, it won't hurt your hand to throw your weight into it." I punched, mimicking his instruction.

"That's my girl!" Soren beamed.

"Run through it a few more times and then I'll show you what I brought for dessert."

"You have dessert?!" I punched again, hitting the bag with a thud.

"Not just any dessert, but Ronnie hooked me up with some of Mrs. Blake's fresh chocolate chip cookies with caramel chips." His brilliant hazel eyes crinkled at the corners when he smiled, and I never wanted to look away.

"That sounds amazing!" I threw a few more punches, making sure I was hitting with enough force, and extended my body the way he taught me.

"Alright, Muhammad Ali. You can be done for today," Soren quipped.

"Thanks for showing me how to do that." I struggled to undo the Velcro on the gloves since my other hand was also covered in a glove. I bit my lip. I couldn't grasp the elastic strap.

"Here, let me help you."

Soren reached for my glove, which made me feel engulfed in him when he was this close. His thumb brushed the inside of my wrist, and my breath caught before he moved to my other hand. He appeared unaffected by our nearness, but there was something in me that was slightly lightheaded around him. I remembered when my attraction to him made me want to run, but now I wondered what it'd be like to stay.

Chapter Thirty-Seven

Soren

I PULLED THE BROWN paper bag out and held it so Sawyer could select a cookie after we settled at the table in the corner of the gym.

"Real talk. What made you want to punch something today?" I asked as I leaned back and settled into my seat. What Sawyer didn't know was I had some questions, and she was not leaving until I got answers. She had circles of exhaustion under her eyes the last two times I'd seen her and I wanted to know why. She bit her lip. One hand held a cookie and the other reached to pull the military tags out of her shirt. She took a deep breath before starting.

"Sometimes I feel like I can't do enough to help kids. Like no matter what I do, it isn't enough. Realistically, I know I'm helping, but I wonder sometimes if it really makes a difference. It's overwhelming sometimes. I mean it always has been, but lately it feels like an uphill battle."

"What parts feel most overwhelming?" I asked. She bobbed her head from side to side in consideration as she chewed another bite.

"The monumental weight of the issues. It's not something that can be fixed with one law or one regulation change. Essentially, you're a hamster on a wheel with no end in sight. Sometimes . . . " She paused and broke off a piece of cookie. I waited. Her eyes were wet with unshed tears, but she wasn't looking at me. She set her cookie on a napkin.

"Can we talk about this but you don't look at me?" She peeked a glance at me. Her cheeks flushed. She steadily rubbed at the tags.

"Sure." I stood, lifted my chair, flipped it around, and straddled it.

"This good?" I asked as I faced away from her.

"Yeah," she replied, and I swore I heard her mumble, "I'm such a freak."

"Sometimes, I don't function well when I get home from a hard day." She hesitated, but I waited. "This is embarrassing to say, but most of the days that are rough end with me under my weighted blankets unable to move, and sometimes I think about what Talia said to me."

"What did Talia say?" I knew she'd been under too much pressure. I could see it in her eyes these last couple of weeks.

"That maybe working in this career field might not be healthy for me because it's so personal. Maybe I'm addicted to the chaos of the way I grew up, the adrenaline rush of it all. I know I want to help kids, but maybe this isn't the best place for me to do that."

"Do you think that maybe she could be right?" She paused so long that I almost thought she wouldn't continue.

"Sometimes. It feels wrong to know there's so much suffering in the world and not do anything about it." Her heart sounded broken simply by giving a voice to the emotions.

"What if 'doing something' looks different from what you thought it did?" I asked. She paused again as if she was thinking.

"I feel like it consumes my life. I don't have a life outside of it, but it's all I've done for six years since I graduated early. It's all I've ever wanted to do. I feel stuck between wanting to make a difference and also not wanting my life to pass me by, especially now that I get to choose what my life looks like." Her voice was barely a whisper.

"Can I turn around?" I asked, desperate to see her face.

My hand gripped the back of the chair, making my knuckles turn white. I could barely stand not touching her.

"Yes." Her voice was small.

I flipped around to face her, my elbows on my knees, and I reached a hand out palm up.

She placed her smaller one in mine. She was learning to trust me, and my heart wanted to sprout wings and soar.

"Thank you for telling me. How about this? Until you figure out what the best path is moving forward, any time you have a rough day, you call me. I can listen, and then I'll find something for you to punch," I promise.

One corner of her mouth tugged up in a smile.

"You're not going to tell me what to do?" Her voice was incredulous.

"No, Sawyer. You are the bravest and smartest person I know. You will know the answer when it's time."

She studied my face, searching for what I wasn't sure. I stood and pulled her into a hug. Her curves melted into my body as she shifted to burrow closer. Her head on my heart.

"Okay," she whispered. I pulled back and clasped her soft face in my hands where I could see her eyes.

"Do we have a deal that you'll call me on the hard days?" I didn't want her carrying this alone.

She nodded.

"Words." Because I knew she'd worry about "bothering" me, which wasn't possible.

"Yes, Cowboy. We have a deal," she agreed.

She didn't call me this often, but when she did, it made my heart skip a beat. I did the most impulsive thing I had in this relationship and pressed my lips to her soft forehead. This beautiful, smart, and brave woman was going to be my undoing. I heard her quick intake of breath before I wrapped my arms around her again. Where she was concerned, I was never letting her go.

Chapter Thirty-Eight

Sawyer

Soren:

Just a heads-up, my parents ambushed me this morning to "help" with wheat harvest. I wanted you to know before you arrived.

Sawyer:

Ambushed? Hmmm should I be worried?

Soren

No, they'll treat you like an angel. I, on the other hand, am preparing myself to be embarrassed no less than twenty-three times today.

Sawyer

Ohhhhh. Embarrassed Soren. I can't wait to see! *insert evil cackle*

Soren

Squinting side eye gif

AFTER NEARLY TWO HOURS in the combine with Soren harvesting wheat, we had finished the fields we were working on, but I hadn't met his parents yet. I saw their RV parked in Soren's drive when I arrived, but they had met up with friends for lunch. Travis was a dutiful cart driver. When the combine bin was full of wheat, we'd stop and offload into a cart pulled by a large green tractor with a cab. Gene drove a semitruck to the grain elevator to unload the last of the wheat harvested. Soren was patient, teaching me all the names of things and how everything worked. It was one of those things I'd never really considered, but once he explained how the combine worked, I was immediately interested in the whole process. It might have helped that my instructor had heart-stopping dark hazel eyes with tiny crinkles at the corners that made me want to brush my lips across them.

"Sawyer?"

I had completely missed him speaking because I was too busy lusting after his attractive . . . eye crinkles. I was such a weirdo. His eye crinkles were now on full display as he looked at me with amusement. His lips tugged at the corner trying to suppress a smile.

"Sorry, what?" I needed help against my attraction to this man.

"Do you want to drive home?" He asked as he gestured to the steering wheel.

"Really?!" He grinned at me.

The tires on the combine were taller than my head when I stood beside them. I had never driven anything this big.

"Yes?" I said, nerves kicking in. "But I don't know how . . . " I glanced at all the buttons and screens.

"If you want, you can sit on my leg. That way if something goes wrong, I'll be right here. I'll handle the gears so all you have to focus on is steering?"

I was nervous, but far too excited about the opportunity to pass it up.

"Okay." I stood up from the small seat to his left that he'd called a "buddy seat," and he scooted back and slapped his left leg.

"Sit here and I'll run everything except the steering wheel."

I timidly sat down, and the warmth of his firm thigh bled through the jeans I was wearing. My right elbow grazed his abs under his shirt. Sitting this way, I was much closer to his face and height. When I turned to look at him, his face was right there. His five o'clock shadow made his eyes appear more consumingly vivid. The warmth of his breath on my cheek sent tingles down my spine. If this were any other person, I would be nervous at his proximity, but Soren Roberts always made me feel safe. In this position, my head could lay on his shoulder, and I impulsively wrapped my arms around his torso. His large hands wrapped around me, and all I could smell was fresh sunshine and spearmint. He was warm and firm, and my knees hit his other thigh as he held me close.

Turning my face to his neck, I whispered, "Thank you for today." Thank you for making me feel safe was what I wanted to say, but my throat was tight.

He pulled me in tighter and all I wanted to do was kiss his neck . . . and so I did. My lips brushed the underside of his jaw where his five o'clock shadow was coming in, and it was sandpaper against the delicate skin of my lips. He stopped breathing and pulled his head back to look at me. His hazel eyes searched mine, and I could see every single one of his individual eyelashes. Something told me he wanted to kiss me, while at the same time, I felt a sense of apprehension telling me to back away. Tugging equally as much was the desire to lean forward and press my lips to his. I wanted Soren to kiss me, but I immediately realized I'd never kissed anyone of my own volition, and I wasn't sure I'd be any good at it. There was a part of me that wanted to be exceptional at kissing if I ever had the opportunity to be kissed by Soren Roberts. His eyes briefly dropped to my lips before bouncing back up to my eyes, but he didn't move. He was waiting on me, and I was paralyzed like I was partially buried in sand. I wanted this, but I didn't want to screw it up. I unwrapped my arms around him and pulled back. All of my inexperienced adult thoughts rushed in yet again. He looked at me as though he was working to understand me, but I didn't understand myself either. I didn't know exactly why I pulled away, but I had, and there wasn't anything I could do now. He sat back, and his hands gripped the armrests of his seat a little too tightly. I swung my knees toward the steering wheel, and he reached for my hands and placed them where they needed to be. The rough texture of his calloused hands sent fire through my body at the touch. As he leaned back, he brushed his lips against my temple and I felt it all the way to my toes. I should have kissed him. If his forehead and temple kisses had this effect on me, what would kissing him be like? My cheeks burned thinking about it, and I wanted to sink into the floor.

"Sawyer?"

I shyly met his eyes as we sat, still parked.

"Is it okay with you that I kiss your forehead? I shouldn't have assumed. I should have asked the other day." His eyes searched mine.

I nodded, my cheeks fully ablaze now.

"I need your words." His voice was gravel.

"I like it." My voice was unnaturally high, and I bit the inside of my cheek.

He must have found what he was looking for because a soft smile tugged at his mouth and he ran a knuckle down my cheek before he pushed a handle and the combine began moving. I was left wondering if having a man ask if he can kiss me was my weakness.

Chapter Thirty-Nine

Sawyer

Driving the combine was even more fun than I had imagined, and Soren was diligent in teaching me everything. A woman in a pastel tracksuit with a face-splitting smile came from the porch as we turned into the lane toward the barn. Her hair was a bright blonde, and it swished around as she exuberantly waved using her whole body. There was an older man sitting much more calmly on the porch swing. He raised his head and stood.

I heard Soren mutter something as he took over driving. I rolled my lips in to suppress a smile because this must be his mom and dad. Admittedly, I was somewhat nervous to meet them, but something about the pastel blue jogging suit moving toward the now parked combine told me I had nothing to fear. She visibly bounced with excitement, and I swore I even saw her clap her hands at one point. The much calmer man had made it to the top of the porch steps and descended at a much more reasonable pace. I stood and collected my water bottle as Soren pushed open the door muttering, "Here we go."

"Soren sweetheart, couldn't you take her on a better date than in a combine?!"

Soren's mom immediately turned to his dad and proclaimed, "He must take after you, Harvey, although you did win me over with combine dates, so that's not saying much for me is it?"

She laughed at her own joke and Harvey walked to her side. As I reached the bottom of the ladder, I was squashed into a hug unlike any I'd ever received and she did not let go. I think if I knew her better, I would have enjoyed it. Tears stung my eyes at what it must be like to be loved by a mom so much. Even if the hug felt like a little too much.

"Gayla, let the girl breathe," the man that I now knew as Harvey reasoned.

Gayla let go and put both of her hands on my cheeks.

"Sweetheart, I can't believe I'm seeing you again after this many years." Her hazel eyes shone with tears, and Soren took my hand. I didn't say anything because I wasn't sure what to say, but there was something in her eyes that made me want to get to know her better. She seemed a little familiar, but I wasn't sure if it was because of the things Soren had shared with me or if I'd simply forgotten the other times I'd seen her before. Something inside of me wanted to remember any memory I had of seeing her, although logically, she had most likely only seen me from a distance. She pulled me in for another fierce squeeze and Soren made the introductions.

I learned that Harvey was similar to Soren, except more quiet. He had a deep kindness behind a quiet smile that simply exuded from him. If anyone could ever be considered the human form of sunshine like Talia, it was Gayla. I knew she and Talia would be fast friends. They both had that gift of making people feel welcome, and appreciating people as they are. We made our way toward the porch after a back-slapping hug between Harvey and Soren and a rib-crushing embrace between Gayla and Soren. After more catching up and visiting, we settled in around the kitchen table to a meal that Gayla prepared, and there was never a moment of awkward silence. There was never a moment where I felt like I didn't belong.

Three hours later and I was driving back home. Soren's parents were everything that parents should be. They were kind and supportive to their son. His mom was hilarious, and his dad was reserved and quiet, but not in a rude way. More of a watchful and shy way. He rarely talked, but he appeared more comfortable in letting his wife do most of the talking. The thing I didn't miss was how his eyes lit up when he looked at her. She'd said they had been married for thirty-eight years, but their love still seemed like a cross between puppy love and two people that knew each other exceptionally well. Gayla had explained that the ranch was from Harvey's side of the family, and they had dedicated twenty-five years to running it. After Abel had passed, they decided they needed a change. Farming and ranching had always been Soren's passion. After he had completed his agriculture degree, they wanted him to feel free to make the changes he wanted without being limited by their opinions. Gayla worked in insurance, most of which involved hurricane damage, therefore allowing them to travel along the southern coastline. Harvey had discovered a love for birdwatching and golfing and those activities kept him busy in retirement. Gayla said that she required more activities in her life and working part-time allowed her to be around people more which she loved. I felt a tinge of pain wondering what it would have been like to grow up with a family that loved each other. Knowing that no matter what hardships you faced, you had a family there to face them with you. I was thankful knowing that Abel had such a loving family for his short life. He had known what it was to be truly loved and cherished, and I imagined that must be the best feeling in the world.

Chapter Forty

Soren

"Thanks, Mom," I said as I closed the door to the dishwasher and pressed start. We had cleared the table long ago, but I had to practically drag Sawyer away from cleaning the whole kitchen so we could visit with my parents. At first, she was hesitant, but as the time passed, she relaxed and grew more comfortable to the point that she asked questions. The tension and apprehension in her shoulders dropped, and she laughed at my mom's antics that I knew she was especially playing into for the benefit of Sawyer.

My mom's eyebrows met, unsure of what I was thanking her for.

"For making Sawyer feel welcome," I explained, and my mom smiled softly.

"Seems like someone should be fussing over that girl." My dad observed quietly. I ran a hand through my hair and tugged at the strands at the bottom. I settled at the dining room table where my dad sat with a cup of decaf coffee.

"If it were up to me, I'd spoil her rotten," I said honestly, studying my hands.

"Oh, sweetheart," my mom responded as she sat beside me and patted my hand.

"What's the hang-up?" my dad asked.

"Sawyer has C-PTSD. She grew up being bounced around in foster care. Some of the places she lived were hell, Dad. I try to tell her how special she is, but it's like she hears the words but they don't make it through her walls all the way. I'm trying to take things slow, but everything inside me wants to run." I scrubbed my face with my hands.

My dad was quiet in his reflective way, mulling over my words.

"Self-worth doubts can run deep, but all you can do is be that steady person that shows her you'll always be there for her," my mom advised as she patted my shoulder, before making her way toward the guest room to get ready for bed.

"Son, I don't say it often enough, but I'm proud of you. The farm is better than it ever has been and you've found a girl that seems real special. You know your mom and I will always be here if you ever need us. You'll know what to do when the time is right." Something shifted in my heart at his words. I blinked away moisture. My dad had a way of saying all that needed to be said with the bare minimum of words. I knew my parents loved me, and all I had ever wanted to do was to make them proud. They had always said they loved me and supported me, even though I felt I had disappointed them with the disaster of my life and the rumors years ago. Was I simply hearing the words and not believing them? Maybe Sawyer and I weren't that different.

I had walls where my parents were concerned. Was it because I was scared to lose them like I had lost Abel? Did I think that keeping them away from me kept them safe? Maybe it was time I simply believed the encouraging words they spoke to me. Maybe it was time I fully realized I was not the same person I had been, and I was capable of loving someone despite the fear of loss. I scrubbed my hand over my eyes as the early morning start to the day wore on me.

"Thank you, Dad, that means a lot. Sawyer's the only woman I've ever wanted, and the possibility of losing her scares the hell out of me." I met his crystal blue eyes, praying he'd have some words of wisdom to tamper the fear I faced.

"Son, loving a woman is always that way. I don't know what I'd do without your mom. I think if we're going to live full lives, we've gotta go out with no regrets. Make sure those around us know we care and leave nothing unsaid." He tipped his coffee cup and stood slowly, stretching his back.

"I'm heading to bed, but let's talk about Abel's foundation tomorrow. I want to hear more about the idea you boys came up with." With that, he patted my shoulder with his weathered hand, rinsed out his coffee cup, and went to bed. Loving Sawyer Brannan was the greatest adventure of my life. I knew that telling her might scare her, so I'd keep loving her quietly until the day she saw that she loved me too.

Chapter Forty-One

Soren

THE RED AND WHITE striped vinyl that covered the booth bench squeaked as I sat. It was aged from having been loved for two generations by the residents of Kennedy. The entire interior of Ronnie's Diner was red, white, and black 1950s-style decor, complete with a jukebox in the corner currently playing Randy Travis. Dad and Mom had approved moving forward with the resource center funding after meeting with Jonah and Lane two days ago. Although I could have decided without them, I wanted to include them in decisions I made with Abel's foundation. 10 percent of the profit I made from the ranch went toward the foundation along with the nest egg Mom and Dad had used to create it. The foundation funded everything from scholarships for kids that attended Kennedy High School, to paying for rehab for those I worked with in AA and beyond. After saying goodbye to Mom and Dad this morning, they loaded up their RV and headed toward Yellowstone for a change of scenery.

George settled across from me as he picked up a menu to scan. We usually met in Lewis City, but I had reached out to him last night, and he said he thought a drive in the country sounded nice.

"Soren, how are ya doing? Who's your friend here?" Tina asked, her apron strings wrapped around her twice because of her petite size. Tina was as much of a staple at Ronnie's Diner as Ronnie himself. She had been working here since I was a child. Her black curly hair was piled on her head with streaks of silver throughout as she turned pointedly to George.

"I'm doing good. How are you doing? This is George." George reached out his hand to shake hers.

"Oh, ya know, just living the dream. Pleasure to meet you, George. I'm Tina. What can I get for you guys?"

Within minutes we were eating cheeseburgers and milkshakes while I had a sneaking suspicion that Tina and George might have flirted more had I not been present, which honestly felt awkward as hell.

"How are you really doing?" George asked when Tina walked away after delivering our cheeseburger baskets. That was how conversations with George always went. He could see through the mess and wanted to know how I was genuinely doing. That was a question I wasn't exactly sure how to answer so I went back to the beginning. I gave him a quick rundown of meeting Sawyer and how things were going for the last two months.

"She sounds like a special person," George remarked, taking a sip of his milkshake.

"She's the one, George, but I haven't told her about AA. I'm scared she'll put her walls up again when they've barely started to fall. I don't know if I can handle the idea of her walking away." George was one of the few people I was brutally honest with, and he always reciprocated.

"You call me if something goes badly, but Soren you just spent ten minutes telling me what a good woman she is. Allow her to see your faults and all. She'll see that you've walked through fire to get to the other side, and if she's as amazing as you say, she'll love you even more for it. My Mildred loved like that before she passed, and real love can change a man," George affirmed.

I took a seat, leaning my back against the corner of Abel's headstone and looked toward the clouds. Right after he passed I had hated being here, but over the years, it became more bearable. There was something about the giant oak tree that provided shade over Abel's grave that was peaceful.

After talking to George about things, I had this peace that everything was going to be okay.

"Hey, bud. I miss you like always. I can't believe you were holding out on me about Sawyer. Although, that would have been a little weird now, considering we're dating. That's what I came to talk to you about. Man, she's remarkable. Sawyer's the bravest person, and she didn't let the shit circumstances of her life turn her bitter. She makes me want that dream I had all but forgotten. She makes me want a wife and kids. To run the ranch like Grandma and Grandpa did." My voice dropped as my nose stung. "Man, I think I'm in love with her." This was the closest I could get to a man-to-man talk with my brother. The wind blew around me and I watched the leaves tremble on the oak near the edge of the cemetery. The years didn't lessen the pain of his loss, but the time did make the reality that he was no longer here more real. I had begun to accept his loss because I was more prepared for his absence. Abel being gone would always be the most excruciating thing in my life, while simultaneously being the biggest catalyst for my drive to make a difference. Because of how completely Abel loved others, it propelled me to manage the ranch with intention, to set that percentage aside every month to invest in our community and those suffering around us. I hadn't told Sawyer about the foundation yet or how much we had done in the community in Abel's honor, but one day I would. I'd share what a difference his life had truly made, but first I had to tell her more about my life, especially since she was becoming a piece I didn't want to live without.

Soren.

photo of circus tickets

Wanna join the circus? *winky face*

Sawyer:

GIF of a woman excitedly clapping hands

Only if you'll be there!

Chapter Forty-Two

Sawyer

Soren held my hand as we walked out of the circus arena, and I was on cloud nine. At one point, Soren had reached over and used his index knuckle under my chin to close my mouth because it was hanging open. The entire show was absolutely magical. The powerful gymnastics, the skilled motorcycle tricks, the graceful dancer who quite literally hung from her waist length hair. I was in a dream and I never wanted to wake up. I couldn't even imagine how magical this would be to experience as a child. Soren opened the passenger door to his truck, and I climbed up.

"It was all so magical," I whispered, still in amazement.

Soren reached to buckle me in as he always did. Initially it used to be weird, and now, I had simply come to expect it. Sometimes I wanted to ask, but I knew that Abel died in a car accident and a deep part of me knew there was a connection. The last thing I wanted to do was cause pain to this man who, for some reason, thought he wanted to date me. Instead of sitting still, I turned toward him and impulsively wrapped my arms around him. I was overwhelmed, and I wanted to say thank you. He had given me the space to be me, and as we spent more time together, I felt the walls I'd built around my heart begin to crumble.

Soren's large hands slid around my ribs as he pulled me close to him. Our height difference was lessened this way, and I turned my face into the crook of his neck. My heart raced as I thought about kissing him, but I was waiting for him to make the first move because the fear of not measuring up was intimidating.

"Pretty Girl?" Soren asked, his stubbled cheek pressed against mine.

"Yeah?"

"I'm going to tell you something, but I don't want you to freak out or think that you have to say it back," he instructed with gravel in his voice. I could feel his heart racing under my palm.

"Okay."

"Sawyer, I love you and I know you might not feel the same about me, but I want you to know." I gasped as my heart pounded in my chest.

He loved me? I cared about him more than any other man I had ever known. The idea of saying "I love you" back felt like there was a hand grasped around my throat cutting off my air supply.

I pulled back more, needing to see his eyes better. His sincere hazel eyes met mine, and I wanted to say those three small words back, but they wouldn't come. I had no context for the type of love he was speaking of, and I wasn't sure if I was capable of it.

"Soren, I care about you so much, but I can't say it back." Tears of frustration pooled in my eyes. Why couldn't I simply say it back? What if I got my hopes up as I had so many times in my life only to not be chosen again? It all was too much to process at the moment. He pressed a kiss to my forehead and pulled me in for another hug, and I buried myself in the solid warmth of his body.

"That's okay, Sawyer. I will love you more than enough for the both of us."

I was wrapped in his arms, and he held me as though I was the most precious thing in the world to him. I wondered why he hadn't kissed me if he really loved me, and I contemplated if I'd ever be able to say it back. I was in college before I'd ever had anyone say those words to me. The words were trapped inside of me, and I wasn't sure if they'd ever come out. Soren deserved someone that would say it back, and what if that someone wasn't me?

I had barely shut the door after Soren dropped me off when my eyes puddled with tears of frustration. Something was wrong with me. How

could I want a man like Soren Roberts who was the best, most thoughtful, and kind man on the planet? I wanted him to kiss me breathless, but
the idea of saying "I love you" nearly made me break out in hives. There
had to be something irreparable about me. I trudged inside, sank into my
comfy chair and buried myself under weighted blankets. Soren couldn't
love me because he didn't completely know me. I'd told him about how
I buried myself under weighted blankets after a difficult day at work, but
he didn't truly realize how much I was debilitated at the end of some
days after work. He didn't know I kept my duplex obsessively organized
because when things were out of place, I wanted to cry. Before I started
going to his house on Sundays, I used to stay in bed all day because I was
emotionally exhausted and drained from my job. He didn't know how
often I turned to how-to videos on the internet to learn basic adulting
skills. He didn't truly understand the shattered pieces of me. I kept the
ugly, undesirable parts of me hidden because once he saw those parts,
he would leave. People always left, and it was only a matter of time. I
fell asleep buried under my weighted blankets, too mentally exhausted
to move. The last thing I thought as I drifted off to sleep was I'd like to be kissed
by someone as handsome and good as Soren Roberts at least once in my
life.

What are you wanting for lunch on Sunday? I'm picking up groceries. I'm thinking breakfast for lunch, which may include chocolate chip waffles?

four hours later

My phone was off because I was in court all morning. Connor's dad got connected with this amazing rehab program and is doing awesome!

That's great news!

That sounds yummy! What do you want me to bring?

Only you.

Chapter Forty-Three

Soren

THE SUN WAS SETTING as Sawyer sat next to me on my front porch swing the following Sunday evening. Her hair was loosely twisted in a messy bun, with little tresses touching her neck and cheeks. She was beautiful, as she always was. I didn't know how much longer I could wait for her to kiss me. I would rather cut off my own legs than move too far, too fast. I would never forgive myself if something I did triggered her trauma response. She was too precious to me to risk making a mistake. Sawyer was warm sunshine and wildflowers. Everything bright and brave, and I was lucky to be near her. Her walls were coming down, and I would be here, waiting, when she finally saw me.

Talia was right the first day I met her. Sawyer was too good for this world, and I'd spend every day trying to make the earth a better place for her.

"Soren?" She pulled me from my thoughts.

Her wide eyes lifted from the coffee table photography book of horses she was flipping through.

"Yeah, Pretty Girl?" She bit her lip. I wished she wouldn't do that.

"I want to ask you something, but can you not look at me?" She raised her brow.

We'd played this game before, so I knew she was going to say something deeply personal to her. She had told me it made her more comfortable, so I closed my eyes.

"Shoot."

"Why don't you touch me more?" She sounded nervous, but she quickly added, "I mean not that you have to or anything, but I like it when you hug me."

I couldn't stop the tug at the corner of my mouth.

"I have been told I'm a world-class hugger." A giggle escaped her mouth at my cockiness.

"Can I look now?" I asked.

"Umm-hmm." Her face was turned down toward her hands as she fidgeted with the military tags. Her cheeks were flushed as I was expecting they would be.

"You're in charge here. I'm following your lead."

Her head shot up. I couldn't tell if she was shocked or surprised. Her mouth moved, but no words came out and then she blurted, "What if I want you to touch me first?"

"How would you like me to touch you?" I asked softly as she studied her nails.

"I've never kissed anybody on my own terms, and I want to know what that feels like."

I searched her downturned face and decided that maybe she was experiencing the same tension I was. I had to ignore her "on my own terms" portion because it made me consider becoming a felon. I could rip someone apart limb from limb. That anger would never leave. I would always feel murderous toward anyone that had laid a hand on her or had ever treated her with anything but the utmost care and respect.

I stood as she looked at me with complete vulnerability in her eyes, and I reached for her hand. She slid her soft hand in mine, and I walked her to the wide porch railing. I reached down, grasped her by the waist, and placed her on the wide ledge, which made us almost eye to eye. I saw her delicate throat swallow at our proximity to each other. I could see her heartbeat racing at the base of her throat.

"Sawyer, remember when I said you can always tell me no?" I asked. She nodded.

"Pretty Girl, I need you to use your words." My voice graveled. I didn't want to do anything she didn't want.

"Yes." She smiled softly.

"Remember that."

I tucked a strand of her glossy hair behind her ear as I leaned in and kissed her jaw under her ear. My lips skimmed down the length of her jaw, beginning by her ear, then her chin. Her skin was as silky as I assumed it would be.

"You're so damn beautiful."

I pulled away and wrapped my hand around the side of her jaw and neck. My thumb brushed between her cheek and ear. I moved to the opposite side to kiss her temple. Lowering my lips, I grazed her jaw as I stopped to place kisses from her ear to the pulse point on her neck. I opened my mouth to taste her there. She was even sweeter than I imagined. A small shiver raced through her body. She was as affected by my presence as I was of hers. I pulled away, wanting to check in, and her eyes met mine.

"Is that okay?" I asked.

"Yes." Her voice was soft.

I was standing between her knees as I reached for her wrists and placed her hands on my obliques in case she thought she needed permission to touch me. I placed my hand back on her neck and leaned to kiss her forehead, trailing kisses from her forehead to her temple. I leaned back, searching her eyes.

"Is this okay?" I asked again.

"Yes," she answered.

I heard a tiny sound of irritation, and then she grabbed my shirt and hauled me closer as her full lips tentatively met mine. I momentarily stopped breathing until she made a whimper that made my self-control crumble to pieces. I groaned and grasped my hand through her hair, knocking it loose as it cascaded down her back. Her hands gripped my shirt tightly, pulling me even closer. The gap between our bodies closed, and a fire stirred deep within me. I ran my tongue across the seam of her mouth and she gasped, giving me entrance to her mouth. Kissing

Sawyer Brannan was better than any kiss I'd ever had. Her hands were fisted in my shirt, tugging me as close as possible before sliding up to wrap around my neck. I left one hand in her hair as the other found her hip. This kiss was like a fireworks show on the 4th of July. It was a World Series, Super Bowl, NBA Finals-winning kind of kiss. All of her curves fit mine perfectly, and I slid my hands under her thighs and carried her to the swing. I sat on the swing, never breaking the kiss while she straddled my lap. I anchored my hands on her hips, refusing to let them roam. I wouldn't do more than kiss her until she told me otherwise. She pulled away from my lips and trailed kisses along my jawline and back to my ear. I flexed my fingers, hoping I wasn't bruising her hips. When she moved to kiss my neck, I couldn't stop the groan in the back of my throat. It was the most sensual sensation, and there was something about her innocent exploration that lit a fire in me. I moved my hands to her shoulders and gently created distance between us.

"Sawyer, we have to slow down," I choked out.

Her hooded eyes and the sound of protest were almost too much for my resistance. Her hair had tumbled down her back in soft waves. The old me wanted nothing more than to pick her up, toss her on my bed, and let her soft innocent exploration continue. I wanted to taste her. To kiss every inch of her soft, strawberry-and-cream scented skin and watch her unravel as I spent all night showing her how much I adored her.

"Maybe we should set boundaries?" I asked, barely holding on to logic.

"Like how far is too far?" she asked back. Her lips swollen from kissing me.

"Yeah, I want you, Sawyer. But I don't want to scare you or make you uncomfortable or move too fast." Her cheeks flushed, and she bit her bottom lip as she searched my eyes, which almost made me come undone again.

"You want me?" she asked incredulously.

"Every single inch of you. From your cute little feet to the top of your beautiful head, but I won't be another man who ignores your boundaries or pushes too far, too fast," I said, watching her closely.

"Okay. But can we kiss one more time?" she asked with a smile.

"Now that I can do," I answered huskily as I dipped my head to kiss her swollen lips. We sat this way for one more lengthy kiss before I pulled back and asked if she wanted to take a ride on the UTV to check on the calves. We talked and held hands the entire time because there was nowhere on the earth I'd rather be than loving Sawyer for the rest of my days. I only hoped that when she saw all the pieces of me, she wouldn't want to leave.

Chapter
Forty-Four

Sawyer

Talia:

Can you come to dinner next Friday?

Sawyer:

Sure, that should be good! Soren is busy, but I'll be there. Can't wait to see my Ava girl and her parents, of course. *winky face*

All I could smell was Soren as I shut his bedroom door. It was masculine with a touch of spearmint. His room mirrored the rest of his house, tidy and minimal, but his bedroom had a darker vibe. A California king-size, four-poster bed in dark wood sat in the middle of the room. On either side were framed antique maps, and his bed had a navy comforter. I wondered absentmindedly if Landry, Jonah's sister, had designed this room as well. Soren had said that she enjoyed interior design and had helped with his remodel. She certainly had a knack for creating beautiful spaces.

Soren had laid out clothes on the bed, along with a towel. I collected those and went toward his bathroom to shower. I noted the spearmint toothpaste and spearmint body wash, which explained everything. After washing the grime from helping all day with sorting cattle, I dried off and folded the sweat pants multiple times over to get them to stay up. I typically spent Sundays with Soren, but after our first kiss last Sunday, I couldn't wait until tomorrow. I wanted to be around him. I had come a day early and helped him sort cattle, which fundamentally meant I watched Soren and six ranch hands sort cattle. I didn't know what I was doing yet, but I was willing to learn. The guys could call out markings on a particular calf or cow, and it was as if they moved as a unit until it was separated to where it needed to be. I had gotten filthy after shadowing

Soren on the ranch all day. The t-shirt he gave me hit me mid-thigh, but I loved wearing his clothes. My hairbrush was in my bag in the family room. I towel-dried my hair as much as I could. When I walked back through the bedroom, that was when I noticed it. On his dresser sat a large aquamarine-tinted glass mason jar and inside were small slips of folded paper. I knew I shouldn't be snooping, and it was none of my business, but there was something about it that pulled at me like a moth to a flame. As I walked closer, I realized these were exactly the same as the slip of paper I had pulled out of his hoodie pocket the first day we met. I tipped my head to peer closer. They were all written in the same pattern as before but the numbers were different on each one.

2954 > 1

2987 > 1

"Everyone knows that 2987 is greater than 1," I whispered to myself. What did this mean? I reached to touch the jar when a voice came through the door.

"Hey, Pretty Girl. I'm making grilled ham and cheese sandwiches with pasta salad. Is that okay with you?" My heart raced in fear that I was almost caught, caught doing what, I wasn't sure.

"Sounds good," I called as I walked to open the door.

Soren had his arms braced above his head on the door frame and my heart caught in my throat. He was the most attractive man I had ever seen, and I had butterflies in my belly. His hazel eyes slowly trailed down my body before coming back up to reach my eyes. Heat ignited in all the places his eyes touched. There was something about the way that he looked at me that I never wanted him to look away. His white tee was taut over his chest, with his arms raised. There was a tiny sliver of his taut lower abdomen showing, and I wanted to run my finger across that skin. My face flushed at the thought.

"I like the way you look in my shirt," he said, biting the corner of his lip. A grin tugged at his mouth. I blushed and rolled the hem of his shirt between my fingers.

"Come on, Pretty Girl."

He reached for my hand and tugged me toward the kitchen where I sat on the counter while he made our grilled ham and cheese. No matter how distracted I got in the ease of conversation, I couldn't forget about the jar all throughout dinner. After eating the best grilled ham and cheese I'd ever had, we settled on the couch where Soren said he'd brush out my hair for me. I sat in front of him on the ottoman while he sat on the edge of the couch, brushing out the tangles in my hair. I knew I had to ask him about the jar and what it meant if I wanted to sleep tonight.

"Soren."

"Hmm." He was thoroughly distracted, running his hand through my hair as he brushed it out.

"When I was in your room earlier, I saw a jar with papers in it. What is that?"

He immediately stopped brushing my hair, and his hands landed on his thighs with a thud. I felt uneasy, but he had always made me feel comfortable talking to him about hard things and I was committed to being as straightforward with him as I could be. He'd given me space to be me. He sat quietly, and when I turned, his eyes were tortured. I wanted to give him an out, but I equally wanted to know what was going on.

Chapter Forty-Five

Soren

I OWED HER AN explanation, and I also feared that the truth would send her running. I ran my hand down my face.

"Can you promise to not run until I finish explaining?" I cleared my throat against the physical reaction to my emotions.

She tipped her head while studying my face.

"Why would I run?"

"Because there's a lot about me you don't fully understand and I'm afraid you'll hate me." Her eyes became guarded, and I was sure she didn't realize it, but she created distance between us and it killed me. This is why I hadn't told her. I had always planned to, but the timing never seemed right to obliterate the fragile trust that someone had placed in you. She had such a delicate trust system as it was, and me explaining the man I used to be could blow it all to pieces. Her demeanor after her shower made sense now. All throughout dinner she was quieter than normal, as though something was concerning her. She was as kind as always, but she didn't have that lightheartedness that she allowed to shine when she was comfortable. I owed her an explanation, and all I could hope was that she'd see who I was now and she wouldn't want to leave.

"May I hold your hand?"

I opened my calloused palm and held it out. She bit her lip and flicked her eyes over my face and posture. I knew she was unsure, but I wasn't sure I could tell this story without touching her. I needed her to be my anchor. After a second, her small hand slipped into mine. I used my index finger on my other hand to draw designs on top of her hand as my elbows were braced on my knees.

"When Abel died, it was my fault." I heard her sharp intake of breath, but I continued to study our hands and draw on her smooth skin. If I stopped, I didn't know if I could start again.

"Abel was extremely safety conscious when we were kids, and I'd always give him such a hard time and tell him to live a little."

A sob burned in my chest, but I would finish this story before I let a single tear fall. Damn my foolish choices. Damn my selfishness. Damn who I used to be. Without my influence, he'd be here. He might be the one holding her hand, and a knife of guilt twisted in my gut at the thought. He would have been a better choice than me.

"When I'd get outside the town limits of Kennedy, I'd always un-buckle my seatbelt because I hated how confining it was. He'd always give me a hard time, and I'd always say, 'We're almost home, loser.' I can still hear him lecturing me." A ghost that haunted all my future choices.

"I had a flat tire late one night, and I'd called him to bring me a tool since I was close to home. He hopped in his truck and made it about a quarter mile away from me when a deer jumped out in front of him. He slammed on his brakes and flew through the windshield because he wasn't wearing a seatbelt." I swallowed, trying to keep talking. "He died in my arms." Her sharp intake of breath drew my eyes up, and for the first time, I noticed the silent tears that dripped from her chin. I reached up and wiped them away.

"Oh, Soren."

"I'm not done yet. I want to tell you everything."

She squeezed my hand in encouragement, and I began drawing patterns again. Jonah and Lane knew this story, but I wasn't sure they really knew how much guilt I still carried. My little brother wasn't here because of me, and if I reflected on that too much, it was suffocating. Even as I sat here, I considered scheduling a meeting with George.

"After I pulled him from the ditch, I completely lost my mind, Sawyer. I became an alcoholic. Whiskey and women were the only things that seemed to dull the ache. I would disappear for a week at a time on benders. I was sleeping with any woman that offered and was drunk more often than sober. My parents tried to help, but it wasn't until a pregnancy scare and Lane punching the hell outta me that something slowed me down enough to sober me."

I wasn't going to tell her Lane's story, but I had never been more grateful for a black eye in my life. Jonah and Lane had saved me in entirely different ways, but their friendship was as close as brothers could be without sharing blood.

I blew out a breath that ended in a bitter laugh.

"That day you were on my porch was like déjà vu. The last time a woman sat on my porch steps, it was to lie and tell me she was pregnant with my baby." I lifted my eyes to hers, which had widened at that statement.

"In the end, she was after money and wasn't pregnant, but the idea that I could have created a child in my whirlwind of damage sobered me. Lane hired a doctor while I detoxed at Jonah's house and then I went through a rehab program. There are still people that were convinced by her lies that I'm a deadbeat dad." She watched my face and for the first time, hers was unreadable. I plunged on because at this point, I wanted everything on the table.

"I'm eight years sober, and I attend AA one night a week for accountability. I try to help other men in the same situation that I was in." I hopped up, startling her, and tugged her hand with mine and led her to my bedroom. She followed willingly until we stood in front of the jar and I reached a hand to pull out a paper.

"I write one of these every morning to remind myself that one day can undo that many days of sobriety, and it's just not worth it."

Her beautiful blue eyes scanned the paper I held, and then she slammed her body into mine. Her arms wrapped around my waist and she buried her face in my chest. I wrapped my body around her as her sobs wet my shirt. I gathered her to me and took two steps to reach the bed until I was sitting against my headboard and she sat in my lap. I knew I had dumped a lot of information on her. It wasn't until I lifted my head from resting against hers that I noticed the tears tracking down my own face. After some time, she wiped at her face, sniffed, and her tears slowed. I scrubbed a hand down my face, wiping away my own tears.

"Soren, you're wrong," she retorted shakily. My muscles tightened at her words. "I don't hate you."

She reached for my hand and pressed a kiss to the palm, causing my heart to catch. She studied me while adding, "I could never hate you."

My eyes bounced between hers, and I took my first deep breath since I told Sawyer my story. Over the next hour, I held Sawyer close to me as I told her about George. How Lane and Jonah held me accountable, and how I volunteered to support other men getting sober. I told her how successful the farm was and that the land that Connor had run away on was mine. I'd been scared to tell her at first because I'd been down the manipulating woman route before. I relished holding her close to me. It reminded me that she trusted me, and I never wanted that to change.

Chapter Forty-Six

Sawyer

GREG STOLE MY LUNCH again. Initially it was annoying and now it ticked me off. I was called in early because one of my kids was in a standoff between the foster parents and police. The teen had stolen the family's minivan, decided to go joyriding, and wrecked the car. It was only a fender bender, and no one was injured, but the family was distrustful of having the teen in their home again. After a two-hour heart to heart, we worked things out and the family said they would try to continue to foster the teen. I could understand their hesitation. As with everything involving situations similar to these, it was always a delicate balance of remembering that they were a teen but also that they were responsible for their actions.

I was exhausted. I hadn't gotten to spend any time with Soren in the last week after he'd told me everything. I was getting pushed to intense limits at work. I hated that I was the only person that truly cared about these kids, but sometimes it seriously felt true. I needed a break. I needed to stop having coworkers that pushed all their extra work off on me. I needed my dang lunch. I was hungry and tired, but I needed to make it a couple more hours. Then I would clock out and turn on "Do Not Disturb" on my phone. I wanted to see Soren, but I was drained. I wasn't sure that it was going to be doable. I unloaded the files in my bag as I finally sat at my desk without my lunch. I hated having hunger pangs. It made me think of things I wanted to forget. What makes a thirty-five-year-old man steal his coworker's lunch? I was leaving in two hours and I didn't have time to go get lunch. I scrounged through my purse, hoping there was a crumbled granola bar at the bottom. There wasn't, and I felt the disappointment acutely as Sharon made her way to my desk.

"Sawyer, honey, can you read these documents for me and tell me what they say? The font is just too small for my eyes." And that was the story of how I left work four hours later instead of two.

By the time I arrived home, exhausted wasn't even the right word to describe how I felt. I had a headache that felt as though it was rooted directly in the middle of my head. I wasn't sure if it was from hunger or lack of hydration or from feeling overwhelmed all day. No doubt the sheer stress from dealing with my coworkers contributed to the already stressful job. I walked in and plopped everything down on the floor, leaving a trail of the aftermath of me as I trudged to the kitchen. I grabbed the cold pitcher of water from the fridge, poured a cup, and reached for over-the-counter meds for my headache. This week sucked the life out of me. I felt like I was eighty-six instead of twenty-six. I had barely swallowed the capsules when my phone began ringing. Talia. Crap. I had forgotten about dinner tonight. There was no way I could function through something that social right now.

"Hey, Tal." I answered.

"Hey, I wanted to see if you were going to be here soon?" she asked hopefully.

"Uhhh . . . I can't make it. I'm sorry." I could sense her disappointment in the pause.

"Ohh . . . something came up?" she asked.

"I've been working since four this morning with a disturbance. I still have a few reports to finish. I'm sorry." Again, another pause. I was the worst friend, but I couldn't imagine leaving my house at this point. My head pounded, and it was almost eight at night.

"Okay. I'll talk to you later." Her voice was heavy with disappointment.

"Are you mad at me?" Talia had never truly been mad at me.

"I guess I'm wondering if your job will always come first, but I already know the answer to that." Her answer gutted me. I knew I missed things from time to time, but my job helped kids. I was making a difference. This was it. This was the moment that Talia didn't stay. I knew it was too good to be true.

"I'm sorry if caring about kids inconveniences you," I bit out, and I heard her catch her gasp. I knew it was unfair, because I'd seen Rob and Talia go above and beyond volunteering at events and buying Christmas gifts for these same kids.

"Saw, you know that's not fair. I really wanted you to be here tonight. But only if you want to be . . . look, I have to go. My family just walked in. Bye."

I could hear the tears in her voice. I knew she hung up hurriedly because she was on the verge of a sob. Tears I put there. I was the worst person. This was why I was completely unlovable. It had been proven to me over and over again. It was a miracle that Talia stuck around as long as she did, but she had a family, and I wasn't it. It was only a matter of time before Soren realized I wasn't worth staying for, either. My hand shook as I lifted the cup to my parched lips. He'd see how broken I was and before long, he'd be gone too. My phone rang. Glancing down, I saw it was Soren.

"Hello."

"Hey, Pretty Girl. How was your day?" I didn't deserve him. I should distance myself now to save him the hassle.

"Uh okay." My tone sounded defeated, even to my own ears.

"Just okay? Want to talk about it?" I could hear him getting ice in a glass. He must be coming in after a long day too.

"Not really." I knew I sounded short.

"Fair enough. If you change your mind, I'm here. Are you getting ready to go to Talia's?"

"No. It's been a long day," I clipped. The pain was too raw to talk about.

"Okay," he drawled. Undeniably confused on why I was being snippy.

"I've been thinking, and this isn't going to work," I rushed out because I wouldn't be able to say the words otherwise. The metal tags bit into my palm. I hadn't even remembered reaching for them.

"What's not going to work out?" He hesitated, sounding suddenly more serious. All background movement silenced as if he had stopped moving altogether.

"Us," I clipped. I hated myself almost as much as he was going to hate me.

"Sawyer, is everything okay?" he asked slowly.

I didn't deserve him. I was a fool to even think for a moment that I did.

"Yeah, I've decided I don't want to do this," I lied.

"'Do this?'" he repeated, and I could hear his uneven breaths through the phone.

I stayed quiet. He knew what I meant.

"If this is because I pushed you too far, please tell me. I don't want to lose us because it's hard for you to tell people how you're feeling sometimes. Is this because of the things I told you?" I didn't deserve him, and after what I was about to say, I never would.

"Look, Soren. This has nothing to do with what you told me. I'm done. I've decided to move on." Silent tears dripped down my chin as my headache blazed. I would never let him think he was the cause.

"Can we talk about this in person?" he tried again.

"No, can't you take a damn hint? I don't want to date you." He sucked in a breath. He had rarely heard me curse and never at him.

After the most excruciating pause in history, he responded, "Okay. I hope you find what you're searching for."

His voice was stiff. All emotion was gone, and I clicked the phone off as a sob tore through me as I hit my knees. I curled into a ball on my cold kitchen floor. I had ruined all the good things in my life in a matter of minutes. It was better to lose them this way than to see the good things walk out on me. It was inevitable. They would leave. I was only speeding up the process.

Chapter
Forty-Seven

Soren

My FIST CONNECTED WITH the bag and a sharp pain tore through my wrist, but I wouldn't stop. I punched until I was a puddle of sweat dripping on the floor. Music raged in my ears from the overhead sound system. I had been completely blindsided, and the only thing that made sense was to beat the hell out of this bag tonight. I was here by myself thanks to having my own all-access key fob from Jonah. What had happened? Sawyer had made it abundantly clear she was done, but I didn't understand why. We had a good thing going—or so I had thought.

Suddenly, the music cut and I jerked around to where the door was. Lane had his usual smirk on. His backward ball cap covered his blond hair that curled out from the edges. His smirk dropped.

"Why so angry?" he called out.

He flipped his keys in his hand. I swiped at my brow and squirted a spray of water in my mouth. I weighed the pros and cons of coming clean and knew it didn't matter. It was a small town, things would be found out, plus I never hid things that significantly mattered from Lane and Jonah. Not since rehab.

"Sawyer called us quits," I retorted.

"Ooft. Didn't see that coming." His head jerked back.

"Yeah, me neither." I tightened my wraps around my wrists.

"Why?" He straddled a nearby weight bench.

"I don't know. Just said she didn't want to date me," I stated.

"Hell, man. I'm sorry." Lane blew out a breath.

"If I understood why, I think I'd be okay. I thought we had a good thing going." I paused. "I thought she was the one." A shadow passed over Lane's face. He was all jokes and laughs, but he never talked about "the one" for him.

"If you think she's the one, don't give up yet, man. Fight for her."

"I don't know if that's a good idea," I hedged.

Lane didn't completely know her history. He didn't know how important it was to respect her ability to control her environment.

"It's a better idea than letting 'the one' walk away," Lane replied solemnly, and without another word, he walked up to me, slapped me on the shoulder and walked out. If anyone knew about that, it was Lane. The reality was, if I didn't try harder to see if we could make a go of this, I would essentially be Lane. Years later, I'd still be in love with a figment of my imagination because she would be gone. I rubbed at my chest. The ache there was unreachable. I couldn't let her simply walk away without a good reason, but I also knew that by crowding her I wouldn't be allowing her to make the choice for herself. As much as I wanted her, I also wanted her to want me, too. No matter how much her words had cut, I couldn't get over the thought that maybe she was simply scared, but how do you prove to someone you'll be there? How do you build that foundation of trust when she'd been through hell? How could I let her know I was here for her but also not come on too strong? I debated multiple ideas and reached for my phone to text the guys. Would it be humbling to get their thoughts on how I could reach Sawyer? Hell, yes. Would it be worth it? Absolutely. Sawyer would always be worth any effort I put forward. When I reached for my phone, the date glowed on the screen, and at that moment, I knew what I would do—and who I could call, someone who might be able to help, perhaps even more.

Day One

Soren:

I love your eyes. From the moment I met you, I thought they were the most beautiful eyes I had ever seen.

Day Two

I love your hair. I love running my fingers through it.

Day Three

I love your brain. You finished college early because you're a badass smarty.

Chapter Forty-Eight

Soren

Lane:

Ribs at my place on Sunday before the game.

Jonah:

I'll be there.

Lane:

Bring Landry and Hope. Hope wants to see her favorite uncle.

Jonah:

eye roll emoji

AFTER THREE HOURS, LANE texted again.

Lane:

Yo, Soren. Are you coming?

Soren:

I'll be there.

I stared at the words on the screen, fully aware that Lane's comment about being Hope's favorite uncle was his way of provoking a reaction from me. Everyone had reached out over the past three days, even Landry. Of course, Lane had shared everything with Jonah and Landry. He knew more small-town gossip than Chet Fagan and his morning coffee crew. Volunteering as the high school football coach made you privy to all the latest news around town.

My desperate hope of being able to have a relationship with Sawyer was dwindling like sand in an hourglass, and I felt as if I were drowning under the weight of losing her. Without the crutch of whiskey, I had to confront every emotion head-on, and it frustrated me to no end. Dammit, I was exhausted from feeling. But it was impossible to silence the pain, especially when I was counting the days I'd been sober this morning like they were etched in stone. I felt hopeless, as if no matter how hard I tried, I might never have been everything she needed. Was life so cruel as to send me this incredible woman to love, only to take her away?

I wanted to be angry at her. I wanted to tell her she had given up on us before we even had a chance. But deep down, I knew that wasn't who Sawyer was. She was scared, and I could hear it in her voice. But that didn't change anything. She had said she didn't want to date me, which left me feeling trapped. I wouldn't force her. I wanted her to choose me just as much as I chose her. A relationship could never succeed long-term if one of us was always running away.

As I pondered these thoughts, the mail carrier drove by, leaving a cloud of gravel dust in his wake. I climbed out of my truck and walked toward the road. The mailbox door creaked open, and beneath a stack of envelopes, I spotted one of the deliveries I had been expecting. I didn't have all the answers, but maybe this package would hold some. Thank God for expedited shipping.

Lane's house was a new custom-built home located outside of Kennedy. The winding gravel driveway left visitors unprepared for the mansion that lay beyond the hedge row of Osage orange trees. The house was entirely hidden from any passerby or nosy neighbor curious about what the residence of a retired MLB pitcher looked like.

The house was situated around a five-acre pond with a fishing pier. Lane insisted on driving his restored powder-blue 1954 Chevy pickup even though he could purchase any vehicle on the market. He appreciated nice things, but he didn't flaunt them. Although he was outgoing, Lane created a sanctuary that provided him with privacy that no other part of his life had allowed him.

I walked in without knocking, precariously balancing two six-packs of soda in glass bottles, a bag of chips, and a crockpot of queso with ground sausage.

"Look, Hopey, it's Uncle Soren," Landry said, smiling at Hope on her hip, who was all gums, slobber, and smiles. Her cheeks were like pink, round apples as Landry reached to take the bag of chips before my tower of food crashed to the floor.

"Thanks, Lands," I said as I lowered everything to the kitchen counter and plugged in the crockpot.

"Hey, man!" Lane called from where he was pulling a pan of ribs from the oven. I raised a hand in greeting. Jonah sat on a bar stool at the high-top counter. Everyone's eyes were on me, even Hope's. I reached to carry Hope, trying to pretend I was feeling better than I was, but Hope burrowed her cheek into the hollow of Landry's neck.

"She's been kind of clingy since she's teething," Landry explained, her dark brown eyes alight with love for her daughter. Although Hope was unexpected, Landry knocked it out of the park as a mom. She had been secretive about who the father was, which killed Jonah because he wanted to rip him limb for limb, but aside from that moment of tension between them, Jonah adored his younger sister. I brushed a knuckle down Hope's cheek, which gained me another smile. Hope's eyes were the brightest blue, which made me think of Sawyer.

"What's everyone been up to?" I asked, settling onto a barstool as Lane finished painting the barbecue glaze on the ribs. Landry tilted her head and blew out a breath to push a stray piece of hair out of her face before Hope's grabby hands could reach it.

"Worrying about you," she said bluntly.

Lane and Jonah turned to her, ready to kick her out. Landry tended to speak her mind, regardless of who was around, which only added to the mystery of Hope's dad. I had rarely been on the receiving end of her ire—it was usually reserved for Lane and Jonah. Lane enjoyed riling her up for fun, while Jonah often overextended himself, or so Landry claimed.

"Men, honestly." She rolled her eyes and tossed her hand in the air, her straight black ponytail fanning out behind her as she surveyed the group. "There's no point in pretending this lunch wasn't planned to check on Soren and make sure he's okay. You can stop pretending."

Lane looked at me sheepishly, biting the corner of his bottom lip while shrugging. Jonah grunted as Landry continued.

"We love you. You're family. How are you really doing? How can we help?" she asked, resting her cheek on Hope's brown tuft of hair. I had never had a little sister, but in all the ways that mattered, Landry had been mine. My chest burned with the knowledge that they would do anything for me, just as they already had. I would return the favor tenfold.

I scrubbed my hands down my thighs, feeling tension ease out of me because we all knew why we were here. We might as well acknowledge it. This was why I had hesitated to come, but this crazy group would have shown up on my front porch if I hadn't.

"I feel like sh—crap," I stumbled over the words since Hope was watching me with her big, round eyes, too young to understand my language. "But I talked to Talia, Sawyer's friend, and I'm hoping this isn't the end. Sawyer's been through a lot, so I need to be patient, but it's hard not talking to her." It was even more challenging that she wasn't trusting me with her fears. Sometimes, I wondered if I was wasting my time being optimistic that Sawyer would change her mind. She could say what she wanted, but I didn't believe her.

"I'm sober. I would reach out if I were struggling with my sobriety." I met all of their somber eyes, trying to reassure them.

"Okay. As long as you know we're here for you," Landry said, and both of my friends nodded, satisfied with my answer.

Desperate to change the subject, I quipped, "Hey, I know a way you can help! I finally caught that bull in the corral that's been fence-hopping. Want to help me load him in the trailer next weekend for the cattle sale?"

There was a mix of laughs and groans, but Lane and Jonah agreed.

"It's been a long few days, but I'm off now and I think I might try to get to bed early," I explained as her crystal blue eyes assessed me.

"Why don't you stay for a minute and eat a fresh peach muffin? The peaches are fresh, straight from Colorado."

Fifteen minutes later, I was sitting at a lawn table under an oak tree with a glass of iced sweet tea and a peach muffin. In a matter of moments, I was telling Mrs. Bailey about the mess that was my life.

"Sawyer, I don't tell a lot of people this, but the reason Gerald and I offer respite is because I spent time in foster care as a child. Five years," she recalled, glancing toward her garden, her silver hair shining in the sunlight.

"It was the worst time of my life, and it left scars that I'll carry till the day the good Lord takes me. That's why we wanted to be a safe place for kiddos to land. Gerald loving me changed my life. I tried to push him away, but he's an ornery one. His love paved the way for me to understand all the other ways I could be loved—and love others. It healed parts of me that felt broken beyond repair." I gasped at her words. That was me. I was broken beyond repair before I was even in kindergarten. I had been abused, assaulted, starved, beaten, and broken, and it had only gotten worse from there. My eyes filled with tears. Soren had tried to love me, and I had pushed him away.

"I'm such a mess. I can't be loved like that right now."

"Oh, so you are only worthy of love when everything is perfect?" she inquired gently as silent tears tracked down my cheeks. She pulled me into her gentle body, and I melted, as if I was hugging a grandparent I had never met. She ran her hand over my head as sobs racked my body. I couldn't hear her clearly, but I thought I heard her softly praying as she held me while I fell apart.

Soft music played as I burrowed in my comfy chair that night. A notebook and pen lay across the arm of the chair as I made a list. Mrs. Bailey had given me some homework. She had stated that if I wanted a different outcome, I needed to do something different. I wasn't sure what the difference was, but I had some ideas. I had done therapy, but it had been years since I had met regularly with my therapist. Especially not since some of the life-altering things I had experienced in the last few months, like processing Abel's death, dating someone for the first time, and the extreme stress of my job. My notebook list included:

- *schedule therapy*

- *consider job change*

- *call Talia*

My fingers stumbled as I considered writing "call Soren," but I didn't think I was brave enough to tackle that one yet. I would start working through this list tomorrow.

Chapter Fifty

Sawyer

It wasn't until I was halfway through my workday that I realized it was my twenty-seventh birthday. I had reached to check something on my phone, and the date across the locked screen stopped me. The reason I had forgotten was because for the last seven years, Talia had woken me up with obnoxiously loud sounds and confetti. Today I woke up to complete silence, aside from Mrs. Beakle mowing her lawn for what felt like the third day this week. Could grass even grow that quickly? I hadn't seen or heard from Talia in five days. I knew she was giving me space. I glanced down when a notification came through on my phone.

Talia

HAPPY BIRTHDAY! I LOVE YOU.

GIF of woman dancing and throwing confetti

Tears flooded my eyes, and I preemptively sniffed, trying to keep them at bay. I knew that I shouldn't have said the things I did, but my desire to make a difference in foster care was unlike anything I had ever experienced. If I didn't help these kids, who would? Was what Talia said true? Did I have an unconscious addiction to the adrenaline rush that I got from the chaos that I knew would be found in this space? I knew I needed to be better at setting boundaries with my coworkers, but that didn't mean I needed to quit my job, right? I kept replaying Talia's words in my head almost as much as I had the hurt I heard in Soren's. How had I managed to hurt the two people that cared the most about me? The other voice I heard in my head was Mrs. Bailey telling me that I should do something different if I wanted a different result. Regardless of if I needed to rethink my dedication to my job or not, I couldn't ignore that it was a Saturday and I wasn't supposed to be working. But here I was, because I couldn't tell my coworker no when they gave me some excuse about having a stomach bug. I had clearly overheard them talking about a concert they wanted to go to in Kansas City this weekend. They didn't have a stomach bug. They were most likely tipsy at the three-day long festival they had talked about for weeks. I was the one they knew would show up because I cared about the kids too much to not show. The more that I contemplated the situation, the more I knew Talia had some valid points. I canceled my plans with her and, most recently, with Soren because I was incapable of telling people that, *Yes, I do care deeply about every child that comes through this office, but I have human needs too.*

I wanted to fix things. Repairing things with Talia felt somewhat possible, but there was no way on earth I could ever feel worthy of a man like Soren Roberts. He deserved so much more than I had to offer. Looking again at Talia's text, I decided to be brave.

Sawyer:

> Thank you! I love you too. Can we talk later?

Almost immediately, she responded.

Talia:

> Of course. 8 p.m. at your place?

Sawyer:

> Perfect. See you then!

It was 6:30 p.m. before I made it home. I looped my work bag over my arm as I carried it inside. My heels clicked on the concrete on the walkway, but I came up short when I realized there was something on my welcome mat. My breath caught as I moved forward. In a jar similar to the blue-green jar that Soren kept on his dresser was a beautiful bouquet of wildflowers. I knew without even looking they were from him. I dropped my bag and reached for the tiny envelope that stuck out of the top of the bouquet.

Slipping the card out, I read, "I'm trying hard to respect your wishes, but a Pretty Girl deserves flowers on her birthday. All my love, Soren."

There weren't enough tissues at Target to dry the tears that followed. How had I screwed up something with the most thoughtful man on the planet? This was further confirmation that he deserved someone better than me. I gathered the jar and my bag in my arm and made my way inside as silent tears rolled down my cheeks. Soren Roberts was a good man, and I had ruined the best thing that had happened in my life. I had always wondered what it felt like to be in love. As I sat buried deep under my weighted blanket in my comfy chair and stared at the second bouquet of the most beautiful flowers I had ever received, I was certain I could explain what both love and brokenheartedness was in vivid detail. Because somewhere along the way, I had fallen in love with the gentle and fierce way that Soren Roberts loved me.

I washed my face before it was time for Talia to come over. There was no hiding my red and puffy eyes, but there was a certainty that these wouldn't be the only tears I shed tonight. I had to repair my relationship with her. Whereas the situation with Soren felt too overwhelming to tackle, I knew that there was a truth to what Talia had said, and I didn't want to toss away eight years of friendship. A knock sounded, and when I went to the door to find Talia holding a small birthday cake and gift bag, the tears flooded my eyes. My words were barely intelligible as I told her I was sorry. She set the cake down on my coffee table and wrapped me in one of her warm hugs.

Chapter Fifty-One

Sawyer

"Tal, I know you're right about me not being able to continue like I am, but I feel stuck. I know I want to make a difference in the lives of children, especially children from hard places, but I also don't want my entire life to be my job."

"What if you could do that without working directly in foster care?" She asked as she licked frosting from her finger.

"I can't turn a blind eye to these kids." I had experienced that.

"What if you still helped kids but in a different way? I saw a job posting the other day that I think would be perfect for you."

"Really? Where at?" I asked taking a bite of my cake.

"It's a new venture in Kennedy, and they are recruiting someone to manage the resources and organize community involvement. I briefly glanced at the website and it sounds as though they are preemptively working with at-risk families in an effort to prevent foster care service from being needed, training caregivers and providing resources for those in need," Talia explained.

"I would love a chance to help families before CPS or foster care is needed if that were possible, but I can't work in Soren's town, Tal." Surely, she understood this.

"Why?"

I hadn't told her about Soren yet. I looked toward the flowers and explained what I had done. She nodded quietly, and I read her the card. I told her how he had texted me everyday since telling me something he loved about me. She simply listened and nodded.

"It seems as though Soren is more than willing to talk this out. I don't understand." She didn't understand and she wouldn't.

"Tal, on no planet would I ever be worthy of someone like Soren Roberts. He deserves someone who isn't damaged like me." Talia tilted her head, studying me.

"Would you let someone say that about me? Would you let someone say I didn't deserve Rob?" Her tone startled me. I squinted my eyes because I knew she was pulling one of her psychology tricks.

"No . . . "

"If you're not okay with someone saying those words to me, why would you be okay saying them about yourself?" She easily took a bite of cake, as if her calm words weren't a punch to the gut.

"Sawyer, this is the thing. While you are negating why you don't belong, there are people who love you, wanting you to be there. I wasn't upset because you couldn't come the other day. I was upset because I wanted you to be a part of a special moment in my life and you weren't there. You are wanted. How will I ever get that through to you?" She remarked all of this in her matter-of-fact voice, but I was hung up on two of her words.

"Special moment?" She reached for the gift bag and handed it to me. I set my cake aside and pulled out a tiny blue onesie that said "My aunt is pretty cool." Talia was pregnant. I squealed with excitement.

"I'm so sorry that I missed your announcement. Tal, I'm excited for you! Truly." I hated that I had missed such a special moment in her life.

"Thank you." She smiled as she patted her still flat belly.

"Is Ava excited?" Ava would be the best big sister.

"As much as she can be. She is having a hard time understanding that it's going to be a few months, but she's made a stack of toys to share," Talia shared with a smile tugging at her lips.

"Of course our sweet girl would."

"I know you don't want to talk about this, but, Sawyer, please promise me you'll think about other jobs. I'm only pushing this because I love you and I want you to have a life outside the chaos of the system. Just because you grew up in the system doesn't mean you have to sacrifice your entire life to it. You can still make a difference in other places. In places that are no less worthy." I searched her eyes. I knew she was speaking the truth with love, but the idea of walking away from the thing I knew best scared me.

"Okay. I'll try." I agreed as I bit the inside of my cheek.

"I can send you the link to that new center that I was talking about. The website and mission statement sound legit. Essentially, it's supposed to be a resource for the town, for everything from tutoring, job interview prep, parenting classes, therapy offices. I'm even thinking of donating an afternoon each week for the free therapy sessions portion."

"Wow. It sounds like an amazing resource for the community." Maybe this would be the right fit.

"You're amazing at multitasking and organization. I think you'd be fantastic at it, plus it had clearly defined hours. It's 9 a.m. to 5 p.m. Monday through Friday. You should check it out. After reading through the information, I got the impression that the heart behind it is genuinely trying to make a difference," Talia said while taking another bite of cake with a smile on her face.

"I'll check it out."

Day Seven

I love your heart. It's brave and compassionate.

Chapter Fifty-Two

Sawyer

ACCORDING TO THE CLOCK on the dashboard, I had been sitting in my Jeep for exactly eight minutes. My palms were sweaty, and my heart was racing. I had never resigned from a job without a backup plan, not that I had much experience with quitting. In college, I worked as a night stocker at a grocery store to make ends meet, but I already had my position at CPS lined up. I always had a plan, but I knew I needed to go through with this. I had enough savings to last through the next six months, but the anxiety of touching those funds made me feel as if my lungs were in a vise, making it hard to breathe. I could do this. I had to.

I took a deep breath, held it for a count of four, and then released it. I had discussed this with my new therapist, Susie. While she didn't tell me what to do, she encouraged me to trust my instincts, since I had already taken the necessary steps, like double-checking my finances. The decision was made, and my lengthy list of pros and cons was evidence of that. I had tucked the list into my purse as a reminder in case I got to the parking lot and lost my nerve. My resignation letter and two weeks' notice were folded neatly inside a white envelope on my passenger seat.

I took another deep breath and jumped into action! I turned off my Jeep, slung my crossbody bag over my shoulder, grabbed the envelope, and speed-walked across the parking lot like I was competing in the Olympics. I yanked open the glass door with a little too much force, my hair blowing back in the rush. I needed to do this quickly before my courage faltered. I didn't stop at my desk before heading to my supervisor's office. I dropped the envelope on her desk before I could second-guess myself. Jill turned from her computer screen, her eyes widening as she took me in.

"Sawyer?" I reached out with a trembling hand to push the envelope toward her.

"Th-this is my two-week's notice. I've decided to make some changes. If it's possible, I'd like to introduce the kids to their new worker." I stumbled over my words, but I wanted to ensure that the transition for the kids was as seamless as possible.

My heart raced in my chest. Those speed walkers may be onto something with their cardio. Jill adjusted her glasses, reached for the envelope, and opened it, glancing up twice as if trying to gauge my sanity. Her eyes skimmed the two pages before rising to meet mine.

"Yes, of course. We will be sad to see you go, but I feel confident you will make a difference wherever you go." Jill looked at me as if she were proud, and I expressed my thanks as I made my way back to my desk. The aftermath of the adrenaline rush still made my hands tremble, but I settled in and pulled up my calendar. I had dozens of children to see in the next two weeks, and I wanted to tell each of them how special they were.

Then I paused, realizing something had shifted within me. There was a lightness in my chest, a fragile spark of hope that everything would be okay.

Chapter Fifty-Three

Sawyer

A WEEK AND A half later, I tugged my dress down as the wind blew and stared at the restored historical building in front of me. It was cut limestone with large white-framed windows. A large sign broadcasted it as The Hope Center, and something about that tugged at my heart, because hope could truly change everything. I clutched the folder with my resume and letters of reference to my chest and walked in. I had corresponded with a man named Will who stated he was an assistant to the individual running the organization. My heels clicked on the newly refinished wood floors as I walked in. Everything was modern with an industrial rustic touch that felt fresh and welcoming. It smelled slightly of fresh paint, and I wondered if it was because of the beautiful mural of the Flint Hills painted on the wall. I was stunned as the two men turned toward me at the sound of my heels. It was Lane and Jonah. They didn't appear to be surprised to see me, though.

"Sawyer," Lane stated.

Lane smiled and walked forward, extending his hand. We shook as I tried to figure out what was going on. Jonah studied me, but didn't extend his hand. His head simply dipped with a nod. His face was always serious; it was difficult to know what he was thinking. Lane was dressed in a suit while Jonah wore nice denim pants, a button-down shirt tucked in at the waist, and a blazer.

"We'll meet in here." Lane pointed with the folder in his hand.

Lane led the way, and I followed. Did he own this place? Why was Jonah here? What was going on and how was Soren? I wanted to thank him for the flowers, but I knew if I contacted him, it would be difficult to cut off contact. I couldn't continue the same way I was. I had scheduled a therapy appointment, and by some miracle, I had been able to have three appointments already, despite being a new client. I had found a wonderful therapist named Susie, who was a recommendation from Talia. She made me think of Soren's mom. She was an avid cyclist and yoga fan, but she had this way of being both kind and blunt and it was exactly what I needed. I needed someone to make me think outside the box, but who also understood that my life experiences were unique.

A spark of hope had ignited in me again. I think that's why the sign outside drew me in. I knew hope changed everything because it had begun to change me. We entered a beautiful meeting room that hosted a long boardroom table with ten rolling chairs around it. Jonah sat on the opposite side while Lane took the seat on the end. I sat on his other side. He flipped open the folder.

"My assistant has been the one to organize these interviews; it wasn't until this morning that I saw exactly who I was interviewing. I'll admit I was surprised to see your name," Lane stated.

I swallowed.

"I was also surprised when I walked in. I didn't realize both of you were connected to this," I responded.

They looked at each other and then Lane announced, "Let's get started."

Lane tapped a pen on the table and proceeded to ask me questions about my experience, making notations on an iPad in front of him. This side of him was in stark contrast to the jokester that loved sports, and it was staggering. After thirty minutes of continuously answering questions with no input from Jonah, I was taken aback when Jonah interrupted.

"Why do you want this job?"

His voice was gruff and his face had that ever-present scowl of concentration. I wanted to run. This whole interview had been a complete shock. I pushed all thoughts of Soren out of my mind. When I considered working in his town and being surrounded by his friends, I didn't think I could do it.

"To be honest, I'm not sure if this job is for me . . . I'm not sure I'll fit into this town."

I paused and looked down. My hands itched to pull the military tags from underneath my shirt. Jonah scoffed. My eyes burned, but I forced myself to finish. I raised my gaze that welled with tears, and met his eyes.

"I just want to make a difference. I want to do whatever I can so that kids don't have to grow up the same way I did," I said, despite the shakiness in my voice.

A shadow passed over Jonah's face, and I willed my tears to stay at bay.

After a pause that felt incredibly long, Lane spoke softly, "Sawyer, thank you for coming today. We will have a decision by Monday of next week. I do feel I should make you aware of one more thing. Soren is on the board and one of the decision makers. Myself, Jonah, and Soren will be overseeing the center. Is that something you would be comfortable with?" I tilted my head.

"Why is Soren not interviewing?" I had to know the answer. Lane immediately turned to Jonah with surprise on his face.

"You don't know?" Lane asked. My back shot ramrod straight.

"Know what?" I blurted as every fiber of my being stood at attention.

"Soren was in an accident. He was moving cattle last week, and a bull rammed him against the panels. He broke five ribs and collapsed a lung," Lane stated. My blood ran cold.

I stood abruptly, sending my rolling chair flying back against the wall.

"Where is he?" I practically yelled.

I had to see him. He was hurt. Everything made sense. He had texted me 'I love you' messages every single day, but a few days ago he had missed a day. Was that when he had been hurt? Lane and Jonah both stood.

"He's resting at home. He got out of the hospital the day before yesterday," Lane explained.

Blood rushed in my ears and I ran. I had to see him. I faintly remembered dropping my folder and running toward the door. I had almost made it to my car when a strong hand grabbed my forearm and spun me around.

"Let me drive," Jonah cut out.

He pulled me to his matte black truck, and I hopped in. Jonah drove as if he knew I needed to lay eyes on Soren soon. Everything hit me all at once. I was running to Soren, not from him. I loved him. I had loved him. I was still in the process of working out my own hang-ups, but with the hope of meeting with Susie and the encouragement from Talia, I knew I could do this. I might always need therapy and reassurance, but I was worth loving. Soren had shown me that every time he had adjusted his pace for me, when he had slowly loved me, waiting for me to catch up. He loved me. I knew that more than anything, and now I wanted to tell him that in return, if he'd let me. I didn't want to face the reality of growing older without him. When Jonah pulled into his drive, the reality of what I had done hit me. I'd run from an interview and left my vehicle, I had no way to leave.

"Oh, shoot. I left my car and ran out of the interview," I blurted out as it hit me. My hands were twisted together.

Jonah chuckled. I wasn't aware he was even capable of that. It almost sounded rusty.

"That you did. I'll have Travis go with me, and he can bring it back." I grabbed my keys and laid them on his center console.

"Thank you," I responded.

Jonah's quiet words stopped me before I shut the door.

"Sawyer, his heart can't handle you walking away again. Please make sure you know exactly how you feel before you make promises." His eyes were earnest and my heart crumbled. I had hurt the man I loved. The weight on my chest was unbearable, but I simply nodded and climbed out of the truck.

Chapter Fifty-Four

Sawyer

I STOOD IN FRONT of the steps that changed my life. It felt full circle that I was here again, and I wondered if I had made a mistake. I glanced at the tire swing where Soren had pushed me under the stars for the first time. I took a breath to calm my heart from racing. I walked up the steps and turned toward the porch swing where Soren had kissed me for the first time. I knocked on the door. I knew Soren was hurt, therefore I was sure he may not be able to open the door. I tried the handle, and it was open.

I called out nervously, "Soren, it's Sawyer."

Complete silence met me. I glanced around and the house was untidy, which was surprising, but I knew that had to be a testament of how much pain he must be in. I could fix that. I walked toward the family room, but he wasn't there. I hesitated to walk toward his bedroom, but that made the most logical sense, especially because of his injuries.

"Hey, Soren. It's me," I called out again as I neared his bedroom. The door was partially open, and he was asleep in the bed. His bare muscular chest was above the blanket, and I could see his ribs were painted with purple bruises. His face had a cut above his brow. My heart clenched. I loved this man, and he had almost been taken from me permanently, and I hadn't even told him how much he meant to me. He needed rest in order to heal, so I gently shut the door and set to work cleaning his home. I put away all the misplaced items, started a load of laundry, and scrubbed the kitchen from top to bottom. Travis had quietly brought my keys inside after retrieving my Jeep, to which I whispered, "Thank you."

He said he was glad to see me, and if Soren asked, he was out checking water for the cattle. It was when I was carrying a rogue sock to the laundry room when I passed by the end table and saw it. A stack of books with colorful tabs sticking out with a highlighter and pen laid on top. It appeared as if he had been studying the books with exceptional detail. The top book snagged my attention as I set down the sock and looked more closely. The title read *How to Love Someone Who Has Experienced Childhood Trauma*. My heart immediately stopped and my nose burned with emotion. I lifted the next book with trembling hands and it was more of the same. Five books, highlighted throughout, with tabs marking sections on how to be supportive of someone you love. *He'd truly loved me.*

As I stacked the books back on the end table, I had an unnerving feeling that I was being watched. I turned and Soren stood at the end of the hallway with a mask of confusion on his face. One hand was braced on the wall and the other wrapped around his bare bruised ribs. Gray sweatpants hung from his narrow waist.

"I see you still make a habit of trespassing." His voice was gravelly from sleep.

"Soren," I whispered as my eyes took him in. He was still the steady, handsome man I knew him to be.

"Sawyer," he countered. My heart sank that he didn't call me Pretty Girl.

My fingers reached for my chain.

"I didn't know you were hurt," I explained, trying to keep my voice from breaking.

My brain raced with all the thoughts going through my head. Cataloging his injuries. Should he be standing? There was a crease in his brow that spoke of pain.

"Sawyer, why are you here?"

His voice had an edge of honesty and pain. Pain I had put there. My eyes welled, and I broke eye contact because I couldn't keep looking at the pain I had caused. I had hurt him, and I wasn't sure if I could ever undo that pain.

"I hurt you." My voice broke and I worked to keep it together. He quietly cleared his throat. I blinked away tears and searched for the right words.

"I knew if I didn't stay away, I would hurt you more deeply. I thought you would leave me, so I left you first."

A tear trailed down my cheek, and I wiped it away immediately and turned away, toward the stack of books. I had to calm my racing heart if I was to be able to keep going. I took a shuddering breath as I felt the warmth of his body behind mine. He didn't touch me, but he didn't have to. His nearness was my undoing. A sob attempted to escape, but I willed myself not to cry as the back of my throat burned with emotion.

"What are you here for?" he asked and I turned to face him.

"You."

His hazel eyes searched mine.

"I'm sorry." My heart raced in my chest. "I'm sorry I pushed you away. I'm sorry I didn't thank you for the flowers. They were beautiful. Every text—" I cut off before a sob broke free.

"Sawyer." One word in his heartbroken voice held multitudes.

"I realized a lot of things lately," I started, needing the weight off my chest. "I realized that I needed more help. I realized that I would never process things the way other people do. I realized I was going to hurt you. I realized I didn't want to. I realized I couldn't keep working in the system that raised me." I took a deep breath as I continued my list. "I realized I love you, and it scares me to death." His brows shot up at the last statement. "I know you have no reason to trust me, and I realize I'm not worthy of your love, but I want to try if you're willing to try with me?" His brow creased.

"Come here." He held out the hand not supporting his ribs. It was only two feet, but it felt like a trek across the Sahara as I stepped into him.

"You're wrong."

My nose burned, but I couldn't look away from his eyes.

"You are worthy of my love by simply being you." My breath shuddered and tears threatened.

"I want to love you how you deserve to be loved, but I don't know how."

"Then we'll do the work together. I know things aren't going to be perfect. We both have more baggage than an airline, but, Pretty Girl, I love you to the absolute core of my soul. I don't want to live without you. You make every day special because you're in it, and I want to spend the rest of my life loving you. Let me love you exactly as you are." His voice was hoarse by the end of it, and I did what I wanted to from the moment I laid eyes on him. I buried my face against his chest as gently as I could and breathed deep. If home were a person, it would be him. I wanted my home to be him.

His hand came up to hold me, but he winced and I backed away.

"I'm sorry. I don't want to hurt you." I glanced toward his bruises.

"Can you help me back to the bed so I can hold you?"

We walked slowly to the bedroom, and I adjusted pillows around him where he could lie back as comfortably as possible. He tugged on my hand again, and I laid on top of his comforter and wrapped myself around his arm, too worried to touch his torso. My face pressed to his biceps, breathing him in. I kissed his warm, sun-tanned skin.

"My lips are jealous of my guns." He smirked. My lips smiled against his skin. I never wanted to be away from him again.

"I love you, Cowboy." I whispered the words as they still felt foreign, but also oh so right.

"I love you, Pretty Girl." His thumb rubbed the back of my hand.

"I scheduled therapy again, and I quit my job. I also dyed the potato salad in my lunchbox with a ton of yellow food dye. Greg had bright yellow teeth for three days." I blurted out a laugh, excited to tell him all the things. Greg was then forced to admit he'd been taking my lunch, saying that it was easier than making his own. He really was the worst. Soren laughed, holding his ribs.

"Atta girl," he remarked. "How do you feel about all of that?" He was always concerned for me.

"My therapist is wonderful. Would you be okay going to a few sessions with me?" I asked.

"Sounds good. We could meet with George too," Soren added, linking one of my hands with his. I hadn't met his sponsor yet, but I wanted to.

"You'd be okay with that?" I asked.

"Anything for my girl," he assured me, and I knew with certainty, I always wanted to be his.

Chapter Fifty-Five

Sawyer

"I'M BEGINNING TO THINK you just want me for my muscles!" Soren remarked with a boyish smirk as he leaned against my pantry door, crossing his arms to emphasize said muscles. I bit my lip, trying to hold back a smile as his teasing tone sent tingles through my body, like tiny butterflies racing through my veins.

"Hmmmm," I said, tapping a finger to my lips. "I hadn't noticed any, but perhaps they would be helpful." My cheeks hurt from the never-ending smile on my face. Before I could blink, Soren swooped in and wrapped his arms around my waist. My hands rested against his firm chest. His hazel eyes blazed as his embrace caused his heart to race beneath my palms.

It had been three weeks since I discovered that stack of books, and every day since then, Soren had wrapped me in his arms and kissed me breathless. No matter how often he did this, it still made my heart feel like it was bubbling over with joy.

"For someone who hasn't noticed any muscles, you sure seem to like the feel of them," Soren remarked, looking down as my hands slowly—very slowly—began to rub over his shoulders until they reached the back of his neck. A blush lit up my face.

"I was simply searching to see if there were any," I replied, my cheeks burning brighter.

"And what are your findings?"

I tilted my head as my hands ran across his shoulders and down his biceps. They were quite firm indeed. Desire stirred within me as I felt the smooth skin at the edge of his t-shirt. He was more tan than when I'd met him, having worked outside so much this spring and early summer.

"There do seem to be a few," I admitted, biting my lip and grinning.

"That's good to know." His eyes traced my face like I wanted his lips to.

"Soren?"

"Yeah?"

"Are you going to kiss me?" I asked breathlessly.

"Always," he whispered before kissing my temple, brushing his lips down my cheek before finding my mouth. We kissed until we were both breathless. Suddenly, the sound of a can dropping to the floor startled us, and we sprang apart, my chest heaving.

A can of green beans rolled out the door and finally came to rest against the baseboard in the kitchen. A laugh bubbled up from my lips, and he chuckled in response. He rested his forehead against mine.

"I love you," I whispered.

"I love you more." Something had shifted inside me, and I no longer doubted his words. Would everything be seen through rose-colored glasses in the future? No, but my confidence in his love for me gave me a freedom I had never experienced before.

"Perhaps I could reward you for your hard work?" I quipped playfully. He kissed my forehead and leaned back.

"I like the sound of this. Let's hear it." He smirked.

"One kiss for every can you carry to the truck?"

"Now that's a reward I'm interested in." His smile made my insides feel warm.

"Shall we shake on it?" I said, stepping out of his arms. I raised my hand to shake his.

"I'd rather kiss on it." He gently grasped my wrist, lifted my open palm to his lips, and kissed it. The stubble on his face felt like sandpaper against my soft skin—gritty and invigorating. My breath hitched at the sensation.

"Sawyer," Soren said more somberly than during our earlier joking.

"Yes?" My eyes bounced between his.

"You know that none of this is necessary, right?" He gestured to the full shelves surrounding us.

"I will always make sure you're taken care of. Always." The intensity in his voice was fierce.

The truth in his eyes calmed my anxiety, and a small smile tugged at my lips because I believed him.

"All these boxes are going to The Hope Center, except for two on the counter. Susie has challenged me to step outside my comfort zone in areas where I feel the safest."

"Why does this area feel the safest?" He tipped his head, studying my face.

"You. You make me feel safe and seen. I see the evidence of love for me every day. I can feel your love. Being loved by you feels like home." And deep in my bones, I meant every word.

Chapter Fifty-Six

Soren

IN THE LAST WEEK with the help of Lane, Jonah, and Travis we moved Sawyer into her studio apartment above the restored hardware store on Main Street. After meeting, we determined that Sawyer was by far the best candidate to be the director of The Hope Center. She was passionate about making a difference and had the qualifications and experience to execute it. Jonah had said he wouldn't consider anyone else. Her eyes shone with excitement every time she talked about ideas she planned to implement once it was open. When I showed her the blueprints for the two acres of land next door to The Hope Center, she cried. We had worked with a team to design a top of the line playground structure with modifications for those in wheelchairs. The walking trail was complete with benches that could be accessed from the sidewalk that ran along the front of the street. To enter the park, you had to walk under a metal arch that read The Abel Roberts Community Park.

In the last three weeks, we had met with Sawyer's therapist weekly and had lunch with George who, interestingly enough, had a date with Tina later that night. Rob, Talia, and their adorable daughter, Ava, had also come out to visit. I would forever be grateful for Talia's book recommendations on how to navigate the challenges of loving someone from a difficult background. Talia had been expecting my call and texted me a list of her recommendations.

Most nights, Sawyer and I would end the night falling asleep while talking on the phone. Something shifted in those weeks we were apart, and now, Sawyer told me that she loved me daily. I answered back enthusiastically, which often ended with us kissing. That had been another huge change since the beginning of our relationship. Sawyer was a complete cuddle bug. We rarely weren't touching if we were in a room together, which I loved, but even more than that, I loved that she loved it too.

She shifted beside me on the porch swing, reminding me precisely how true that was. Her head was lying on my thigh as she laid on her back reading, one knee crossed over the other, her cute bare feet on full display. My hand was threaded through her soft hair.

"Enjoying your book?" I asked.

"Yeah, I've read it at least a dozen times, but I still love it," she declared, bookmarking a beloved edition of *Anne of Green Gables* and

laying it on her stomach. "I thought of something to disagree about."
Her tone was playful.

"Oh yeah? Let's hear it." I quipped.

"I think you owe me a kiss," she teased, laying the book on the table
and sitting up. Her blonde hair spilled over her shoulder.

"Is that so?" My lips tugged into a smile. "But how exactly is this a
disagreement?"

"That you didn't kiss me sooner, and now the kiss is late."

She smirked, knowing exactly how ridiculous it sounded. I found her
waist and tugged her until her knees were straddling my hips.

"So now I owe a late fee for kisses with more kisses?" I clarified as I
kissed her smooth skin below her left ear. Her involuntary shiver lit a fire
in me.

"Yep," she attempted to quip, but her breath caught as my lips
skimmed her neck.

"You win. I'm a man that always pays his dues." I kissed the pulse
point at her neck.

I kissed one eyelid, then the other as her soft hands glided across my
shoulders, pulling me closer.

"I love your eyes."

I kissed her chin.

"I love your chin."

I kissed her nose.

"I love your adorable nose."

She smiled, completely lost in my touch as her eyes fell shut.

"I love your lips," I said before my lips found hers. I moved my left
hand from her waist to her hair as the other hand grasped her waist. My
thumb slid under the hem of her shirt to her soft skin as I tugged her

closer. I was never letting her go. She didn't know it yet, but there was an engagement ring in my top dresser drawer that I was holding for the right moment. When you found someone like Sawyer, you didn't let them go. I would spend my life showing her, in big ways and small ways, exactly how much she was cherished and adored.

Abel had shared his light with Sawyer decades ago, but no matter the distance, light did what it always does. It traveled the vastness of time, no matter the expanse, and was still creating luminosity years later because in the end, that was the magic of light. The ability to go the distance for the ones that we love. Regardless of the hurdles of our pasts or our fears of the future, we were determined that light would always lead the way.

Epilogue

Sawyer

(Five Years Later)

I CHECKED THE APP on my phone again to confirm that the delivery was today. I had ordered something special to celebrate our anniversary, and I wanted to intercept the package before Soren saw it. The company used these obnoxious hot pink boxes, and I knew he'd recognize the box because I'd bought things from there before. I glanced out the window again, but there was no delivery truck. I plucked the last apple streusel muffin from the tin and placed it in the container. It was Friday afternoon, and I was baking for our family style brunch tomorrow morning. Lane, Jonah, Talia, Travis, Landry, The Baileys, and George were all bringing their families over, along with a few others.

I heard the crunch of gravel indicating that someone had driven up. I untied the floral apron I wore over my cut-off denim shorts and spun around to turn off the oven. I made it to the front door right on time to see the delivery driver hand Soren the hot pink box. *Ugh!* I stood, hands on my hips in the frame of the front door as he sauntered toward me with a cocky smile on his face.

"I see that you got me something," he quipped as his eyes twinkled and my belly dipped. Why was my husband so hot? It really made it difficult to stay upset at him for ruining his own surprise.

"Maybe. Maybe not," I quipped back, reaching for the box that he held slightly out of reach. I narrowed my eyes at him, barely keeping a straight face.

"How can I turn it into a maybe?" he asked with a grin and a wink.

"A good place to start would be to give me the box," I explained in a stern voice, tilting my head to the side. I smiled, despite trying to appear cross. He passed over the box, but something seemed too easy about it. I immediately tucked the box behind my back as if that would wipe it from his memory, and he hadn't just had it in his hand.

"So, how was your day?" I asked, backing away into the house as if nothing had happened. Soren stalked toward me, playing along as he tapped the door with his boot to close it, never letting his eyes leave me.

"Pretty good. It got a whole lot better when the nice delivery driver handed me that box." My belly dropped again at the hooded look in his eyes. My husband was sexy and there wasn't any point in denying that fact.

"What makes you think I wasn't buying it for someone else? It could be a gift," I reasoned, but we both knew that wasn't true.

"I wasn't aware you bought lingerie for other people." He smirked. I had backed up all the way until I bumped against the family room wall. His forearm landed beside my face as he leaned down. His warm breath teased the hairs at my neck as he whispered in my ear with his husky voice.

"My favorite thing is when you're wearing nothing at all."

I couldn't stop the chill bumps that skated across my body at his words or the blush that spread across my cheeks. I wanted him as much as he wanted me. He kissed below my ear and the box slipped from my fingers to the floor. My breaths came quicker. I felt his chuckle as his lips pressed against my neck, loving the bite of his five o'clock shadow against my soft skin. His calloused hands found my curves, and I hopped up on instinct, wrapping my legs around his waist, my hands buried in his thick chestnut hair. Soren pressed me against the wall as his lips found mine. His chest rising and falling in quick rapid pants. He kissed me hungrily and I melted at his touch. His hands gripped under my thighs, carrying me as we kissed and whispered sweet nothings, bumping our way down the hall toward our bedroom. My surprise delivery was completely forgotten because Soren did in fact prefer me in nothing at all. He loved me so completely, but more than anything, he made his heart my home. I never had to worry about how he felt about me because he had always made it clear by choosing me first over and over and over again. We learned together that the secrets we'd kept and the lies we believed weren't true, because the magic of light would always guide us back to each other where we'd always belonged.

Acknowledgements

Hannah Grace: This book would not exist without you. Thank you doesn't seem like enough words to express how much your being in my corner has meant to me. Love you forever.

Mr. Abitz: You will forever be the greatest love of my life. It is an absolute honor to be on this journey of life with you. Thank you for choosing me even when I put my cold feet on you in the middle of the night.

My Children: May you always live and love as fearlessly as you were created to. May Light always lead the way, and may you always have a thorough understanding of how deeply you are loved.

Stacy: I am so incredibly thankful for you. Thank you for listening to my ridiculously long voice messages and not telling me I'm crazy even though we both know that's questionable.

Katie: I feel lucky to have you as a cousin and friend. Thank you for being my sounding board and laughing when things are complete chaos. This journey of parenthood is the rollercoaster ride of a lifetime and I'm so glad I get to experience it with you.

My Library Co-Workers and Friends: I am incredibly blessed to live in a small town that truly cares about its neighbors, treasures books, and loves reading. Thank you for welcoming this Southern girl into the Heartland!

Beta Readers: Jenah, Bridget, Hannah, Jayden, Chloe: Y'all are the real MVPs! Thank you for being encouraging, honest, and kind. Your comments fueled the fire that kept me going. I'm not sure I'll ever have the right words to express how much I appreciate you.

My Parents: I know it was hard to choose a favorite child but no worries I won't tell the others. *winky face* I love you to the moon and back!

My siblings, nieces, nephews, brother-in-laws, sister-in-laws, mother-in-law: I love you and I mean it.

Bookstagram Fam: I am forever grateful to sit at the table with the coolest kids (AKA authors and bookstagrammers) on the internet. The fact that there's a place on the internet dedicated to a love of reading fills my heart with overflowing joy. I feel honored to know each of you.

Jordan: For loving gas station cake as much as I do.

Gail and Loretta: Thank you for providing caffeine after many late night writing sessions. You're the best neighbors a girl could ask for.

Dolly Parton The Cat: Thanks for warming my feet as I edited.

Johnny Cash The Kitten: For being cute.

Jesus: Without You, I am nothing.

About the Author

Born and raised in south Mississippi, Jordan has always loved reading. At the age of nine, she declared to her mom that she wanted to write books when she grew up, but it wasn't until after telling her children they could be anything they dreamed of that she realized she wasn't chasing her own dreams. Jordan is a lover of libraries, family farms, antiquing with her husband, advocating for children in foster care, and being a lifelong learner. Jordan resides with her husband and three children on their third-generation family farm in rural Kansas. And yes, her cats are named Dolly Parton and Johnny Cash. Her passion is to write stories that show the magic of love that brings hope and healing.

Let's Stay Connected

The best ways to keep up with the latest releases and bookish news are through Jordan's newsletter and Instagram!

www.authorjordanabitz.com

&

www.instagram.com/authorjordanabitz

www.ingramcontent.com/pod-product-compliance
Lightning Source LLC
Chambersburg PA
CBHW031316280626
47169CB00019B/1638